In Such a World

Book One

Mine

to

Avenge

A Novel by T.J. Hux

This novel is a work of fiction.
Any references to matters of historical record;
to real people, living or dead; or to real places are intended
solely to give the story a setting in historical reality.
Other names, characters, places, and incidents are the
product of the author's imagination and their resemblance,
if any, to real-life counterparts is entirely coincidental.

ISBN-13: 978-1541327726
ISBN-10: 1541327721

Front cover image: Item 23505323 US Capitol, Flag, Eagle
Textured Liz Van Steenburgh Dreamstime.com

Table of Contents

To my loving and encouraging wife, Brenda, for her support of my strange imagination.

The only thing necessary for the triumph of evil is for good men to do nothing.

*   - Edmund Burke*

"Do not take revenge, my dear friends, but leave room for God's wrath, for it is written: "It is mine to avenge; I will repay," says the Lord. On the contrary:

> *"If your enemy is hungry, feed him; if he is thirsty, give him something to drink. In doing this, you will heap burning coals on his head."*

Do not be overcome by evil, but overcome evil with good."

*   - Paul, Romans 12:19-21* New International Version

Prologue

The slight tremor in his hand wasn't the only manifestation of his anxiety. Though still in the cool of the morning, his shirt was damp with perspiration. Three antacids had not been able to soothe his aching stomach. At the age of only thirty-two, lines of stress were being etched into his face, a fact pointed out to him by his wife just last evening.

He cursed his trembling hand as he signed the document he had prepared. One last cursory overview of its content, then he quickly deposited it into the manila envelope and sealed it. Hurriedly he reached into the center desk drawer and withdrew his personal wax seal. Lighting the candle, he poured the melted wax over the envelope and depressed the stamp into it, holding it firmly in place while the wax hardened, then cleanly removed the stamp and returned the implements to the drawer. He knew the stamp would do nothing to prevent the wrong eyes from viewing the contents of the envelope, but there wasn't much chance the envelope would find its way to his desired recipient anyway.

Michael Claypool had first noticed that he was under surveillance two days ago, when he spotted the medium-height Colombian following him after he had left the U.S. embassy compound in Bogotá. That man had made an amateur's mistake but the others were far more professional. So much so that he wondered if he were just being paranoid. The man on the motor scooter? The woman at the open-air market? No, he wasn't being paranoid. Not with the knowledge in his head and in his hands.

1

Would anyone understand what he was about to do? How could they, unless they could see the big picture? Yet had he even seen the big picture? No, he had merely seen a glimpse of a small corner of it but that was enough to frighten him into his present course of action. Maybe when the story hit the newspapers and the dust settled, he could explain and return to a safe, quiet life. Hopefully.

But that wouldn't happen if he didn't find sanctuary for himself and his wife. How could he have put her in so much danger? When the State Department ordered him to the U.S. Embassy in Bogotá, it seemed like a thrilling opportunity for them to explore the world. After arriving in Bogotá, Claypool discovered that most of the contacts he would need to complete his assignment lived in the vicinity of Cali. After only a week in Bogotá, the Claypools leased a spacious suite in Cali and Michael went to work. They had only been in Colombia for eight months and now he feared they would never leave alive. Drug lords and revolutionaries aside, the source of his fear came from sources much closer to home.

"Marie! Are you ready?" he called to his wife who was sitting at the vanity in the powder room.

"Almost, dear," she answered with a hint of annoyance in her voice. She knew something was troubling her husband, but he wouldn't tell her anything. Now, he was hurrying her to pack for a trip she knew nothing about. "Pack enough for several days," was all he would say.

After insuring that her make-up and hair were acceptable, she emerged from the powder room and found Michael on the small balcony which overlooked much of the city of Cali. She moved up quietly behind him and placed her hand on his shoulder, only to retract it when he flinched at the touch.

"Mike, what is going on? I've never seen you so edgy," she asked, her eyebrows furrowed with concern.

"You startled me, that's all. Are you ready?"

2

She turned away in frustration. Why wouldn't he talk to her? "My bag's packed. Ready when you are to go wherever we're going," she said with unveiled disapproval.

It took five hours to navigate the narrow, winding mountain roads that stretched between Cali and Colombia's coastal city of Buena Ventura. Michael tried to control his growing desperation as he faced the usual congestion of 'chicken buses', produce trucks, peasants on bicycles, and one herd of sheep that stalled traffic for forty-five minutes as they crossed the highway. After completing the 95 miles, he parked the rented Ford Explorer in the parking garage of one of Buena Ventura's luxurious shopping malls. They walked three blocks to the nearest Post Office where he mailed the envelope, sending it on its way with a prayer, its contents his only hope. From there he hailed a taxi, having to fend off another inquiry from his wife about his strange behavior. He finally promised that he would explain everything that night, but for the time being she would have to trust him. She was no longer just worried, she was scared.

In the eighties, at the height of the "drug wars," Colombia was nothing short of a war zone. In the 1990's, Colombia had stabilized, or so it had seemed. When the opportunity for an assignment in Colombia had presented itself in the fall of 2001, moving to Colombia had seemed like the perfect opportunity for the Claypools. For Michael, it meant more than a huge promotion. The assignment opened the door to future posts in high level offices. For Marie, it gave her the chance to live out her compassion volunteering with as many humanitarian organizations as she desired.

The presumed political stability was shattered shortly after their arrival in Bogotá. She wondered now whether the drug wars were about to resume. In the eight months that they had been in the country, there had been several assassinations of government officials, judges, and numerous bombings. Michael had insisted that Marie return to the States to live with her parents until things settled down, but she had adamantly refused, insisting that what God had joined together would not be separated – not even by drug lords.

But why would Michael be so fearful now? She had noticed the change in his demeanor two weeks ago but his fearfulness and distance from her had only grown. And if there were danger, why not seek safety inside the embassy compound? Well, at least now he had promised her answers.

Twenty minutes later the taxi deposited the Claypools in the parking lot of Buena Ventura's most exclusive marina. Michael looked around nervously. He tensed when he thought he saw someone suddenly turn away from his gaze. Another tail? It didn't matter now. In a few moments, he would be safe, or so he hoped. Jumping in bed with the enemy seemed a strange way to find safety but then again, who was the real enemy?

Suddenly, four men appeared at the gate to the marina. By now it was 2:00 p.m. and the cool of the morning was a cherished memory. The combination of heat and humidity was draining, yet each of the men at the gate wore casual, light colored sport coats over their shirts and slacks. There was only one reason for the sport coats: the weapons concealed beneath were both reassuring and troubling.

One of the men stepped away from the others and approached. "Señor Claypool?" he asked, already knowing the answer. Michael nodded without a word. "Come with me, please, I will take you to your host," he said politely, taking the bag from Michael's shoulder.

He led them through the gate, where the remaining three men positioned themselves strategically around the couple, one on each side, the other guarding the rear. They followed their leader down to the docks and to a very expensive cabin cruiser where two more armed men greeted them.

Marie was trembling now, terrified and in total confusion. "Honey, where are we..." she whispered, only to be cut off as her husband put his finger to her lips.

"Later, I promise," he whispered, helping her onto the boat.

The boat sped them across the bay, along the breakwater pier, and out to the open ocean. They cruised over the calm seas, heading approximately fifteen miles north. They seemed to be heading toward a white spot on the northern horizon, toward the southern edge of the Gulf of Panama.

Michael and Marie focused on that white spot and watched it grow as they sped toward it. The 160' yacht seemed to dwarf the 30' cabin cruiser as it came alongside the luxury vessel. Another much smaller yacht was anchored about one hundred yards further out to sea. The Claypools would soon learn that the magnificent yacht boasted a master suite, eight staterooms, a formal dining room and living room, a recreation and fitness room, Jacuzzi and sauna, helicopter pad, not to mention quarters for her eight-person crew and ten security personnel. The bridge was fully equipped with the latest marine GPS system, digital cellular communication system (encryption equipment and security devices included), as well as state-of-the-art radar and sonar systems.

At the top of the gangplank their host awaited his guests. "Welcome aboard my home at sea," Rodrigo Mantazar announced magnanimously, his arms outstretched in welcome. Instantly, a crewmember appeared and gathered up the Claypool's three pieces of luggage. "You must be parched in this heat! Allow me to serve you some refreshments. Would you follow me?"

After an hour of hors d'oeurvres, drinks, and awkward conversation, Michael decided it was time to get down to business. Politely, he suggested that Marie retire to their stateroom while he and Rodrigo discussed their current situation. Reluctantly she agreed, knowing that he owed one whopper of an explanation. She knew who their host was and more importantly, how he could afford a yacht that she guessed cost over $20,000,000.

Once alone, Rodrigo Mantazar studied his guest. "So, you require my protection?" he asked with a trace of suspicion.

Michael locked eyes with him. His fears had concerned getting to Mantazar. Now that he and Marie were safely aboard, he was calm, confident, and angry. "Señor Mantazar, I want you to understand that under other circumstances I would be doing everything within my power to bring you to justice. I appreciate your hospitality and I am humbled to admit that I need your protection for my wife but know that I am not your friend. If we live through this, I will hunt you and bring you down."

Rodrigo Mantazar stared coldly into Claypool's eyes. Neither blinked. Finally, Mantazar burst into laughter. "Señor Claypool, I appreciate your candor. If we should live through this, I will watch my back. May I suggest now that we focus on the situation at hand and hope we live to worry about the future?"

Michael raised his glass. "To a temporary alliance?"

Rodrigo grinned and raised his glass in return. "Agreed."

They spoke for over an hour, analyzing and strategizing. Finally, Mantazar rose to refill his drink. "Señor Claypool, you were right to come to me. I suggest you remain as my guest until this problem is resolved."

Claypool cursed the circumstances that had brought him to this place. "Thank you," he managed to say.

Again, Rodrigo laughed, "That must have been difficult."

For the first time in many days, Michael Claypool's face broke into a spontaneous smile. "You have no idea."

"Since we will be sharing this galleon for the near future, may I suggest that we at least pretend to be friends—for now? It will make life so much more pleasant for everyone." Rodrigo Mantazar had not met anyone in years who was willing to lock eyes with him and defy him to his face. He respected his guest. It was a shame that one day he would have to kill him.

Again, Michael grinned. "Agreed. If you would excuse me, I have work to do."

"Oh? And what would that be?"

"Explaining all this to Marie."

"Ah! Good luck, Señor. You will need it, I believe."

Chapter One

July 13, 2003
Pacific Ocean, off the South American Coast

The night was black over the waters off the Pacific coast of Colombia. Storm clouds now hid what dim light the crescent moon had offered earlier in the evening. The darkness seemed fiendishly appropriate considering the evil that had been committed that night.

Rhythmically the hull of the small naval craft struck the rolling waves as it sped across the water, heading out to sea, away from the nightmare her passengers had both inflicted and experienced.

"What the hell happened back there, Preacher?" a weary and disheartened young warrior whispered. They were the first audible words spoken since the beginning of the mission, seven hours ago. Behind them and to the south, the lights of Buena Ventura, Colombia, slowly faded into the distance.

Lieutenant Matthew 'Preacher' Pierson, U.S. Naval Special Warfare Development Group (DEVGRU), popularly known as SEAL Team Six, leaned back against the engine cover of the high speed, 24' Rigid Inflatable Boat (RIB) as it sped him and his beleaguered unit to the safety of the USS assault ship *Nassau*, which was currently cruising 60 miles off the Pacific coast of Colombia.

The whispered question snapped the Lieutenant's thoughts back to the present. He looked at the young SEAL's sweat-smeared camouflaged face, then into his eyes. In that moment, he realized he needed an answer to the question, not only for himself but also for his team. Someone would provide those answers, one way or another. "I don't know, but I sure as hell intend to find out," he finally answered.

Pierson's shirt was soaked with blood that was not his own and his mind was already playing back the events of the past hours as though recorded on video tape. He could hear the voices in his mind—calling, screaming, crying. He could still see the face of his target and the dead man's wife sobbing over him. He had killed the man. Killed? It was murder, his conscience accused. He had put two bullets into the target's head. He had only been following orders, he tried to rationalize, but to no avail. As the scene played back over and over through his mind, the only word he could comprehend was a question. Why? The question seemed to swell with urgency and rage each time he relived the scene.

Leaning lifelessly against the inflatable hull of the boat was the body of one of his men, one of his friends. His life ended two hours earlier when a single bullet struck him in the back, shattering his spine and exploding his heart. Pierson had helped to pull his lifeless body through the water for two miles to the rendezvous point where the RIB extracted his team from the water.

Two and a half hours later, the SEAL RIB was recovered by the *Nassau*. Without so much as a word to anyone, they were escorted to the aft helo deck of the assault ship where they boarded a waiting Sikorsky SH-60 Seahawk. After another hour and one-hundred-eighty nautical miles, the helicopter deposited the team on the deck of the aircraft carrier USS *Enterprise*.

Lieutenant Pierson's feet had barely hit the flight deck of the aircraft carrier when he saw Admiral James T. Bartle, PACOM (Pacific Command) Director of Operations, emerge from the superstructure of the flight deck known as the island. He would provide the answers. He was the one who had sent them on the deadly mission.

Pierson was on the verge of charging the Admiral when a strong hand gripped his shoulder and spun him around. The hand belonged to Master Chief Warren 'Pepper' Adler. Pierson's eyes were filled with anger as they met those of the closest friend he had ever known. "Remember, Lieutenant, we're SEALs. We don't need to understand the orders, just obey 'em."

Pierson tore away without a word in reply. Marching double time, he met the Admiral midway between the island and the helicopter. The men of his unit positioned themselves behind him.

"We will begin debriefing immediately. Have your men stow their gear and report to the CO's conference room. I'll take the video," the Admiral announced, referring to the mini-cam video filmed to establish the target's positive identity and confirm that the mission had indeed been completed.

"Excuse me, Sir!" Lieutenant Pierson interrupted, almost shouting. "I demand to know just what the hell this mission was all about!" he growled.

"Take that tone again with me, Lieutenant, and I'll have you..."

"Sir, we lost a good man on this mission! Now, I want to know who the hell our target was!" Pierson interrupted again, now clearly risking insubordination.

Pepper Adler again grabbed his Lieutenant's arm. "Back off, man...," he whispered in his friend's ear, only to be ignored.

"Your mission is over. Now stand down or I'll have you thrown in the brig!" Admiral Bartle ordered, scowling. Other senior officers of the carrier were now gathering at the sound of the raised voices.

"He was an American, Sir! I'll ask you one more time. Who was our target?"

His own anger now flaring, the Admiral stared coldly at the insubordinate junior officer before him. After a moment of hesitation and a deep breath, the Admiral collected himself. "Lieutenant, not another word until we're in the debriefing room." Breaking eye contact with the angry SEAL, he turned his attention to the others of the unit. "The

10

rest of you get yourselves cleaned up and be ready for debriefing in one hour. You follow me!" he ordered, stabbing his finger at Pierson.

Three minutes later Admiral Bartle and Lieutenant Pierson entered the debriefing room. Admiral Bartle ordered his aides to wait outside.

"Who was our target?" Pierson demanded.

The Admiral studied his face for a moment before answering. "Lieutenant, your mission briefing gave you all the information you needed about your targets. Target number one—Rodrigo Mantazar, renegade member of Colombia's surviving drug Cartel; target number two—José Gutierrez, Mantazar's commanding officer; and target number three—Miguel Sanchez, Mantazar's 'intelligence officer'."

"Sanchez wasn't Colombian! He was an American! He was shouting at us in English—he knew we were coming, he was trying to stop us!" Pierson exploded. "Now, who the hell was he?"

"You're already on thin ice, Lieutenant!" Bartle exploded, and then quickly calmed himself. "You signaled that all three targets had been eliminated. Your job is done. Now, get yourself cleaned up and be back here for the formal debriefing. That is all. You're dismissed." The Admiral took a step toward the door.

"Excuse me, Sir!" Pierson hissed. "Sanchez was not who you said he was and I am not leaving until you tell me why you had us kill him!"

"You're this far from the brig!" the Admiral snapped, holding his thumb and forefinger inches from Pierson's face.

"If you don't give me some answers...," Pierson stopped himself but not in time.

"Are you threatening me, Lieutenant?" the Admiral asked incredulously as he opened the door.

11

"Sir, I double-tapped him in the head right in front of his wife! Now I want to know why you sent us to take out an American?"

"You're a SEAL, Lieutenant. You're trained to kill, not ask questions," Admiral Bartle sneered contemptuously.

Anger, guilt, and grief suddenly overwhelmed him. Pierson exploded. He slammed his fist into the Admiral's face, while his right leg whipped the Admiral's feet from under him. In a split second, Pierson was straddling him, his hands clenched around Bartle's collar. "Who the hell did you send us to kill?" he hissed.

Suddenly, there were hands grabbing him, pulling him off the stunned and bloodied Admiral. Pierson turned to defend himself when someone struck him across the back of the head. He collapsed on the deck with searing pain in his head and white light blinding his eyes. He tried to order his body to move, but it refused. Vaguely he was aware of the punches and kicks that began raining down on him. Then, on the verge of unconsciousness, he heard a familiar voice.

"Next man to hit him answers to me!" the voice of Pepper Adler boomed. He had broken away from the rest of the unit and had followed Pierson and the Admiral unnoticed to the hall just around the corner from the debriefing room. He had been waiting for Pierson when the commotion began.

The Admiral's aides turned at the sound of the voice and immediately lost all enthusiasm for continuing the beating. Even if they hadn't heard of Adler's reputation, merely his size and the deadly look in his eyes would have been enough to unnerve all but the most zealous and foolish would-be opponents.

Suddenly two Marines burst into the room with their pistols drawn.

"Put those damn things away!" Adler barked. "He's not causing any more trouble."

The Admiral's aides turned their attention to their ward and helped him to his feet. With blood dripping from his shredded lower lip, Bartle looked with fury at the face of his now unconscious attacker, then turned his scornful gaze upon Adler. "That man tried to kill me!" he accused.

Adler calmly shook his head. "I doubt that, sir. If Pierson had wanted you dead, you'd be dead."

Further enraged, Bartle knelt beside Pierson, grabbing his collar and jerking his limp body from the floor. "You're going to rot in the brig, you son of a bitch!" he cursed, then dropped him mercilessly back on the deck. "Have this man shackled and placed under armed guard. If anyone tries to see him, shoot them!" he snarled to the Marines.

Pepper Adler watched helplessly as they dragged his friend away. "I won't be able to get you out of this one," he whispered.

August 25, 2003   Dam Neck, Virginia

The small café was just off General Booth Boulevard, not far from the main gate of Dam Neck Naval Air Station. The two friends stared into their cups of steaming coffee, both wrestling within themselves to discern what needed to be said and what should remain unspoken. They had exhausted pleasantries and small talk after greeting each other at the door of the Lendy's Café and waiting for their coffee to be poured. It was their first time to see each other since the deadly mission just six weeks before.

"You heard they're splitting up the team?" Pepper Adler said, breaking the silence.

"I figured they would," Pierson responded without looking up. "Any word on where you're heading?" The thought of breaking up the team he and Pepper had built was just one more reminder of the shame he had brought on himself and his team.

13

Not only had Pierson's General Court Martial been conducted in record time—due to pressure from Admiral Bartle and others in authority—but his immediate discharge was also highly irregular, given that charges against him usually carried a mandatory incarceration, not to mention that SEALs often spent up to six months of "down time" before being unleashed on the civilian world. At Admiral Bartle's insistence, Lieutenant Pierson had been prosecuted for an Article 90 crime, Assaulting or Willfully Disobeying a Superior Commissioned Officer, with aggravating circumstances: intent to kill. If convicted, the sentence during wartime could be the death penalty or anything less at the discretion of the court.

Fighting the Admiral's influence and aided by his client's pair of bronze stars, Purple Heart, and outstanding service record, Pierson's Judge Advocate General (JAG) attorney had plea-bargained for the dishonorable discharge, without time in prison. Admiral Bartle had lobbied for the maximum sentence, but he settled for the verdict, wanting to end the matter quickly.

Yet what seemed to the Admiral to be a mere slap on the wrist, to a young man like Preacher Pierson, a dishonorable discharge was a far more severe punishment than time in prison. As he had once failed and disappointed his parents and family, he had now failed the Navy, and himself.

"They're keeping me with Red Squadron. Guess I'll be breaking in a new lieutenant." Adler offered a forced smile, then quickly returned his gaze to the steam rising from his cup. "Hey Matt, I want you to know I would have come to see you in the brig, but we – the whole team – was ordered not to have any contact with you. In fact, when they announced the verdict of your trial, word came down from on high that we are supposed to report any attempt you make to contact us." Adler paused to sip his coffee. "In fact, this little meeting we're having is a direct violation of orders."

14

"Glad to see your attitude toward direct orders hasn't changed," Pierson said with a genuine smile. "Thanks for this, Pep."

Another awkward moment of silence followed until Adler finally found the words he was searching for. "You know, Sir, trying to rip the head off an admiral has got to be one of the stupidest things a SEAL has ever done, but I want you to know, in my eyes there isn't an ounce of dishonorable blood in your body. I mean that."

"Thanks, Pepper, it helps."

The story behind Warren Adler's nickname was somewhat of a legend among the members of the Naval Special Warfare Community. The legend involved a proverbial shotgun wedding and dozens of freckle-like scars on the six foot-five-inch tall sailor's buttocks. He studied his friend, trying to read his expression, his eyes. "Preacher, you gonna be alright?"

"Not till I get some answers." Pierson paused to take in a deep breath and looked away. "You know Pepper, I'm even starting to have nightmares—like some little kid! I keep seeing the faces, know what I mean? Hell, maybe Bartle doesn't know any more than we do, but I've got to find out, somehow, from someone."

"Your problem is you think too much, you always have... Sir," Pepper Adler added as an afterthought. "What's it going to change if you find out 'Sanchez' really was an American? He was a guest on the yacht of a Cartel member. Personally, I don't care if it's an American or a Colombian drug runner – a dirt bag's a dirt bag."

"Pepper, before we began to extract, I grabbed his wallet off the nightstand," Pierson said, reaching for his own. From it he withdrew a laminated identification card and handed it across the table to his friend. The extra time it had taken to grab the wallet had allowed one of Mantazar's soldiers to get off one shot – the shot that killed their teammate.

"Oh, shit...," Pepper said on his next exhale. The card had once belonged to a Michael Claypool and identified him as an employee of the U.S. State Department.

"This is what he was reaching for when I drilled him, Pepper. If he had sold out and was working for Mantazar or the Cartel, why the hell wouldn't Intel have just told us we were taking down a traitor? It's been done before..."

Adler stared long and hard at the dead man's ID. When he finally spoke, his voice was tight, controlled. "Anyone else know you've got this?"

Pierson shook his head. "No, but they know I know his name—how else do you think I was able to get off without time in the brig? Somebody does not want this investigated."

"Walk away from this one, man. Walk away and don't ever look back."

"You know I can't do that. I've got to..."

"Got to, what? Get yourself killed? Will that clear your conscience?" Adler snapped, instantly regretting the words when he saw the pain in his friend's eyes. Pierson looked away, out the window, watching the traffic on the highway.

Adler cursed at himself. He never had the gift of diplomacy. He decided to change tack. "I know what you mean about the faces, though. Sometimes, I wake up in the middle of the night, covered in sweat, afraid to shut my eyes again. Nancy tries, but she doesn't understand." He now looked up from his coffee to make eye contact with his friend. "Matt, I want you to do something for me. Whenever those faces start to haunt you, whenever that damn court martial gets you questioning yourself, I want you to remember how you saved my ass in the Philippines and remember the face of that little girl in Afghanistan that you took a round in the shoulder to save. It doesn't matter what a stinking piece of paper says or even what happened that night. You've proven yourself. You've shown what kind of heart you have."

With his eyes focus down at the table, Pierson slowly shook his head. "Thanks again, Pep. You've always been there for me. I'm gonna miss you."

Both men recognized that they were coming dangerously close to becoming emotional. "Well, somebody had to change your diapers, but you'll have to handle that yourself from now on." Pepper grinned and quickly glanced around the diner, suddenly aware that a customer at the counter had been watching them. He hadn't told his friend that the order to have no contact with Pierson had come with a warning that anyone caught breaking the order would be busted out of SEAL Team Six and possibly out of the Teams altogether.

"Hey Matt, this coffee sucks. Let's get out of here."

Pierson looked at him, knowing something wasn't right. They paid the check, left the diner and walked toward Matt's burgundy 2001 Eddie Bauer Ford Explorer. Arriving at the SUV, Matt turned to his friend, sensing their time together would be short. He knew the risk his friend was taking by meeting him at all. "Pepper, once again you've put your ass on the line for me. Thanks, I really appreciate it, but you should go. I don't want you getting in any more trouble because of me. Go easy on your next lieutenant."

"Oh, don't you worry about that. I'll be gentle with him," Pepper vowed with a purely devious grin.

"I'll pray for him!" Matt managed a laugh as he opened the driver's door and slid into the black leather seat.

"You be careful with that prayer stuff! I don't want you to turn into some militant religious zealot that me and the boys will have to deal with!"

Prior to joining the Navy, Matthew Pierson had earned a Bachelor of Arts degree in Religious Studies from the Northwest Lutheran University in Tacoma, Washington. When that particular tidbit of personal trivia was learned by his fellow Basic Underwater Demolition/SEAL (BUD/S) cadets years before, they had dubbed him with the nickname "Preacher." In fact, Pierson had once considered entering seminary and becoming a pastor in the Lutheran Church, yet those thoughts seemed a lifetime away. Though he admitted it to no one, hearing the nickname tended to stir uncomfortable feelings and memories that he preferred to leave in his past, especially now.

"Don't worry, I think I'll become a pacifist."

"Not bloody likely!" Pepper laughed as Matt started the car and shifted into reverse. Before the car could move, however, Adler reached in and grabbed Pierson's left shoulder, causing him to wince slightly as his friend's fingers dug into the year-old scars. Slipping the gear shift back into neutral, Pierson looked out the open window into his friend's face. Pepper was wearing his "game face" and making no attempt to conceal his concern.

"Hey, Matt, you remember hearing about Willy Moulitor?"

"One of the guys from Six, a few years ahead of us, right?"

"Yeah. He was court-martialed, too."

"What are you getting at?"

"He was found dead six weeks after the hearing. Throat cut."

"Are you saying that someone's gonna come after me?"

"Look, all I'm saying is that sometimes the guys who make the rules don't always let guys like you and me just walk away. Watch your back, Sir," he said, releasing his grip on his friend's shoulder.

It happened so fast that Pepper didn't see it coming. With one swift motion, Pierson had dropped his right hand to the seat, retrieved, raised, and aimed a 9mm Browning Hi Power pistol at his friend's chest. "I was just kidding about the pacifist part," Pierson said with an evil grin.

18

"You son of a bitch..., Sir!" Adler cursed, respectfully, as he let out a long breath.

"Thanks, Pep, I'll be careful," Pierson said, still grinning like a schoolboy. With that, he stepped on the gas and popped the clutch, sending the SUV backward, the tires squealing. Smoothly shifting into first, the tires again screeched as he shot forward, pulling out of the parking lot and darting across the highway, heading north.

At the age of 27, Pierson was on his own, a chapter in his life now closed. Someday he would consider returning to his home and his family but there were other matters that needed his attention. First, he had to find answers. And then...retribution? He would cross that bridge when he came to it.

Only then would he consider returning home to search for a new career and a new life. Maybe then the faces that haunted his nights wouldn't follow him.

Chapter Two

September 27, 2003 Bogotá, Colombia

Two months had passed since the last rebel bombing in Bogotá and the streets were bustling with activity. The downtown streets were filled with a curious combination of ancient smoke-belching vehicles, buses coming in from the country filled with peasant farmers carrying their produce to market, bicycles, pedestrians, and an occasional luxury vehicle. The chorus of vehicular horns played the melody of a city that endures – drug lords and rebels, corruption and poverty, tragedy and grief. The presence of tourists in the midst of the throng of locals gave testimony to the resilience of life and the short-lived memory of people whose primary concern in life is simply survival.

Moving his way along the crowded sidewalks, Matthew Pierson scanned the street in front of him, his eyes taking in details – people, vehicles, police, the bank across the street, the store to his left, the restaurant at the end of the block. He was confident no one was following him; there was no reason to, yet. Even if someone was interested in his activities, they would have had a difficult time keeping up with him.

His shaggy, sandy-blonde hair, khaki utility pants, loose fitting linen shirt, hiking boots, and camera bag made him barely recognizable as the dishonorably discharged ex-SEAL. After his discharge from the Navy, Pierson had spent three weeks setting up his new life. A modest apartment in Newark, New Jersey, and a security job at one of Manhattan's newest and most elite nightclubs, The After Market, a club founded by the heir of a telecom fortune and his former BUD/S classmate. He won the position by putting two former bouncers in the hospital. He worked at the club for three weeks and then, after some expensive arrangements with the manager of the club, he disappeared.

Traveling from New York to Singapore using an authentic, though false U.S. passport, he then traveled from Singapore to Sydney, Australia, using an Australian passport and the identity of Jonathan Dunham, a freelance photojournalist with press credentials from the Melbourne Gazette. From Sydney, he flew to Mexico City and from there to Bogotá, arriving the evening before, exhausted from one week of steady travel.

Walking felt good, loosening the tension in his unexercised muscles. He moved with purpose, as one familiar with the city though he had never been to Bogotá before. The major avenues, the general layout of the city, and the route to his destination had been memorized from the international map software loaded on the laptop that he carried in his backpack. Though he could have taken a taxi or even public transportation, he chose to walk, giving his mind and senses a chance to take in the city, to feel its pulse and to analyze its overt security measures.

As he expected, the ominous presence of heavily armed police officers on virtually every corner of downtown Bogotá diminished as he moved further from the wealth and power of the central city and into the working-class neighborhoods. High walls guarded every house, with jagged pieces of broken glass mortared onto the top to discourage intruders. Every four blocks or so he passed small, family-owned *Tiendes*, which sold water, soda, and non-perishables to their neighborhood. In the three miles of his walk, he passed three Catholic Churches whose grandeur stood in stark contrast to the poverty of the neighborhoods around them. On one street corner, over a hundred people stood patiently in line to receive the services offered at a medical clinic sponsored by an American evangelical mission organization.

21

Three more blocks and the counterfeit photojournalist arrived at his destination. A small mission church sponsored by the Lutheran Church of Finland stood halfway up the steep hill, surrounded by small houses and shacks that needed no walls for security. The occupants of these homes had nothing to steal. These people, the countless poor of Colombia, were the people that the Finnish missionaries had come to serve and live out the gospel of God's love.

Pierson knocked on the weathered double doors of the church, noting the peeling paint and rotten wood. When no one answered, he walked around the side of the building, peering over the fence that enclosed a small courtyard behind the church. An old, stooped Colombian woman was there, tending the garden that belonged to the missionary and his family.

"Excuse me, please," he called in intentionally poor Spanish. "Could you tell me where I could find Pastor Luakkannan?" Though Pierson spoke Spanish fluently, as well as German, he had learned that his language skills could often be best used when concealed.

The woman answered slowly out of respect for the attempt the stranger had made to use her native language. "He is in the house, just behind the garden," she answered, moving toward the gate and inviting the visitor into the garden. "I will bring him to you," she said.

Moments later, Pastor Mikko Luakkannan entered the garden, staring hard at the stranger and making no attempt to conceal his suspicions. As an outspoken activist on behalf of the poor of Bogotá, he and his mission had been harassed, surveyed, and even threatened by local drug dealers, Catholic priests, and paramilitary branches of the Colombian government. He had lived with his family in the same house in the poor outskirts of Bogotá for six years – two of his children had been born within those same walls – and for the last two years the Finnish Lutheran Church had

22

been pleading with him to leave Bogotá, believing that the dangers had grown to unacceptable levels. Yet Pastor Luakkannan and his wife truly invested their lives to work for justice and mercy for the poor and stubbornly refused.

"What can I do for you?" he asked in English, assuming his visitor to be an American.

"Goo' day," Pierson said, extending his hand. "I'm John Dunham with the Melbourne Gazette. I've come to do a story on your mission here. Would it be possible to 'ave a bit of a talk with you and some of the people your mission is helping?"

"We have telephones here in Bogotá. If you wanted an interview, you could have called and made a proper appointment," the missionary answered, unveiling further his suspicions.

Recognizing that his cover and the questions he needed to ask would never escape the pastor's intuition, Pierson changed tactics and decided to gamble. "All right, Pastor, no games. I cannot tell you who I am, but I am here to investigate the murder of an American who worked out of the U.S. Embassy here in Bogotá and in Cali. He was murdered back in July. His name was Michael Claypool."

The pastor, though described by friends and foes alike as wise as a serpent, looked confused. "What possibly would I know about a murder – his or anyone's?"

"Look, Pastor Luakkannan, I don't expect you to know who did it or why. What I expect you do know is the political terrain in Colombia these days. Your reputation is that you, perhaps more than any foreigner in Columbia, know the people. I need information, a place to start. What factions are warring in the cartel? Who has been making the power moves lately?"

The missionary stared intensely at his uninvited visitor. "Who do you work for?" he finally asked.

Pierson knew Luakkannan would sense a lie. "I'm working for myself, that's why I need what you know to get started."

Luakkannan nodded. "I remember reading about the man you are talking about. The papers said he died in a terrible auto accident in the mountains outside of Buena Ventura. I remember no mention of murder."

Pierson's mind flashed back to that dark night only months ago. "It was murder."

"So, are you here for vengeance? Was he a relative of yours? A friend?"

Pierson looked to the ground, the familiar current of guilt, shame, and anger swirling through his heart. "I killed him," Pierson said, his voice barely audible. "I want to know why."

September 29, 2003 Cali, Colombia

The villa belonging to Helena Estabar stood perched atop a series of cliffs in the hills south of Cali. With its beige stucco walls and terracotta tile roof, the mansion had the appearance of a Spanish castle of centuries ago. Indeed, it was the modern equivalent to a fortress of old, though its armaments were state of the art. The security detail was comprised of fifteen men commanded by a loyal soldier who once guarded Helena's late father. The rest were the most loyal men money could buy, and Helena paid them handsomely.

Two of these men met Pierson at the main gate of the villa. He had parked the old Volkswagen he had purchased to the side of the gate, deciding to walk from the gate to the mansion, leaving his only means of escape outside the reinforced steel gate. If this visit didn't go well, he wanted the car on the free side of the walled compound. The two

24

guards checked his identification, frisked him professionally head to foot, and then radioed to the main house for final clearance. The radio crackled, and the two motioned for their "guest" to proceed toward the main house, each guard assuming strategic positions on his flanks. As they made their way up the driveway, Pierson reflected on the proficiency of Helena Estabar's security that he had just observed. He hoped the meeting would go well.

Helena met him at the wide open, eight-foot-high, double mahogany front doors of the mansion. At the age of forty-seven she was strikingly beautiful. She could easily have passed for thirty without a line on her face or any sign of gray in her auburn hair. Her green eyes were alive with curiosity and suspicion.

"Welcome, Mr. Dunham – if that is your real name. Before I invite you in and extend to you my hospitality, I want to inform you that you will not leave my villa alive unless I am satisfied with our conversation. I have given my men orders to kill you at my command. So, here are the rules for our discussion. I do not need to know your real name – I will respect your wishes to remain anonymous to me. Yet, I will insist that you answer whatever other questions I ask and I would strongly suggest that your answers be truthful. My men are very experienced in extracting the truth from liars. If your answers satisfy me, you will be free to ask your questions. My answers, if I choose to offer them, will also be honest. Are you understanding me, Mr. Dunham?"

"Perfectly," Pierson answered, again hoping that the conversation would go well.

Helena guided him through the mansion with the grace that would be extended to an old, trusted friend. She clearly had no fear of him; she was in her castle and she was in control. She could afford to be gracious. After a ten minute tour of the "public" areas of the house, they were seated on the patio which overlooked the large swimming pool and beyond to the valley below.

25

"So, Mr. Dunham, you are not really an Australian journalist, are you?" she asked, already knowing the answer.

"No." She waited for him to continue but he simply met her gaze. "Your rules, remember?" he finally said.

Her eyes flashed with anger, yet a smile appeared on her face. "Yes, my rules. You said on the phone that you wanted to speak to me about the death of my ex-husband. What do you know about him?"

"I know who he was, what he did, and most importantly, how he died."

Helena stared at him indifferently, though the memory of her ex-husband still brought pain to her heart. Though they had divorced, which was virtually unheard of in the predominantly Catholic nation of Colombia—and particularly among the wives of the Cartel members—she had never hated him; she simply could not put up with his "habits." Her father's own fortune and the influence of his political connections had allowed her the luxury of divorce. Still, when news of Rodrigo's murder reached her, she had wept bitterly and vowed vengeance on those who had killed him.

"Anyone who knows how to read a newspaper can tell you how he died," she snapped.

"Newspapers don't always get the facts straight."

"And you know the 'facts'?"

"Some of them."

"How do you know?"

Pierson knew the conversation would come to this point. His answer would either earn him a bullet in the back of the head or the answers he was seeking. "I was there," he said flatly, his eyes locked with hers.

At the motions of her wrist one of her guards jammed the muzzle of an automatic pistol into the back of Pierson's head. "You killed my husband?" she demanded with fury in her eyes.

"No, but I was part of the team that did. We had three targets. I eliminated the third, Michael Claypool, a member of the U.S. State Department assigned to Colombia. I know why we were sent to take out your husband. I want to know what his connection was to Michael Claypool. I came to you because I believe you might have some answers."

"You're an American. A soldier, yes? Your government sent you to kill my husband, that is what you are telling me?"

Pierson held up his finger, "Rule number one. I've told you as much as I am going to about myself." He heard the hammer of a pistol being pulled back into firing position.

Helena stared at him for what seemed an eternity. Finally, she waved her hand dismissively and the pistol was withdrawn from his head, the hammer lowered to a safe position. "So, you think you know why you were sent to murder my husband?"

"No offense, ma'am, but he was a drug dealer."

She reached across the table and struck his face. Pierson didn't flinch. The guard stepped in, leveling his weapon at Pierson's head.

"Yes, he was a 'drug dealer' according to you Americans. But tell me, why him? Why Rodrigo Mantazar, and not Felipe Chavez, or Silvano Guzman, or Antonio Ramirez? There are many members of the Cartel who sleep very peacefully in their beds with the blessing of your government!" she accused. Her intelligent, dangerous eyes studied him, analyzing, drawing conclusions in her own mind. "Now I see. You are here because you think that maybe you killed an innocent man, this Michael Claypool? You want me to give you information so you can do what? Appease your guilty conscience? Assure yourself that this man was also a drug dealer and deserved to die? How pathetic!" She spat out the words.

Pierson winced at the words as though he had been struck. Involuntarily, he turned his eyes away. "My

27

conscience is mine to live and die with. You want to know who was behind your husband's killing. I want to know if the man I killed was innocent. That about sums it up."

She leaned forward in her chair, bringing her face closer to his, her own emotions confused. Should she hate this man and have him killed? She could not have pity on him. His guilt was a sign of weakness and disgrace to a soldier. Yet there was something... perhaps she could use him. She wanted vengeance for her ex-husband.

"And suppose this man you killed was 'innocent'... what will you do then?"

Pierson returned her gaze. "I don't know," he said honestly.

"Will you kill the people who sent you on your mission?"

"Maybe," he answered with ice in his eyes.

Helena Estabar reappraised the soldier. Yes, he knows what it is like to kill. Yes, she concluded to herself, he will kill again. Slowly she began to smile, her eyes flashing a signal to the security guard standing next to Pierson. The guard's gun moved.

Pierson caught the glance and attacked. From his seated position, he seized the guard's gun hand with both of his own, using the guard's weight to pull himself up. Pivoting to his left, he rose from the chair, twisting the gun hand away from himself and sharply downward. Instinctively, the guard focused his attention on freeing his hand to use the weapon he held. It was a common mistake, and it cost him. With his left hand still clamped like a vise on the guard's wrist, Pierson withdrew his right hand and stabbed his fingers into the guard's throat, using a technique known as a spear hand. Suddenly unable to breathe, the guard's grip on the pistol loosened momentarily and Pierson wrenched the weapon from his hand, and in one quick, smooth motion, spun around the table, and brought the barrel of the pistol to Helena's forehead.

"Tell them to drop their weapons!" he ordered. Four other guards had appeared instantly at the disturbance, their weapons locked on Pierson. "They can take me but there's no way I'll miss taking you with me!" The guards hesitated, nervously adjusting their grip on their weapons, looking to their employer and to each other for some signal.

A man with a silver streak in his black hair calmly entered the room and walked purposefully toward Pierson, a pistol in his hand, though he did not raise it. "You're a dead man," he said calmly.

Helena looked into Pierson's eyes and laughed. "Put your weapons away," she commanded her security detail, a full smile on her face. Pierson kept the pistol touching her forehead, his eyes meeting her smile with deadly malice. "Put them away, now! I really believe this man would kill me," she repeated, now obviously amused, obviously satisfied with the test she had just staged.

Slowly her security force obeyed, except for the man with the silver-streaked hair. "Stephan, I was testing this man's resolve. Put your gun away. I wish to discuss business with Mr. Dunham."

Reluctantly, the man who had protected Helena her entire life obeyed the order, though his eyes reinforced his earlier message to Pierson. "Pepé, help him!" he ordered, pointing to the guard who was on his knees clutching his throat as his face began to turn blue.

"Mr. Dunham, or whatever your name is, you, too, can lower your weapon. My men will not harm you until I give them permission."

Pierson didn't move. He hated being manipulated. He hated knowing how easily he could have pulled the trigger.

"I have a proposal for you, that will allow you to find your answers and more importantly, to walk out of here alive."

"I'm listening," Pierson answered, without removing the weapon from her forehead. Though she was still smiling, her eyes betrayed a slight hint of fear. That was good, Pierson thought, because he would have killed her.

October 2, 2003   Cali, Colombia

The tool shed at the northeast corner of Helena Estabar's estate reeked of blood, sweat, and urine. The heat of the day, combined with the bodily fluids that had been spilled, created an odor as horrible as the violence that had been committed within the walls over the past twelve hours. Estabar's security men had been interrogating their prisoner in the most inhumane ways they could imagine. Now they were taking a break, allowing themselves the chance to rest from their "work" and breathe fresh air. They were also allowing their victim time to reflect on the next round of torture that awaited him, if he continued to be stubborn.

Sitting on the ground, his back leaning against the wall of the shack, Pierson listened to the sounds of moaning coming from the other side of the wall. He closed his eyes tightly, as if that would shut out the sounds. Helena Estabar had given him the information he needed to understand why Michael Claypool had been murdered. "Representatives" of the government of the United States of America had negotiated an unofficial treaty with members of the Colombian drug Cartel, allowing a certain quota of cocaine to be brought into the United States, thus regulating the supply of the drug, stabilizing the street price, and therefore reducing drug-related violence. The Cartel would be able to sleep better knowing that their profits, though somewhat curtailed, were secure and that the American military and the Drug Enforcement Agency personnel would be hunting the drug lords that refused to sign the treaty, not them. The U.S. received critical intelligence on the other drug lords allowing the seizure of major drug shipments and high-profile arrests and of course, those U.S. officials involved in the treaty were handsomely compensated.

Pierson's fears had been confirmed; Michael Claypool was innocent. Rodrigo Mantazar had refused to sign on to the treaty and became a threat, not only to the Cartel, but also to the Americans who had brokered the treaty. Claypool had learned enough of the plot to get scared, really scared and had sought refuge with Mantazar, believing that the drug lord could provide protection until the American conspirators could be brought to justice. Pierson's team had been sent in not to take down a drug lord, but to remove the competition for their drug-dealing allies and to eliminate a potential security breach. The scenario was clear. What he lacked now were the names of those involved in the conspiracy. Pierson already suspected one name: Admiral James Bartle. He wanted the rest.

Again, the now familiar combination of anger and guilt surged within him, each emotion battling for control of his actions. Springing to his feet, he moved quickly around the corner and opened the door to the shed, instantly having to suppress his gag reflex at the stench. For the first time since they had abducted the senior member of the U.S. Embassy staff, Pierson looked at him closely, lying in a pool of his own blood and urine. For a moment, he was moved with pity and shame that he was involved in doing this to another human being. But as he looked at the battered and mutilated body of Richard Maier, the memories of that horrible night began to play through his mind again as they had done a thousand times before. Claypool lying dead, unarmed, with two bullets in his head, his wife kneeling beside him, sobbing, pleading, screaming. The face of his dead teammate, the fight with Admiral Bartle, the court martial, the guilt, the shame; all these flashing through his mind in a matter of seconds.

His anger began to gain control. Reaching down, he grabbed the barely conscious man by the hair, jerking his

31

head off the floor. Maier moaned and brought his arms up to protect his head from the blows that he expected would come.

"You haven't met me, yet," Pierson said with his perfected German accent. If Maier survived his trip to Helena Estabar's villa, the presence of a German interrogator in Colombia would throw a curve at the investigators. Lifting him from the floor by the hair, Pierson threw Maier onto the wooden workbench and roughly turned him so that he lay across the table on his back with his head hanging over the edge. Maier tried to struggle, but his body had no strength left to resist. Pierson grabbed a length of rope from the wall and secured him to the table. Maier's eyes were filled with fear and horror as what little consciousness remained in him contemplated the unknown suffering that was about to come.

"Answer my questions and your suffering will stop and you will live, do you understand?" Pierson said with the same German accent. "Who ordered Michael Claypool's murder?"

Richard Maier stared up at Pierson with defiance in his eyes.

"Who authorized the treaty with the Cartel?"

This time Maier made an effort to speak, cursing his new torturer.

"Very well," Pierson said, stepping away from the workbench to retrieve the tools he needed. When he returned, he placed a towel over his victim's nose and mouth, but carefully left his eyes uncovered. Seeing the panic growing in Maier's eyes, he said, "This will not hurt nearly as much as what those other brutes have done to you. Unfortunately, this will only stop when you answer my questions, or when you die." Again, he stepped away.

Maier tried desperately to turn his head, to see what was coming, to somehow brace himself. He heard the sound of water running, splattering on the floor. He saw the hose. Suddenly he began to drown.

Twenty minutes after he had entered the shack, Pierson emerged from within having learned what he needed to know. As he walked across the manicured lawn toward the mansion belonging to Helena Estabar, he became strangely aware that the shadow that had seemed to hover over his soul since that horrible night had deepened to total darkness. Somehow, he sensed in his soul that he had just crossed some forbidden line. Where it would lead, he did not know. Could he ever cross back over? He quickly pushed the thoughts from his mind. He could not allow distractions, least of all from his conscience.

Chapter Three

December 17, 2003   Tegucigalpa, Honduras

The Embassy of the United States of America in Tegucigalpa, Honduras, like U.S. embassies around the world, had completed a security overhaul in response to the embassy bombings in Kenya and Tanzania in the spring of 1998. The perimeter wall of the compound had been heightened and reinforced; concrete barriers had been erected in front of the main entrance and surrounding the perimeter of the compound to prevent vehicular bombs from being parked one square block in any direction. Additional video surveillance systems and electronic fencing made the compound a fortress that would repel virtually any terrorist attacks. While inside its perimeter, Embassy personnel and their families were safer than on the streets of most American cities. Of course, once outside the compound, security depended entirely on lightly armed security details and the infinitely corruptible Tegucigalpa Police Force.

General Alexander Lehman's chauffeured Mercedes passed through the main gate of the embassy at 11:43 hours after a brief meeting with the newly appointed U.S. Ambassador to Honduras, Julio Gustavo. As the Commanding Officer of the U.S. Army Forces in Central America, Lehman frequented the embassies of each Central American country to keep fully abreast of the current political stability in each country that he was assigned to "protect." Prior to the meeting this morning, he had never met the new ambassador, knowing him only by reputation which did little to quiet the slight nervousness he felt before the meeting. He had been assured that Ambassador Gustavo would not interfere with Lehman's operations, yet one could never be sure until the issues could be addressed face to face.

The General exhaled softly as the Mercedes pulled into traffic. Slow-moving cars and hundreds of Honduran pedestrians and bicyclists filled the streets. It took twenty minutes to travel through the narrow streets of Tegucigalpa toward the restaurant El Paradiso. Arriving in front of the restaurant, Lehman's security escorts exited the vehicle and immediately surveyed the street for any sign of danger.

It happened so fast there was no time to react. A cyclist, approaching from behind the sedan, suddenly withdrew a pistol from beneath his faded denim jacket, swiftly bringing it to bear on the nearest escort and fired one shot, the bullet striking the Corporal squarely between the eyes. On other side of the Mercedes, the second escort reached for his service pistol at his hip. It hadn't cleared the holster when the cyclist's second bullet struck him in the chest, the impact knocking him off his feet.

From inside the vehicle, Lehman hesitated for a moment, deciding whether to lunge and close the driver's side rear door that the first escort had left open or to draw his own pistol. He reached for his pistol and shouted to the driver, "Go! Go! Go!" But there was nowhere for the driver to go. The stoplight at the corner ahead was red and other cars had closed him in. Realizing that they were trapped, the driver reached for his own pistol.

Neither occupant had time to raise their weapons. The cyclist crashed his bike into the open door. Reaching in with the pistol, he fired into the back of the driver's head, then swung the pistol, bringing it to bear on the general's forehead, not two feet away. "Drop it on the seat!" the attacker hissed.

Lehman's eyes bore furiously into his attacker's, and what he saw in those eyes convinced the old soldier to comply. He dropped the pistol on the seat.

The light at the corner turned green and traffic began to move. "Climb over and drive. Now!"

Knowing from his eyes that his assailant would not hesitate to kill him, he obeyed, pushing aside the body of the driver. Approaching sirens could be heard in the distance and somewhere unseen a police officer was frantically blowing his whistle.

Two hours later, General Lehman's Mercedes was found abandoned in a narrow alley in a much poorer neighborhood of Tegucigalpa. Three days later, his mutilated body was found in the dump on the southeast side of the city. On his bloodied chest was a scrap of paper, held in place by a framing nail that had been driven into his sternum. Written on it were the Hebrew letters, גֹּאֵל הַדָּם which spelled the words, *Go-el Hadam.* Investigators soon learned its meaning: Avenger of Blood.

January 28, 2004   London, England

Dressed as a civilian in a tailored Armani suit, Admiral James Bartle stood behind the ornate, armored glass front doors of London's exclusive Wiltshire Hotel. Newly appointed to the Joint Chiefs of Staff, he was in London for a top-secret meeting with his NATO naval counterparts. His sudden promotion had sparked curiosity and frustration in the naval command, Bartle having been chosen ahead of several others in line for the position. He was flanked on both sides by his personal aides, who in truth were his security detail. Like their charge, they were dressed in formal civilian wear though their military demeanor could not be concealed by the clothes. Each man stood ramrod straight, their eyes soberly scanning the sidewalk and street below for any potential threat.

This was his first official visit to England in his current position. Few, apart from the other Chiefs, the White

House, and a handful of high-ranking Senators, knew he was there. Far fewer knew the reason for his trip.

Through the thick glass doors his aides surveyed the street outside. On the corner, half a block up the street, a constable was dutifully observing the foot traffic on his beat. Down the street, another constable appeared to be giving directions to a lost pedestrian. Across the street, two men in casual attire sat in a dark colored sedan, their heads slowly turning left to right, scanning the street. The man in the passenger seat momentarily locked eyes with one of Bartle's aides and gave a subtle nod. The aide, in turn nodded to the driver of the limousine that was parked on the street just five steps and a sidewalk away. Slowly, cautiously, the driver stepped out the vehicle and opened the rear door with one hand, the other hand hidden under his suit coat.

Swiftly the aides pushed the heavy hotel doors open and stepped through, their eyes scanning the building across the street, the windows, the rooftop. They exchanged a quick glance. "It's clear, Admiral," said the one on the right side.

Admiral Bartle stepped through the doors as his aides moved into position to become his human shield. The single bullet struck the Admiral just behind his right temple as he cleared the third step. The Admiral was dead before his aides even heard the shot.

As the crime scene investigators scoured the scene for clues, a young detective from Scotland Yard found the clue that sent off a shock wave that was felt at the highest levels of the United States government. In a planter on the south side of the front entrance of the hotel was a small, rolled up piece of paper, about the size and shape of a cigarette. Quite sure it was nothing more than garbage— probably that some American had left—the detective picked it up and unrolled it. It contained just two words: *Go-el Hadam*.

January 29, 2004   Washington, D.C. The Pentagon

"Commander Denzer to see you, sir," the secretary of Admiral Lewis Mattison, Director of Naval Intelligence, announced over the intercom. The attractive young Ensign raised her eyes from the phone in time to catch Commander Joshua Denzer's appreciative gaze. She smiled bashfully, waiting for the Admiral's reply. "Send him in," she heard over the intercom, the voice breaking the awkward moment. "The Admiral will see you now," she informed the commander, offering him another smile.

Admiral Mattison cared little for formalities and true to his reputation, he got straight to business, even neglecting to return the commander's salute, much less offering a greeting. "You said you found something on Admiral Bartle's assassination. Let's have it."

Denzer cleared his throat. "Sir, I noticed something in Admiral Bartle's career jacket that I thought might be worth following up on. On July 13, 2003, an officer with SEAL Team Six, Matthew Pierson, attacked the Admiral during a debriefing session on board the Enterprise." Denzer reached across the Admiral's desk and handed him a copy of the file. "The SEAL was court-martialed on charges of assaulting an officer with intent to kill. He was convicted and given a dishonorable discharge without time in military prison or anything else. Judging from the dates, somebody must have fast-tracked the hearing. It was over and done by the end of August, right before Admiral Bartle was selected for the Joint Chiefs of Staff." Denzer paused to turn pages in the file, catching sight of Admiral Mattison's impatient look. "What's interesting about this SEAL is that prior to signing up, he earned a Bachelor's Degree in Religious Studies from Northwest Lutheran College in Tacoma, Washington. Admiral, he studied a year of Greek and one semester of Hebrew."

"*Go-el*," Admiral Mattison said softly.

"CIA's been trying to connect the attacks to Israel or some militant Jewish group, but Israel would never bite the hand that feeds them and what Jewish group would have something against high-ranking American officers? It doesn't make any sense. But if the assassin happened to simply have studied Hebrew. . ." He paused again and flipped through the pages of his copy of the report. "Here's one more thing. Prior to General Lehman's abduction and murder last December, a senior attaché from our embassy in Bogotá was abducted and tortured, then released. Turned out he was CIA and the guy who broke him was an Anglo who spoke German as well as Spanish. The fact that he spoke German has confused the hell out of the investigators down there. Turns out this SEAL is fluent in German and Spanish – was an exchange student in Germany for one year in high school and did missionary building projects in Mexico while in high school and college through his church. It's nothing solid, but there sure are a lot of coincidences."

"What you've got on Pierson is thin, but it's better than anything I've heard anyone else come up with. Do some digging and find out where he's been and what he's been doing since his discharge. Consult back with me when you come up with anything."

"Sir, I, uh, already took the initiative to start tracking him down. After his discharge, he moved up to Newark, New Jersey, and set himself up in a small apartment in the north end. Apparently, he got a job as a security guard at a nightclub in Manhattan after putting two of the bouncers in the hospital. Yesterday, I sent a pair of my men up there to see what they could turn up. One of my men interviewed the club's manager, who claimed that Pierson hadn't missed a shift since he started at the beginning of September. But when they asked around the bar, they found out that Pierson had disappeared for about two weeks around the end of September and didn't show up for his shift ten days ago. He hasn't been seen since."

"So, the manager is covering for him? What's his connection to Pierson?"

"Nothing that we've been able to find yet."

"Well find out – and find Pierson!" Mattison snapped, the scenario unfolding before him making him even more irritable. Calming himself slightly, he added, "Good work, Commander. I want reports every step of the way."

"And when we find him?"

Mattison's eyes locked onto his. "Bring him in or take him out if you can't."

Denzer nodded, paused, and shifted his feet uncomfortably, knowing the implication of the question he had to ask next. "Should I send a report to the other agencies?" Denzer asked hesitantly, referring to the FBI, CIA, and newly formed Department of Homeland Security.

The Admiral had already been calculating the repercussions on the Navy, the SEAL Teams, and the morale of the country itself if it reached the public that one of their own elite soldiers had gone rogue and was attacking his own country. Mattison leaned forward across his desk, stabbing his finger at him. "Commander, I want you to bury that information and bury the records of that SEAL and the whole damned court-martial. If it turns out that Pierson is innocent, then nothing's lost. If we get something solid on him, we can always turn the information over or take him out ourselves. But I want you to understand this up front, Commander. No matter what, that SEAL will not become an embarrassment to the Navy. Am I making myself clear?"

"Perfectly, sir," Denzer replied, having anticipated the answer.

"All right, dismissed – and be sure to notify me immediately if anything turns up."

As the Commander exited the office, Admiral Mattison thumbed through the file of Lieutenant Matthew Pierson. Two bronze stars, a purple heart. "He must have been a hell of a SEAL at one time," he mused. A fleeting thought ran through his mind: "I wonder what Bartle did to piss him off?" thinking of the court-martial. But that was immaterial. What mattered now was finding out if the SEAL had turned – and stopping him, one way or another.

February 23, 2004   Berlin, Germany

With the reunification of Germany, the world witnessed the rebirth of Berlin's grand Hotel Adlon. On August 23, 1997, the president of the Federal Republic of Germany opened the new Hotel Adlon, a Kempinski Hotel and resort, directly opposite the Brandenburg Gate, reviving the high standards of luxury and service that had made the original hotel so famous. Once offering luxurious, temporary housing to political, economic, and military leaders through two world wars and the Cold War, the rebuilt Hotel Adlon now offered its services to a new generation of the powerful and influential.

The concierge of Hotel Adlon steeled himself when he saw the expression on the face of one of the guests of his hotel who had been waiting for him for all of 45 seconds – an unforgivable crime in the mind of the guest. *"Guten tag, mein Herr,"* he greeted politely.

"Ms. Rackl's limousine was supposed to be here five minutes ago!" senior aide to the Deputy U.S Secretary of Foreign Affairs snapped, not even bothering to use his fluent German.

"I am so sorry. I will find out where it is immediately." The concierge turned aside and picked up the telephone.

The aide leaned against the counter, his body language conveying his impatience. He looked over his shoulder, across the lobby to the sitting room where Deputy

U.S. Secretary of Foreign Affairs, Anita Rackl, sat waiting on a divan, her two-person security detail casually standing nearby, relaxed while still inside the protection of the security systems of the hotel.

There were relatively few of the patrons of the hotel present in the lobby at that time of the afternoon. Still there were enough people strolling through or reading papers in the sitting room that no one noticed the woman who emerged cautiously from one of the main elevators of the hotel. Struggling to control her nerves, she made her way across the lobby to the Concierge Desk. Stepping up to the desk beside the sharply dressed man, she set her briefcase on the ground, next to the case belonging to the other guest.

"Excuse me, please," she called in German to the concierge who was still on the phone. Both the concierge himself and the sharply dressed man looked at her with annoyance, quickly drawing conclusions about her character and occupation. The concierge raised his chin at her as if to give her permission to speak.

"I'm just returning my room key," she said.

"Keys are returned at the registration desk," the concierge answered curtly, turning his back on her and his attention to the telephone.

Reaching down, she retrieved the briefcase that was identical to her own, leaving hers in its place. Her nerves made her forget to stop at the registration desk, taking a path straight toward the front doors of the hotel.

Inside the security room of the hotel, the security supervisor was faithfully watching the bank of video surveillance monitors from where he could view literally every hall and area of the resort at his discretion. The monitor that was displaying the portion of the foyer that contained the Concierge Desk caught his attention. He noticed the woman walking away from the desk. She was in a hurry. He watched her look back over her shoulder. She was nervous. He noticed the briefcase in her hand; he quickly appraised her appearance. Quite possibly a prostitute, but not of the level of refinement the guests of the Hotel Adlon usually preferred. The briefcase seemed out of place. The instincts he had learned to trust as a police officer prior to his injury warned him that something was very wrong. He grabbed the microphone that instantly connected him to his security team. "Unit One, intercept the woman heading to the main entrance."

Still holding the telephone, the concierge noticed that the limousine he was inquiring about was just pulling up to the entrance of the Hotel. "*Mein Herr*, your limousine is here," the concierge said, relieved that the annoying patron would be leaving his desk.

Had the aide not been so frustrated at the tardiness of the limousine, he might have noticed that the briefcase he now carried weighed one pound more than his own. He walked briskly across to the sitting room. Out of the corner of his eye, he noticed two security guards moving swiftly toward the entrance of the hotel. Through the glass doors he saw the limousine waiting at the curb, the chauffeur standing alongside, waiting to open the door for his passengers when they arrived.

*   *   *   *   *   *   *

From his vantage point between the columns of the Brandenburg Gate, the man now known to the world as *Go-el* watched the main entrance of the Hotel Adlon. The doorman opened the massive, armored glass doors and a woman walked out on to the sidewalk. She held in her hand a briefcase that from the distance appeared to be identical to the one he had given to her. *Go-el* hoped she had picked up the right case when, and if, she had made the switch.

He had chosen her with as much care as the limited time for his current operation allowed. He had found her in Berlin's red light district. She was a prostitute and a heroin addict. She was desperate enough that she was willing to do anything – anything for money to buy the drug that had become her life. When he met her she was dirty; her clothes that of a common street whore and her body smelled of cheap perfume and sweat. Yet beneath the layers of makeup, he saw that when cleaned up, she would be somewhat attractive. Not to the standards of the professional women who serviced their clients at the Hotel Adlon, but close enough for his purposes. He had purchased her, brought her to his room in a hotel in another part of Berlin, bathed her and dressed her in more appropriate clothing. The next day, he gave her a key to a room at the Hotel Adlon, along with the briefcase, her instructions, 1,000 Euros, and the promise of 2,000 more when she brought him the stolen briefcase. In her mind, all she was doing was stealing a briefcase.

*   *   *   *   *   *   *

"The limousine is here, Ms. Rackl," the aide announced, rejoining his party in the sitting room. Anita Rackl rose and walked beside her aide with one of her bodyguards moving into position ahead of her, the other taking up the rear guard.

Suddenly, two security guards from the hotel rushed out through the main doors of the hotel and descended on the suspicious woman, each grabbing an arm and virtually lifting her off her feet. Though the assassin was too far to see the details of her expression, he saw enough to recognize the panic, her head turning left and right looking for help, looking for him.

*   *   *   *   *   *   *

The Deputy U.S. Secretary of Foreign Affairs, Anita Rackl, and her three escorts were in the lobby, adjacent to the registration desk. It was 16:37 and a small group of

44

tourists, eight in all, had just entered the Hotel Adlon, pausing just inside the doors to take in the opulent splendor of the foyer. Checking into the hotel at the registration desk were three businessmen – two from England, one American. In the sitting room, a Japanese couple sat waiting for the rest of their tour group to arrive for the dinner event. Several individual guests were passing through, either coming from or returning to their rooms. Three employees were at the registration desk—the concierge, two bellhops, one custodian. . .

*   *   *   *   *   *   *

Seeing the prostitute struggle, he knew his original plan was no longer an option. The plan had been that Rackl's aide would carry the four pounds of plastic explosive into the limousine. He would then have followed the limousine from a safe distance until it was on the Autobahn, away from congested traffic and collateral damage.

Any moment, security personnel within the Hotel would stop the Deputy Secretary of Foreign Affairs and her party. They would be smart enough not to open the briefcase. The bomb disposal unit would be called, his operation a failure. He waited a precious moment, hoping the security guards would wrestle the whore back into the lobby of the hotel, into the killing radius of the bomb. But the woman continued to struggle in panic. Reaching his hand into his jacket pocket, he took hold of the radio detonator and depressed the button.

From his vantage point 150 meters away, the assassin felt the concussion of the blast strike his body with amazing force, causing him to stumble backward. There was no great orange fireball as in Hollywood thrillers, simply a bright flash and a massive blast, the effect of the bomb's sheer power exploding out in every direction. The armored doors of the hotel were literally blown off their hinges, the waiting

45

limousine flipped on its side. The damage to the unprotected interior of the Hotel Adlon was severe. *Go-el* reflected on the collateral damage inside. It would complicate things, of that he was sure.

His eyes darted back to the prostitute and the two security guards. They were rolling on the ground, dazed. Their eardrums had been blown by the concussion of the blast. Instinctively, the assassin began moving toward them, reaching into his jacket and taking hold of his silenced pistol. He could not let her live. She had seen him. She knew two of his current aliases. Sirens could already be heard approaching. Policemen on foot rushed from their surrounding patrol routes in the Brandenburg Plaza and from Wilhelm Strasse.

Go-el stopped in his tracks, not 50 meters from the woman, the witness, as the first officer reached her, followed immediately by two other uniformed officers. He cursed, knowing that there was nothing he could do now. It was time to leave Germany.

*   *   *   *   *   *   *

Three hours later, as the German counter terrorism experts searched the shattered lobby of the Hotel Adlon, a young criminologist in his first year with the Krisenreaktionskrafte (KRK, Crisis Reaction Force) discovered a small piece of metal, the size and shape of military dog tags, embedded in the mahogany veneer of what used to be the Concierge Desk. On it were stamped four familiar letters: GO-EL

Chapter Four

It had gone off perfectly, yet Stanley Harverson was reminded that perfection did not exist in this world as he stared at the smoldering cigarette in the ashtray. Fifteen minutes, no more, yet it might as well have been fifteen hours or even days for all it mattered now. His prey had vanished, leaving behind nothing more than a dying cigarette.

Once a linebacker for the fighting Irish of Notre Dame, now at the age of fifty-three, Harverson held a PhD in Political Science, a Masters in Criminology, and was currently the Chief of the Counter-Terrorist Department for the Western Europe Sector of the Central Intelligence Agency. Watching the smoke rise from the ash tray, Harverson found himself wishing for the days when his enemies were as easy to identify as the color of their jerseys.

He was seated at a small table in the kitchen of a one bedroom apartment on the fourth floor of a building that provided housing to students attending the University of Heidelberg. Most of the students residing in this building were enrolled in the Theology Department, as was the tenant that Harverson and members of Germany's KRK had come to apprehend.

"The Theology Department, of all things," Harverson reflected again. It was a strange place to come hunting for an international assassin.

"*Herr* Harverson," a voice called from across the room, startling him back to attention. Looking away from the cigarette and across the kitchen, Harverson immediately recognized the man who had called his name.

Harverson excused his way around two crime scene technicians who were hopelessly searching for clues that would shed light on the hunted terrorist. He met the man who had called his name in the doorway between the kitchen and living room.

"Ah, *Herr* Harverson, the CIA appears to be once again, uh, how do you say it? 'Chasing its tail,' yes?" the old man said with accented sarcasm.

"He was here, Helmut, not fifteen minutes ago! He knew we were coming; there's no other way he could have escaped," Harverson snapped back defensively, the truth of his German counterpart's words hitting their mark. "He even had time to leave us his cigarette as a souvenir."

"I would wager that you will find no traces of saliva on your souvenir for a DNA sample. It is another message, another little trick in his game," Helmut Osterhagen announced as though the fact had already been proven. "You will find very little here, I am afraid."

As much as Harverson resented the smugness of the aged Intelligence Officer, his own intuition had reached the same conclusion. "Maybe we will get lucky with the road blocks or at the railroad station. Have your units been deployed?"

"Of course, but you know they will produce nothing, not with the skills of this one," he said, motioning to the smoldering cigarette as though it represented the man who ignited it.

"We've lost him," Harverson said with a fatalism that he instantly regretted.

Slowly a thin, devious smile began to appear on the wiry old man's face. An intelligence officer himself since the end of the Second World War (though some speculate that his training and the early years of his career actually began during the war with the Gestapo), he was now ninety-one and a living legend in the intelligence community. Opportunity had presented itself for a comfortable retirement years ago, but Helmut Osterhagen could no more retire than renounce his Aryan roots and there was no protest from anyone in the German Intelligence Service. Even at his age his brilliant analytical mind, his years of experience and contacts, and his career record assured his position as long as he desired to keep it.

"*Herr* Osterhagen, I know how you enjoy it when we Americans stumble, but I don't find anything even remotely amusing about this! In the last two months, he's abducted, tortured, and murdered one of our generals in Honduras, assassinated Admiral Bartle in London—who happened to be on the Joint Chiefs of Staff—and just yesterday he blew the hell out one of your fancy resorts right in Berlin!" Harverson snapped.

Still with the thin smile on his aged face, Osterhagen motioned with his hand for the American to follow. "Come with me, *bitte*," he politely ordered.

In the living room, the assault team members from the Crisis Reaction Force were quickly securing their weapons and packing their assault gear in order to disappear until their services were needed elsewhere. Working their way past the remainder of the crime team and the German police officers, Harverson and the veteran agent left the apartment and entered the fragile-looking elevator at the end of the hall. Once inside, Harverson faced his colleague.

"All right, what do you want?" the American demanded.

Holding a finger to his lips, Osterhagen answered, "Not here," and began shuffling his aged legs toward a neighborhood park across the street.

Eventually arriving at a vacant bench, the old man motioned for the American to sit, then slowly lowered himself beside him. The thin smile was still firmly fixed on his narrow face.

"My friend, your prey may not remain as elusive as you fear." Osterhagen paused, whether to collect his thoughts or for dramatic effect, Harverson could not tell, nor did he care.

"Get to the point, Osterhagen," Harverson snapped impatiently.

The old man's eyes flashed with irritation. He was about to deliver a gift to his colleague and the American's impatience was annoying. "*Herr* Harverson, allowing that little prostitute to live was never part of *Go-el's* plan. From her we learned two of his aliases. One led nowhere as you know. The other led us here, to an apartment belonging to the University of Heidelberg, occupied by a student named Christoph Speilmann, a student enrolled in the Department of Theology. As you said yourself, only fifteen minutes earlier, we might have had him.

"You're not telling me anything I don't already know," Harverson interrupted impatiently.

Osterhagen offered a patronizing smile. "No, I suppose I am not but perhaps we should begin to put the clues we have learned together. Your assassin leaves a curious calling card with each of his attacks. *Go-el*, the Hebrew word referring to a family relation's responsibility to provide for their less fortunate relatives – marrying the widow of a deceased brother—or avenging the death of a family member. '*Go-el Hadam*' specifies the responsibility to avenge murder. This assassin – or his benefactor – is declaring that each of these attacks is personal, related in some way to a crime committed against someone close to him or to those who hired him. Find what ties the attacks together and you will be close to your prey."

Harverson grunted his agreement and more effectively concealed his impatience.

"Now, this prostitute survives the bombing at the Hotel Adlon and we learn from her that she had been given a key to a room reserved by a fictitious German businessman, Dieter Schwartz, a name that led us nowhere and reveals nothing about your assassin. But it was the name

50

he used at the other, less reputable hotel, that led us here. He never intended for the prostitute to live, to lead us back to that hotel. Christoph Speilmann, theology student from Heidelberg—that was an elaborately developed alias. No doubt our discovering it will at least complicate his plans." The old man paused again, drawing a handkerchief and coughing productively into it, then returning it to the chest pocket of his sport coat.

"Now then, *Herr* Harverson, what are the languages a theologian must know? German, of course, for much of the Reformation's writing came from Germany, but the foundational languages are Latin, Greek, Aramaic, and Hebrew— *Go-el, Herr* Harverson. Your assassin has an unhealthy interest in theology and so we learn that *Go-el* is more than a message, it reveals the background and motive of the killer."

Harverson held up his hand to interrupt. "*Herr* Osterhagen, putting these pieces together helps us get a picture of the man we are hunting, but so far you haven't told me anything that will get me any closer to putting him in a body bag! I've known you long enough to know that you know something I don't, so spill it!"

Osterhagen chuckled. "Yes, yes. There is one other thing. It was a great mistake not to kill the prostitute. While she was in the Hotel Berliner Haus with Herr Speilmann, she remembered hearing him make a telephone call – on a cell phone, of course. It surprised her to hear him speaking English – speaking so clearly that she says he sounded just like an American, though his German had convinced her that he was a native of our country, from Bavaria, she thought. I am afraid the girl never progressed far enough in school to learn English, but the little dear remembered one detail that will set you on your chase. Lufthansa to New York, she remembers hearing him say."

Harverson's face flushed, his pulse quickened. "You're saying he's heading to New York?"

The old man shrugged. "Either he has finished his work here in Europe and will continue in your country, or his quest has been fulfilled, his revenge exacted and he will disappear, perhaps even returning to the life of a theologian, a rabbi, a priest?"

His mind racing, already formulating a strategy in his mind, Harverson swallowed his pride and asked for his esteemed colleague's opinion, something moments ago he would never have considered. "*Herr* Osterhagen, you've given us a place to start, but if he gets past us in New York, where do we look for him? There are many religions and denominations in our country, each with its own seminaries and schools. Where would you start?"

Osterhagen had anticipated the question. "To attempt an investigation so broad and diverse would waste time which, if his work is not finished, you do not have. The State Church here in Germany is called the Evangelical Christian Church of Germany, founded more than five hundred years ago by Martin Luther. The Lutherans, as they are called in your country, have a close partnership with the Church here in Germany. Students frequently travel to study in one country or the other. Though it is only a... how do you say... a hunch, a guess, I would start there, with the Lutherans."

Harverson shook his head. "That's as good a guess as any but why would an international terrorist use a Church organization as a cover? Personal motives, religious beliefs or not, what benefit could it provide? I'm sorry, *Herr* Osterhagen, but this guy is a professional and there is a practical reason for everything he does. A theology student? I can't see it."

"Think, *Herr* Harverson!" the German said. "Every denomination has churches, schools, retreat centers, conferences throughout its country if not throughout the world. Priests and pastors, Christian people who value and work for peace? Some are political but how many are anarchists, let alone terrorists? In our country, we have theology students of every age. A phantom could infiltrate and move freely, attending conferences and lectures, visiting churches and retreats, trusted by his peers, always above suspicion." Osterhagen pulled himself off the park bench as quickly as his arthritic legs could lift him. "*Herr* Harverson, my friend, I think our phantom will like the Lutherans. Follow it through and see where it leads. Maybe you'll catch more than your tail someday," he said with a thin, mocking smile.

Though appreciative of the information Osterhagen had provided, Harverson was still in no mood for levity. "Yeah, that's right, if he's heading to New York, he's not your problem anymore, is he?"

The smile suddenly vanished from the old man's face. "Do not forget that this *Go-el* killed eight Germans yesterday on German soil. He is my problem and if he ever comes back to Germany, I will catch him and put a bullet in his head myself!"

With that, the old man rose unsteadily, turned and walked away, in the opposite direction from where they had come.

"Hiding within the Church," Stan thought to himself. He recalled what he knew of Osterhagen, his record, his reputation. His instincts had served him well for many years. "Maybe the guy is a genius."

February 24, 2004   North of Nuremberg

"Zurich National Bank," said the receptionist of the second largest bank in the world.

"I would like to verify a deposit to account number seven-three-three-eight-five-two-nine-four. The amount of the deposit is 250,000 pounds sterling."

"Just one moment, please."

On the other end of the line, a man waited in a phone booth inside a restaurant just off the *Autobahn*, north of Nuremberg. The restaurant was busy this Tuesday morning as commuters and tourists stopped for breakfast and coffee. A waitress wove her way between the tables, trying to keep up with the demands of customers. A group of students were eating toast and marmalade while studying their books. A couple of motorcyclists in black leathers came through the doors and stood nearby, waiting to be seated.

Jeffrey Atkins, at least that was the name printed on his current passport, casually, carefully, surveyed each person, his alert eyes taking in every detail, searching for anything abnormal, any sign of danger.

"Yes, sir, the deposit has been made. Is there anything else I can help you with?"

"No, thank you, you've been most helpful. Good day to you, miss," he said with a flawless upper-class British accent.

Hanging up the phone, he surveyed the restaurant one more time. Satisfied, he pushed open the heavy glass door and stepped out toward the parking lot. A gust of cold wind caused him to shudder momentarily. The sensation of cold seemed strangely appropriate he thought. Though no one could have seen it, he smiled darkly inside.

Across the parking lot a white Volkswagen Jetta was now parked next to the green BMW 320i, which he had driven from Heidelberg. Seeing the keys in the ignition of the Jetta, he entered the car, started it, and backed out of the parking place. Within minutes, he was heading west toward Frankfurt, to the International Airport to be specific.

It was time to go back to school.

Winter was especially severe this year. Snow was piled along the streets of Washington D.C. and an icy wind whistled through the bare trees. In a normal year, there would have been several mid-winter thaws to look forward to but when the snow began to fall last November, the cold had settled in to stay. Few things had been normal this year.

With battles of words raging between the political parties over the continuing war with Iraq and the threat of continued terrorist attacks, with a national economy that was struggling to emerge from recession, it was not only the weather in the nation's capital that was cold and gloomy. It seemed that the weather only reflected or perhaps magnified, the mood of the city.

Yet for all the gloom of the city, the atmosphere in the back-corner booth of the restaurant Equis was more sullen still. The three occupants of the booth were intensely engaged in a conversation which an observer could correctly have concluded involved matters of life and death.

Henry Morganson, the current Deputy Director of Operations for the Central Intelligence Agency (DDO), and Frank Rucker, the Director of the Federal Bureau of Investigation, sat beside each other and across the table from Stan Harverson, who had arrived in Washington only two hours earlier. Though only 15:00 in D.C., Harverson's body was still convinced that the time was really 01:00 and it was – at least in Germany. Weary from the travel and near sleepless week that preceded it, Harverson now recounted to his superiors the essence of the events of the previous week, focusing specifically on his conversation with Helmut Osterhagen.

"I've never actually met Osterhagen, but I know him by reputation," Morganson said between drags from his cigarette. "So, he thinks our man is coming to play in our yard and he's somehow hiding within the Lutheran Church.

More good news," he added, glancing sideways at his FBI counter-part.

What should have been the beginning of his "golden years" at the age of fifty-seven, Hank Morganson was a heart attack waiting to happen, at least that's what his coworkers believed. At least fifty pounds overweight, he suffered from the combined stresses of a thankless, 24-hour-a-day job and the knowledge that he would probably never be able to finish his distinguished career at the CIA.

It was widely known throughout "the Family" that it wouldn't be long before he was given the axe. Though the fault was not his, Morganson had been saddled with the blame for the botched information that had sent a DELTA force assault team searching for the Bosnian war criminal Radivan Brosverich to the home of an embarrassingly innocent Bosnian citizen who happened to be a delegate to the Peace Council. Thankfully, no one had been hurt in the raid, but someone would have to pay for the embarrassment and Henry Morganson was the man. He would have thought it unfair had he not seen it happen to so many others during the course of his career.

Now, on what could well be one of his last days with the CIA, Morganson was sitting in for the Director of Operations of the CIA, who was ironically briefing the President on the latest information from human resources in Baghdad. Yet as close to burnout as he may have been, Henry could feel the wheels of his keen mind begin to turn as he listened to Stan's report.

"After we raided the apartment in Heidelberg, he just disappeared, which isn't hard to do when no one knows who you are or what you look like. Still, between the Germans and our people, we should've come up with something if he was still in Germany. I think he flew the coop."

"So, you're saying he's already here in the States?" the FBI man demanded.

"All I'm saying is that he vanished in Germany and our best and only lead is that he was discussing with someone a Lufthansa flight to New York. I think we must proceed as though he is already here. Europe will continue the hunt across the pond. I'll keep a few people on it so as not to tip our hand, but I say we focus our efforts here in the States, starting with every passenger on every Lufthansa flight into New York. Maybe we'll get lucky and won't need plan B."

"Plan B? Let's hear it," Morganson said with a trace of resignation in his voice.

Stan cleared his throat. It was time to stick out his neck. Downing a shot of water, Harverson looked squarely in the eyes of his superior. "Let's begin with what we know. First, we have the word *Go-el* and Christoph Speilmann's interest in theology. Like Osterhagen said, this is something personal. The victims had something in common. We need to find out what.

"Second, we can't afford to assume that he's finished his work and returned home to disappear into a normal life. My gut tells me we haven't seen the last of *Go-el* and the attacks are getting bolder and more destructive." He paused just long enough for another swallow of water. "The third point is the one that disturbs me the most. Our *Go-el* has got good information. Too good. In all three attacks, he's getting inside information on us, on the Germans, and probably the Brits too. Think about it. No one was supposed to know about Admiral Bartle's meeting with the Brits; it was supposed to be top secret. Only a handful of people knew about Rackl's trip to Berlin or its purpose. We must conclude that he's got a source either from within the Agency, in the White House, or among the top military brass. My guess is that it's one of the first two options. The first two attacks were on military personnel. Maybe I'm too naive but I just don't think a military person would be involved with that kind of attack on their own, but I guess when you're talking about treason and terrorism, things don't always make sense, do they?"

Frank Rucker nodded his head and softly grunted his agreement—at least on that last point. He had been listening intently to Stan's report and conclusions while using his fork to pick at the remnants of the poached salmon he had ordered an hour earlier.

With a law degree from Harvard to launch him into his career as a prosecuting attorney, Frank had discovered a gift and passion for investigation. After five years working for the Chicago District Attorney's office, Frank had applied to the FBI academy. Early achievements and three front-page successful stings on organized crime had won Frank the dubious identity as the FBI's golden boy. The athletic, blonde-haired and blue-eyed family man was now, only thirty-six, the youngest person ever to be promoted to the FBI's top job. In marked contrast to the man sitting next to him, Rucker's career seemed firmly set in the fast lane and it didn't appear that there was anything foreseeable to slow him down.

"Assuming that your three assumptions are correct, we are still left to hunt a man who has no identity, no description, and no predictable modus operandi. We have no idea who he works for, what his goals or motives are – other than revenge—or what his next target is likely to be. We can assume he has highly placed sources of information but we don't know where or who. Not much to go on, Stan," Rucker replied without enthusiasm.

"Look, Frank, I am well aware of how much we don't know about this guy. I have been hunting him across the pond since Bartle was hit. Besides, you're the Bureau's 'golden boy', I thought you'd enjoy a little challenge," Stan countered.

Morganson now lifted his gaze from the glass of Coke he held in his hand, which seemed to have captivated his attention. "Let's stick to business. Going back to your

58

plan B…" he locked eyes with Stan, gesturing with his hand for him to get on with it.

It was the moment Harverson had been waiting for. He took one more gulp of water and then leaned forward across the table, supporting himself on his elbows, ready to unveil his plan. "To begin, we need a Task Force made up of counter-terrorist types from both the CIA and FBI. I've got names to recommend for the CIA element of the team. I figure the team will need a total of eight people. Any more and we run the risk of drawing the attention of whoever's leaking information. The Task Force begins with basic investigative work, something I'm sure you're familiar with, Frank," he jabbed.

"The Department of Homeland Security is set up to do exactly what you're asking. Why not turn it over to them and let them run it," Morganson challenged.

"Two reasons: First, Homeland Security is brand new, still organizing and suffering from severe tunnel vision when it comes to threats from al-Qaida. The second reason goes back to security. Homeland Security has too many new people that I don't know. Whoever is on the task force, I want to know with absolute confidence that I can trust them. The Task Force itself and the circle of those who know about it, needs to be small and tight."

Perturbed, Rucker interrupted. "Stan, you know as well as I do that the CIA is absolutely prohibited from operating on US soil. Even if I were to allow it, we still need a place to start and at least so far, you haven't given us anything."

Accepting the rebuke, Stan continued. "After talking to Osterhagen, I went back and double-checked his information about Christoph Speilmann. Speilmann was registered as a student in the theology department of the Heidelberg University. He had just transferred to Heidelberg for the winter quarter from a university in northern Germany where no one had ever heard of him. His classes had only

59

been in session for one week before he disappeared, so no one really knew him. Descriptions were so general they could describe thousands."

Rucker shook his head. "No one from the apartment building could give anything?" he exclaimed to no one in particular. "Do these theology students live with their heads buried so far in their books that they can't even describe him?"

"We did get a few general descriptions. From his enrollment forms his supposed age is 25. Light brown hair, brown-green eyes, somewhere between 173 and 190 centimeters—between 5'8" and 6'1" that is. One neighbor noticed that he exercised a lot. One of his female classmates said she thought he was kind of attractive. The problem is that the description provided by the clerk at the Berliner Haus where Speilmann planned the bombing estimated Speilmann to be in his fifties, with black hair streaked with gray, and dark eyes. He walked with a slight limp and one of his shoulders was slumped. In short, whatever physical descriptions we were able to get conflict and don't help us."

"Tinted contacts and hair color, some discreetly applied makeup and a person can become someone altogether different," Morganson interjected again. "We do that kind of thing from time to time in the Agency," Henry gave a quick wink and smirk to his FBI counter-part. "You're right, Stan, we can't rely on any of the physical descriptions. This *Go-el* does seem to be a phantom or at least a chameleon."

"But over there they think he's German, right?" Rucker concluded.

"Just because of his fluency and northern accent. If he's as good as I think, he'll be able to adopt many accents if he knows the language," Stan countered.

"My guess is that he's an American, a seriously disgruntled American," Morganson interjected. "Foreign terrorist groups target Americans in general. If Osterhagen

60

is right, *Go-el* has a personal grudge against very specific Americans."

"So, where does that leave us?" Rucker demanded, impatiently.

"Frank, it may not be much, but start putting the pieces together. You're supposed to be good at that, remember?" Harverson knew he could get away with the jab. After all, he didn't work for Rucker. "We have evidence that he's on his way here. We know in Germany he established an elaborate cover as a theology student. The Lutheran Church is the closest denomination to the State Church in Germany. Osterhagen thinks we should start there. As much as I hate to admit it, I agree with him. I think we start with the Lutherans."

"I was afraid that's what you were getting to," Rucker grimaced. "So, you want to put together a task force, a mix of Bureau and spooks, to investigate students attending Lutheran schools and seminaries? Do you have any idea what would hit the fan if it got out that the government of the United States of America was running a covert, widespread investigation of Christian theology students?"

"First of all, Frank, we're not going to investigate all Lutheran theology students. European and American universities always have student exchange programs. Seminaries do the same and Lutherans have their roots in Germany. We start by putting together a list of all foreign students studying at American Lutheran Seminaries. We'll focus on them first. Then we'll run a check on any American students who have traveled or studied in Europe this last year. When we narrow down a list of suspects, we slip in operatives from the Task Force to the suspect seminaries. Their cover will be the same as *Go-el's*, if we're on the right track."

Frank stared thoughtfully across the table into Harverson's eyes. He had worked very hard to get where he was today. If an investigation like this went bad, the ramifications would be. . . he didn't want to think about it. He searched his mind for another plan, any other plan. Yet as much as he hated to admit it, the spook across the table from him was right. If they handled the investigation well, it was the best chance of tracking down this assassin, hopefully before he could strike again.

"That's the plan," Stan offered, breaking the tense silence. He knew that it was now completely out of his hands. The DDO and the FBI Director would have to make the decisions from here. He lowered his eyes to his own plate and waited.

"Who do you want on the Task Force from our side?" Morganson asked. Though his stress-lined face displayed no emotion at all, inside Henry began to feel a twinge of excitement, something he hadn't experienced for a long time. Perhaps this would be his last operation but he was going to make it work. One last chance to redeem the mediocre career that epitomized his life. He would make it work. He would get this so called phantom.

"Will Siefeldt, from our counter-terrorism department is a good man and he's offered me advice more than once on how to hunt this guy. He should head up our end of things. Patricia Knodell is one of the best researchers we've got, and she can go undercover if needed. Jed Michaelson is a computer genius and Tim Parnel can do leg work and slip in and out of anywhere, if you know what I mean. They'll work well together."

"One problem, Stan. Will's a good man but I want you to head up our end of things. You're the one who's been tracking him, you're the one with the contacts in Europe," Morganson decided.

Stan shook his head vehemently. "Henry, I can't, I have five other investigations I'm running! I can't just..."

Morganson held up his hand to halt Harverson's protest. "Assign someone else from your department to take over for you until this is finished. This is your plan, remember? See it through." And if it fails, you'll take the rap, not me, he thought to himself. "All right, Frank, it's up to you. You gonna play ball with us on this one or not?"

Another thoughtful moment passed without words. Finally, Frank let out a long breath. "Yeah, I'm in," he said with a distinct lack of enthusiasm. Something like this, he thought again, could ruin his whole career. "I want to lay down some ground rules from the start. Henry, I agree with you. Stan, I want you on the Task Force but this is going to be an FBI investigation from the get-go. Domestic stuff is our concern. I'll get Austin Torvick to head up the team. He's one of my top guys in counter-terrorism. I'll check personnel and try to dig up three guys who can pass for college grads."

"Don't worry about their ages so much. From what I've checked out, the average age at most seminaries these days is about thirty-five and you better make sure that at least one of those agents is a woman. Over fifty percent of seminarians are female these days. We wouldn't want our Task Force to be behind the times, would we?" Harverson pointed out.

"Women in seminary?" Henry asked, genuinely astonished.

"Jeez, Henry, how long has it been since you've been to a church?" Stan asked with a slight grin. He hadn't been in a church himself for… he didn't remember.

Henry thought about the question for a moment. It was…well, long enough that he couldn't remember. Maybe that's a little too long, Henry offered a repentant thought.

"All right, it's set. Stan, be at my office by 08:00 tomorrow and we'll start assembling the team. Henry, run it past your boss, but don't give him too much. If this guy does have someone on the inside, we want to keep this as quiet as possible." With that, he slid easily out of the booth and stood next to the table. "By the way, thanks for lunch. I'll let you two fight for the check."

Stan and Henry looked at each other and shrugged. One way or another, Uncle Sam would be buying this lunch.

Chapter Five

The fifty-acre estate belonging to Arthur Collin Rossford commanded a breathtaking view of the rocky New Hampshire coast and the mighty Atlantic Ocean. The main house, though significantly smaller, was designed to reflect the architecture of England's legendary Buckingham Palace. Designed by a French architect, the building had originally been built in France, only to be immediately disassembled and shipped piece by piece across the Atlantic, where it was reassembled in its present location in 1893. Commanding a majestic view of the powerful Atlantic Ocean, the stone-walled miniature palace was the crowning jewel of the estate.

Two hundred yards north stood a much smaller, 7,000 square foot guest house, where Rachel, Arthur Rossford's thirty-five-year-old daughter, currently resided with her husband, Samuel, and six-year-old daughter Annalisa.

The third primary structure of the estate was located approximately a quarter mile off Highway One. The gatehouse itself was made of precision cut stone, reflecting the other buildings of the estate. Being the entrance to the estate, those wishing to visit the New England palace would have to drive through the gatehouse archway. In keeping with its historic purpose, the gatehouse was home to the security force that protected the estate. A handful of other structures were scattered around the estate, including garages, a green house, a workshop, and a groundskeeper's residence.

Rossford had purchased the estate twelve years before as an eleven-million-dollar gift to his wife on her seventieth birthday. The couple enjoyed only two of their fifty-five years of marriage on the estate. Without warning, his beloved Anne was diagnosed with cancer and six months later she was dead. For all his power, wealth, and influence with those who held high offices in the Federal government, there had been nothing for him to do but simply hold her, love her, and watch her slowly die.

The estate had become for him a tomb filled with short memories and unfulfilled dreams until his daughter Rachel and her family moved into the guesthouse a year ago. The sound of a little girl's laughter echoing off the marble floor and walls brought joy again into the mansion and a little life back into the heart of the eighty-two-year-old multi-millionaire.

Arthur Rossford was sitting in his home study at his beautiful, hand-made, rosewood desk, trying to force his mind to concentrate on his monthly task of analyzing the month-end reports of the fourteen corporations that he either owned completely, or was the majority stockholder. The report he held in his hand was still the first one. He had been holding it for forty-five minutes, unable to stay focused, unconcerned with the explanations accompanying the $ 2.3 million one month loss. In ordinary times, the entire monthly chore took only two to three hours, but now, today, he wondered if he would even finish one.

Tossing down the report, pushing his chair away from the desk and turning to face the windows, Rossford let out a quiet sigh as he took in the view. The large, manicured lawn stretched out to the edge of the cliffs and beyond them, the Atlantic Ocean stretched out toward the horizon. White caps dotted the ocean as the strong northeastern wind swept over the waters, reaching the shore and whipping through the trees and shrubbery of his vast backyard. At any other time the beauty of the scene would have brought him at least a sense of satisfaction, but not since Monday, not since Berlin.

66

Arthur had been visiting the corporate offices of Val Tech Enterprises, a company like most in the technology industry that had been all but decimated by the recession of 2000 and continued to struggle for survival. Rossford had spent the morning meeting with the Val Tech Board of Directors and their attorneys to formalize plans for his impending purchase of the company. It was during a tour of the facility in the afternoon that he heard the news. The executives – he could not even remember their names now – were showing him the employee lounge where a 72-inch LED television showing Headline News was positioned in the corner of the room with several employees gathered around, listening attentively. The volume had already been adjusted to be heard over the din of other conversations.

"Among the dead is Anita Rackl, the Deputy U.S. Secretary of Foreign Affairs, who had been working in Berlin this week to secure the support of the German Chancellor for a new United Nations resolution backing the use of force against Saddam Hussein. Three members of Secretary Rackl's staff were also killed in the explosion, bringing the total casualties from this bombing to thirteen dead, twenty-three wounded. . ."

Rossford remembered the wave of nausea that came over him; the feeble excuses he made to dismiss himself from the remainder of the tour. Still, two days later, all he could do was shake his head and ask himself how it could have happened. An act of terrorism; it was nothing more and nothing less.

Official reports voiced suspicions that the attack may have been carried out by al-Qaida, or perhaps by Iraqi agents trying to frustrate the determined U.S. efforts to bring down Saddam Hussein's regime. But Arthur Rossford knew who was behind the bombing and why. His money had paid for it.

The awareness of what he had done haunted him. Though he had never been a religious man, he now found himself praying, begging God to forgive him for what he had done, for the people he had killed. Even Anita Rackl, the one who had been the target—the one who, two days ago, Rossford had believed deserved death—now even her death plagued his conscience. Who had appointed him to be her judge, jury, and executioner? And now, his quest for vengeance had claimed the lives of twelve innocent people and one who only God had the right to judge.

Spinning impulsively in his chair, pulling himself back up to his desk, Rossford took hold of the phone and dialed a memorized number. Though the phone itself was an antique from the 1920's made of wood and brass, the electronics within were state of the art, including line scanning, scrambling, and electronic surveillance jamming equipment. Despite its appearance, the telephone in Rossford's hand was as secure as those used by the President of the United States.

He listened as the phone rang, drumming his fingers on the desk impatiently. Rossford was always a man to make swift, decisive decisions. This one had taken him two days to make but now that it was settled in his mind, it was time for action. He was about to hang up after the eighth ring when suddenly his call was answered.

"Yeah?" the voice answered. The receiver of the call knew that only four other people knew this specific private number.

"Rossford here."

"Hey, old buddy," Massachusetts Senator Glen Barnell answered hesitantly, aware that his aides were working around him and were within earshot. "What can I do for you?"

"I'm pulling the plug on it, Glen. We've got to stop."

The Senator took the phone away from his head and held it to his chest for a moment while he sighed and collected his thoughts. Somehow, he had known that the call would come. "Art, is this about Berlin?"

"You're damn right it is!" Rossford snapped, sensing a note of patronization in the voice on the other end of the line.

"Listen, Art, I'm as upset about it as you are, but. . ."

"But nothing, Glen! Call the others and set up a meeting before the end of the week. Tell Seabrook to have his man stand down. Pay him whatever it takes to get him to disappear. We'll figure the rest out when we meet."

"Listen, Art, wait..." Barnell tried to protest, only to have his objection answered by a loud click.

Rossford had slammed the receiver down into its cradle. Making a decision, taking a positive step toward resolution at least eased the guilt, yet he feared in his heart that it would never really leave him. He raised his head at the sound of his granddaughter's voice, calling for him from the hall outside his office. Another bit of comfort he thought as he rose from his desk, walked to the double mahogany doors and opened them, catching Annalisa in his arms as she jumped to him.

March 19, 2004   Minneapolis, Minnesota

Sitting alone at his desk in the cubicle that was his office in the *Go-el* Task Force Headquarters located on the third floor of a 1960's era girder and glass office complex near downtown Minneapolis, Stan Harverson rested his head in his hands and rubbed his temples with his fingers to ward off the approaching headache.

Having learned that Minnesota was considered the heart of "Lutherland," the Task Force had decided to set up

69

its headquarters in the Twin Cities, conveniently close to the largest Lutheran seminary in North America.

Just less than two weeks old, the *Go-el* Task Force, or its sarcastically dubbed nickname, "Operation Snipe Hunt," was quickly turning into a mild nightmare. Ironically, Stan had to chuckle at himself that he had expected anything less. The team consisted of eight people, four from the ranks of the CIA, chosen not so much for their compatibility as for their individual expertise, and four from the FBI, also chosen to fill the anticipated, predetermined needs of the group.

Had he taken time to think it through beforehand, he knew that he shouldn't be surprised by the result he was now experiencing. The rivalry between "Spooks" and "Feebs" aside, the personality clashes were magnified by the fact that these highly-trained, highly-motivated professionals had been chosen for a task that to this point, was based on speculation and a theory.

In the thirteen days since the Task Force had been authorized, the team had been assembled, briefed, and established their operating headquarters. Not only did Minneapolis house the largest Lutheran theological seminary in the States, but also the state of Minnesota itself had the highest concentration of Lutherans. The fear of *Go-el's* sources of information from the highest levels of the military and intelligence communities made it necessary for the Task Force to work independently from their parent agencies, accountable only to Frank Rucker from the FBI and Henry Morganson from the CIA.

Stan reflected on the composition of the team. Besides himself there were three others from the CIA. Tim Parnel and Jed Michaelson were two field agents who were opposite in personality yet close friends after having worked together on projects in several undesirable corners of the globe. Parnel should have been an actor; good looking, physically fit, charming, and able to adapt to virtually any cover role that was required of him. He had the grace and

70

skill of a cat burglar and he would be the first to go in undercover if the investigation ever developed enough of a lead to warrant it.

His partner in crime (literally, at times, in their line of work), Jed Michaelson, was overweight and out of shape (Stan wondered how he had ever passed the physical requirements at the Farm), cynical, and sometimes even hostile. He was a slob, irreverent, and deeply sarcastic. But he was a brilliant analyst and a computer hacker who could rival any in the world. Stan often wondered whether the CIA academy, or what was referred to as "the Farm," had simply dropped the physical requirements considering his special gifts.

Then there was Pat Knodell. She and Stan had worked together on assignments going back to the end of the Cold War. She was a researcher. What knowledge and information she didn't already carry in her head, she knew how to find. Time and again she had saved the lives of agents in the field by her thoroughness. Over the years, they had become close friends, and at this point, being able to work with her again was the only bright point of the Task Force for him.

If the investigation was simply up to the team he had assembled from the CIA, Stan would have breathed easier. It was working with unknowns from the FBI that troubled him.

Austin Torvick was the Task Force leader, due to Frank Rucker's insistence that the Task Force be controlled by the FBI. Though ten years younger than Harverson, Austin Torvick, at forty-seven, could have passed for sixty. His hair was already completely grey, and his face creased by the years of hard work and hard smoking. To say that Austin took his work to heart would be an understatement. Having worked in the FBI's Domestic Counter-Terrorism Department since the late 1980's, his job confronted him daily with the horror of what human beings are capable of doing to one another. The unending task of fighting terrorism had entered his soul. Austin's lean frame carried a man with a mission in life.

From Torvick's reputation and their acquaintance so far on the task force, Stan liked what he saw. The only problem was authority. Already it was becoming apparent that in this group of eight, there was one too many chiefs to lead the Indians. Naturally, Stan's people turned to him for orders while those from the bureau turned to Torvick. It was a tricky tightrope walk to guide the Task Force, yet not undermine Torvick's authority.

Susan Belcourt was thirty-seven years old and an eleven-year veteran with the Bureau. Her record was impressive – seven years in the FBI's New York office on the Organized Crime Unit, where she had spent a total of two years undercover on various cases. She served three years in Chicago adding another high-profile sting to her resume. Most recently she had been assigned as an agent liaison with the newly formed Department of Homeland Security, which gave her unique access to information from the Defense Intelligence Agencies, the DEA, ATF, and the National Security Agency.

Physically, Belcourt had the body of a disciplined runner and a lean, weathered face that gave her a rugged beauty that projected strength. Of all the members of the task force, she had the street smarts to educate the Task Force in the delicacies of undercover work. She was an asset.

The other two members from the Bureau, Bill Kampo and Brenda LeToure, were Harverson's greatest source of concern. Both were young and relatively inexperienced; Kampo with three years in the FBI and LeToure with only one. Torvick had chosen them for three reasons: At twenty-nine and twenty-seven, their ages allowed them to fit the profile of many seminary students; both were currently in between assignments and were easily transferred without much notice in their offices, but chiefly they were brought on because of their background in the Lutheran Church. Kampo was a Lutheran pastor's kid, raised in the church and knew Lutheran church culture thoroughly. LeToure was raised by Lutheran parents and attended Concordia, a Lutheran college in Moorhead, Minnesota, before going on to law school and then to the FBI academy.

LeToure seemed sharp and he could see potential in her, but her mid-western innocence and her religious background put her at odds with Michaelson, who continually harassed her with sarcasm and prejudice for her faith. Stan worried about her maturity, having yet to see evidence that she was tough enough to stand up for herself. If she couldn't carry herself here with the Task Force, he shuddered to think of sending a rookie into the field, especially with the potential of undercover work.

But Kampo was the real thorn in his side. He was bright, good looking, muscular, and had graduated at the top of his class at the FBI Academy. The problem with him was that he knew it and it showed. Whatever great potential he may or may not have as an agent, his arrogance was certainly not winning him any friends on the Task Force. Stan chuckled as he wondered how many of his colleagues felt the same about him when he had been a rookie.

March 29, 2004   Minneapolis, Minnesota

Ten days passed before their wait was over and the new reality offered little comfort. Stan Harverson stared out the window at the bustling street below. Watching the traffic below, Stan listened while Pat Knodell, the Task Force lead researcher, read the fax that had just come in on the secured line while the office TV was broadcasting the Headline News coverage of the same story. Harverson, once again wondered why the CIA didn't do more recruiting at news agencies.

"Congressman William Deshaw of Ohio was shot and killed outside his Columbus residence at 08:15 CST. A single, fatal shot entered the victim's left temple, exit wound on the opposite side. Still trying to determine caliber, though likely 30.06, fired from long range. Initial crime scene investigation has revealed no physical evidence. The search of the Congressman's office at the state capitol revealed one 30.06 caliber cartridge standing upright on the Congressman's desk. The word *Go-el* was etched onto the casing. FBI has been investigating Deshaw for possible violations of federal racketeering laws. Will send information as it comes in."

"Well, now we know," Harverson said as he turned from the window to face the other members of the task force. The team had been together for just over one month when the news of *Go-el's* first hit on U.S. soil began to reach the public. There was no sense of personal vindication. In his line of work, being right usually meant that someone had died, or would die soon. It offered little satisfaction.

Though the room was silent now, a strange energy was growing and stirring in each of the men and women present. Until this moment, they had been researching Lutheran seminaries and organizations, compiling lists of potential suspects, and running background checks. All their long hours and efforts were based on thin information and a few hunches. They were not even sure that the man they hunted was even in the country. Just like that, things had changed. He was here. He had struck.

Bill Kampo pushed his chair away from his work station and walked to the wall map of the United States of America. Long ago, they had placed pins and labels on the

74

locations of every Lutheran institution throughout the nation, excluding individual congregations, at least for the time being. His eyes quickly scanned the map. Suddenly he stabbed the map with his finger. "Trinity Lutheran Seminary, Columbus, Ohio."

The energy level rose again. "Alright, boys and girls, we now have a real case to solve," Austin Torvick announced. "Bill! I want you and Susan on the next flight to Columbus. Bill, use your shield and check out what the local cops have got; Susan, go to the Seminary as a perspective student, keep your cover, we don't want to tip our hand. Pat, who do we have on our suspect list from Trinity?"

Smoothly Pat slid into her computer chair and immediately began typing in commands. Within seconds, all the research compiled on Trinity Lutheran Seminary was available to her.

"Let's see... okay, here we go. We've got a total of five foreign students studying there this semester. Two doctoral students from Kenya—we can rule them out, they've been there all year. One exchange from Sweden, Madds Andersson, just enrolled for one semester—better check him out. Finally, there's a married couple from Germany, Dieter and Gabriele Zibermann-Fitzbaun. I suppose they're a possibility, but they've been enrolled since, ah, February of last year, so they're doubtful."

"Did we put anyone else on the list?" Stan questioned.

"Well, the background checks we did revealed three students with criminal records and two who had defaulted on previous student loans. Eight others have been arrested at various protest rallies, but that's about it. I'll print this up for you."

"Thanks, Pat," Harverson offered. She never failed to amaze him. They had worked together for twenty-one years and she had never once disappointed him. Many a field agent owed their lives to the thorough research of this forty-seven-year-old one-time homecoming queen. Though neither she nor Stan had ever married, and many had often wondered about their private relationship, the two had never been more than friends. They respected each other and valued their friendship too much to risk it all for an affair that might drive them apart. Still, though, Stan had to admit to himself that he loved her more than any woman he had ever known.

Just then the jpeg images of the 30.06 cartridge appeared on each computer screen. "What do you think, Stan? Any doubts about who's behind this hit?" Torvick asked.

Stan glanced at the images and shook his head.

"I've got to admit it, Stan, when Rucker assigned me to this Task Force, I thought I was going on the biggest snipe hunt of my life! You've got good instincts, Stan. You may have given us a head start on this *Go-el* bastard."

"Susan, we're booked on a flight to Columbus which leaves at 11:15. If we leave now, we'll have just enough time to stop at the hotel and pick up some personal stuff," Bill Kampo suggested.

Kampo was secretly cursing Torvick for pairing him with Susan Belcourt. Though he got along fine with Susan, who he guessed to be at least thirty-seven, (eight years his senior), he desperately would have preferred to have been paired off with the other junior member of the Task Force, Brenda LeToure, who had captivated his attention from the first time he saw her. Like many PK's (pastor's kids), Kampo had begun his rebellion against his moral upbringing in college, where he learned to pursue and conquer the women he set his sights on. From the day they met, he had pursued her relentlessly.

Though Bill had not bothered to find out, Brenda had earned her place on the Task Force because of her family background in the Lutheran Church. Though a rookie, the fact that she had graduated from the FBI academy at the top of her class had also helped secure her position on the Task Force.

Bill tried to sneak an anonymous glance at her while standing and putting on his sport coat. She was sitting at her desk, eagerly studying the text on her computer screen, her back to him. Her light brown hair hung just below her shoulders, the loose curls reflecting the blonde highlights.

Suddenly she spun around in her chair, catching the glance that Bill had hoped to pass unnoticed. She returned a subtle but clear look of what could easily have been interpreted as disgust. "I just punched up the Columbus Community On-line Calendar. Trinity Seminary will be concluding a three-day theological conference on Liberation Theology today. It was open to the public. Mr. Harverson, didn't the report from your investigations in Europe say that each attack happened while a theological conference was taking place in the city?" Brenda asked, already knowing the answer.

"Right. Bill, when you get to Columbus, get a list of everyone who attended that conference and fax it to us immediately. That could be our best lead yet! Good work, Brenda," Stan said, feeling his pulse beginning to race at the thought of closing in on *Go-el*.

"Come on, Bill!" Susan ordered. "We've got work to do." Playfully, she grabbed his arm and pulled him toward the door. Bill paused for one more glance at the target of his growing infatuation. Immediately he felt another tug on his arm.

Once outside the door, Susan turned her head so she could see her partner's face as they walked down the hall toward the elevator. "Go easy on her, Bill. She's a sweetheart but if you push too hard, she could grow fangs."

Bill stopped in his tracks. "How did you...?" he started to ask.

"Come on, Bill. I've been an agent for eleven years, I'm supposed to notice things. Besides, you're not as subtle as you think," she added with a wink.

Back in the office, Austin had pulled Stan into the only private office in their government-leased facility. "Have you heard anything from Tim or Jed?" he asked. Tim Parnel had been sent by the Task Force to go undercover, posing as a student at the Seattle Lutheran Bible College, an under-graduate level Bible school. A German student with a history of political activism had transferred there for the spring semester—a lead that warranted close investigation.

Jed Michaelson, on the other hand, couldn't break his way out of a paper bag, but could hack his way into virtually any computer system. He had been sent to search the files of the headquarters of the Evangelical Lutheran Church in America on Higgins Road in Chicago. Set up in a small, one-bedroom suburban Chicago apartment, Jed's current assignment involved spending ten hours a day sitting in front of his computer, breaking into church files, gathering information—unofficially of course—on anyone or anything that might lead to Go-el.

"Jed checked in yesterday afternoon about 16:00 with nothing to report other than he was running out of Twinkies. Tim's supposed to check in this evening."

"You think with the hit this morning we should call 'em back in?" Torvick asked.

Harverson shook his head. "Jed's almost gathered all he can in Chicago, so I'd say let him finish. Tim hasn't found anything conclusive about our suspect there," he paused, trying to recall the name from the thirty-four the Task Force was investigating. "Claus Braun might be clean, but Tim says there are some things that make him suspicious—nothing tangible. Says he's got a 'gut' feeling. I say we leave him there for now. If we pull him out now, we'd never get him in again."

Now, as Stan surveyed the man in charge of this task force, he could see that something had changed in the man, just in the twenty minutes since the announcement of the assassination had arrived. Before, his work on the Task Force had been abstract, tracking down ideas rather than real people. Now there was a real attack which meant there was a real terrorist at work here in the States. It seemed the lines in Austin Torvick's face had grown deeper, his presence more intense, almost severe.

Stan had already turned to leave the office when he stopped. "Hey, Austin, we're going to get this guy, I promise you."

Austin returned Stan's gaze and nodded his head. "I know we will."

Chapter Six

March 30, 2004   **Seattle, Washington**

Calling from the closet-like phone booth at the bottom of the stairway leading from the receptionist desk of the Seattle Lutheran Bible College (SLBC) in Washington, Tim Parnel waited while the phone continued ringing. "Where are they?" he asked no one. On the seventh ring, his patience was finally rewarded by the sound of a familiar voice.

"Emil and Brown Insurance. How may I help you?"

"My diagnosis is terminal and I need insurance, can you help?" Tim completed the code, and in doing so identified himself. Though Tim often felt such codes were far more valuable for the melodramatic effect they had on those using them, still the use of such codes was the simplest way of establishing and verifying identities.

"Hi, Tim! How are things going out there in Washington?"

Tim recognized the voice immediately. "If it isn't the lovely Miss LeToure! Things are wet here in Washington, and they have been wet since I've been here, thank you," he said playfully. "And how are things in the heart of 'God's country'?" Though many found the phrase offensive, a sizable contingent of SLBC students came from Minnesota and stubbornly clung to the erroneous depiction of their home state.

"Oh, we're just sitting around, enjoying a beautiful winter day, that's all. I suppose you want to talk to Stan?"

"Well, of course I'd rather talk to you, but I must earn my keep. Is he in?"

"Is he ever not? He's been here sixteen hours a day since we started and he was here all night sifting through information on the Deshaw assassination."

"Deshaw? Congressman Deshaw was assassinated? When?"

"Yesterday morning, 08:15. Don't you get any news at that school?"

"I've had my nose in the Bible all day, what can I say? Does Stan think the assassin is our guy?"

"Ninety-nine percent sure. A 30.06 cartridge with the word *Go-el* etched on it was found standing upright on Deshaw's office desk."

"Jeez!" Timothy exhaled as he processed the information. "Well, I guess that means I've been barking up the wrong tree."

"You on to something?"

"Well, I thought I was. I guess I better check in with Stan anyway."

"Alright, I'll connect you. Stay dry out there!" she teased.

A moment later it was Stan on the other end of the line. "Okay, Tim, what 'cha got?"

"Hi, Stan! It's good to hear your voice too. Things are wet out here and I think I'm catching a cold. How are you?"

"Cut the crap, Tim. You got anything?"

"Well, I thought I did until Brenda told me about Deshaw. The guy I've been looking at was right here at the Bible school this whole week."

"Claus Braun? What've you got on him?"

"It's not him. I think he's clean, actually. I kind of stumbled on to someone, though. I overheard this guy talking to some other students about a trip he took to Europe last fall. Said he had a Eurail pass and traveled all over—specifically England and Germany."

"Is that all?"

81

"That's what got me started, anyway. I did a little snooping, and I tell you Stan, even knowing he isn't our guy, he gives me the willies. I don't have anything solid – don't worry, I haven't done anything illegal... yet. It'll sound stupid, but it's his eyes." He paused, waiting to hear the sneering rebuke, but it didn't come.

"Go on," Harverson ordered.

Surprised, Tim continued. "I've never met anyone like him. He can smile, laugh, and joke with the other students; he can discuss theology with the sincerity of a priest, but the whole time his eyes are cold, penetrating." Parnel paused to search for words to describe something that could not be described. "You'll laugh, Stan, but when I've looked into his eyes, I see death." Again, Tim expected ridicule, but it didn't come.

"I've seen the look before, Tim. What's the name he's using?"

"Jeff, Jeff Atkins."

"All right. We'll run a check from our end, but I want you to stay on him."

"But he couldn't have been in Columbus. He was here."

"I know, but let's not jump to any conclusions. See what you can find."

"Why, Stan! Are you authorizing me to break the law?" he chided.

Though he knew the line was secure, Stan cringed at the implications of the joke. "I'm not asking you to do anything illegal if you don't get caught."

"Right, boss. Don't worry. I haven't been caught, yet."

"Tim, don't forget those eyes. Even if this guy isn't our man, he's dangerous. Watch yourself."

"Ah, boss, I didn't know you cared."

"I don't. I just don't want you to screw things up for the rest of us."

82

"Got 'cha, Stan. I'll check back in three days. "Terminally ill, out."

March 30, 2004   Manhattan, New York

Arthur Rossford entered the national headquarters of the People Alert Foundation wearing his usual, custom-fit gray tweed business suit with his yet unread daily edition of the New York Times tucked neatly under his arm. The Foundation's headquarters were located on the twenty-fourth floor of the Condé Nast Building, one of New York's many high rises. In continuity with People Alert's grass roots image, the building had been specially chosen for its simplicity and functionality.

Though he would never describe himself as a religious man, Rossford considered himself a moralist; one who prided himself on living according to the laws of God and man. His moral standards and work ethic made for little tolerance for corruption or inefficiency on any level. His idealism led to the birth of his personal brainchild, The People Alert Foundation.

On the surface, it was just one of the many government watch dog groups which had sprung up across the country. But watchdog organizations required patience, a commodity which Rossford had never possessed. The People Alert Foundation was what he liked to a call an "attack dog" organization. Not content with the painfully slow and unpredictable election process, People Alert was founded specifically to expose and root out political and moral corruption in government, military, and civil leaders. In its three-year history, over 200 political and public officials from 34 states had been forced from office after People Alert made public scores of allegations ranging from statutory rape to racketeering to "conspiracy to defraud the American people."

The fact that no one challenged The People Alert Foundation's use of criminal methods which violated the civil rights of its targets, or victims, as some saw it, only revealed the level of frustration the public felt toward its government officials. Illegal phone taps and surveillance seemed to be justified in pursuit of the unending challenge of government clean-up. Though these methods, along with bugging homes and offices and occasional break-ins, were officially denied by the organization, most public officials and law enforcement agencies suspected People Alert's methods. The strange thing was that nobody was doing anything about it! The public was either willingly unaware, indifferent, or outright supportive. Officials found themselves in a dilemma. If they acted against People Alert, they risked losing their public support, or worse, becoming a target of the attack dog group themselves.

Following his ritual, he greeted all the volunteers and the handful of paid employees with warmth and concern, though everyone noticed again that there was something wrong with the Founder. He didn't have the usual spring in his step which both friend and foe had parodied over the years. The warm smile with which he greeted one and all was strained, forced. Was there something wrong or something missing? The questions had been buffeted around the lunch tables in the cafeteria for the past two weeks.

Indeed, there was something different about Mr. Rossford. Though only those closest to him could have diagnosed his condition, he was a changed man. Gone was the absolute self-confidence which had propelled him through his life. He had never been an arrogant man, yet his self-assurance had frustrated many a business adversary. Never one to question his own decisions or motives, he had lived 71 years on this earth never having experienced the uncertainty of regret, much less the anguish of guilt.

Finally, after all his years, Arthur Collin Rossford had considered his own heart, and the results had made the most profound change that the he had ever experienced in his life. More than acknowledging his guilt in the deaths of fifteen people, three of them quite intentionally, he now looked at his life in a way unknown to him before. The confidence and high moral standards which had been his pride were now revealed to be little more than deep-seated self-righteousness which had blinded him to his own selfishness and ambition.

In his attempt to come to terms with his role in the bombing in Berlin, Rossford experienced a profound transformation. He couldn't change his past but he could change his future. With the guidance of a local Episcopalian priest from North Hampton, New Hampshire, Arthur had come to see himself through the eyes of God. Never having been dependent upon anyone, he suddenly found himself totally and absolutely dependent upon the grace of God.

With these fundamental changes in the way he looked at himself and the world, Rossford's relationship had also changed with the People Alert Foundation. Always its chief spokesperson and benefactor, he had increasingly backed away from involvement in the day to day activities of the Foundation. Though outwardly he still believed in the primary motives of People Alert, inwardly he could no longer condone the tactics he had once urged.

In addition to taking personal steps to amend his life, Arthur had sought, ironically enough, to "clean up" the Foundation, only to find that his three other associate directors remained firmly committed to the Foundation's covert tactics. They had agreed to break all contact with Go-el and limit People Alert's range of tactics.

Today, as he weaved his way through the maze of work stations and their constantly ringing phones, Arthur paused by the desk of his secretary.

"Any messages for me, Marge?"

85

"Not from today, Mr. Rossford," Marge Neyland answered while her inquisitive eyes studied her boss.

"Ah, Mr. Rossford, I hope you don't mind my asking, but. . . have you been feeling okay lately? It's just that. . ."

"No, Marge, I don't mind you asking. I guess you could say I've had a lot on my mind lately, that's all, but thanks for your concern."

With a genuinely warm smile he turned to enter his intentionally modest cubicle office, comprised of two moveable, floor-to-ceiling prefab walls attached in the southwest corner. Inside, the walls were decorated with a collection of photos, awards, and framed newspaper clippings which celebrated People Alert's many successes and accreditations. Two functional chairs were positioned in front of a simple oak desk, on which stood a few neatly arranged personal pictures.

Slipping into his desk chair, he paused, as was his unconscious habit, to survey the photographs of the handful of loved ones in his life. Following his ritual, he began with the first picture on the left of the desk. In truth, he didn't need to see the picture for the image and memory were forever etched in his mind. His daughter, at the age of seventeen, standing on the north rim of the Grand Canyon, wearing a beautiful smile across her face. The next picture displayed again his daughter, from a year ago, standing alongside her husband and their then, five-year-old daughter.

Arthur's eyes then subconsciously shifted across the desk to the right corner, where a lone picture stood encased in an antique silver frame. The all-too-familiar flood of love and grief washed through Arthur's heart as he stared at the image of his wife, dead now for the past eight years.

Arthur concluded the silent ritual by absent-mindedly exhaling a long, slow breath. He then turned to his morning paper. Immediately his eyes locked on the front-page cover story.

86

"Congressman Deshaw Assassinated," the headline proclaimed in bold letters. Fighting the growing sense of dread that was invading his soul, he hurriedly read the article. Skimming past the details of the assassination, he frantically searched for the one detail he intuitively knew the story would contain. The fifth paragraph confirmed the premonition.

> "Unconfirmed reports indicate a 30.06 cartridge with the word *Go-el* etched onto it was found standing upright on the congressman's desk in his Columbus office, linking the assassination to the deaths of eight U.S. military personnel and American citizens in Europe, along with nine international victims."

Arthur lowered the paper and stared out the window across the hazy New York skyline. Unconsciously he began massaging his temples. There was only one conclusion he could reach. The order for the assassination must have come from what Rossford had named the Core, the People Alert Foundation's secretive board of directors that controlled all the Foundation's covert operations.

Congressman Deshaw had been the next name on the Claypool list, the list of individuals that *Go-el* was created to eliminate. With painful clarity, Arthur Rossford realized that there had been a coup d'état within his own Foundation and he had been so self-absorbed with his own personal anguish that he hadn't even known. With equal clarity, Arthur now knew what he had to do. He picked up the phone, punching the first button on the automatic dialer.

"Senator Barnell's office," a receptionist answered with only a faint trace of monotony in her nasal voice.

"Yes, this is Arthur Rossford. Connect me with the Senator immediately, please."

"I'm sorry but the Senator has requested..."

"Tell Senator Barnell I need to talk to him. Now!" he interrupted.

"I'll see if he can accept your call," the receptionist answered curtly.

Less than a minute later, Glen Barnell, senator from Massachusetts and also member of the Senate Intelligence Committee, was on the line.

"Arthur! It's good to hear from you. My secretary said that it sounded urgent. What can I do for you?"

"Who authorized the hit on Deshaw?" Rossford demanded.

"Arthur, this is an open line!"

"I don't give a damn what line this is! I want an answer, now!"

"Arthur, I will not discuss this over the phone. Can you meet me later?"

"That won't be necessary, Glen. As of right now the Core is disbanded and all People Alert funds will be frozen."

"Arthur, you can't do that. The Foundation's by-laws clearly state that decisions involving the use of funds must be made by a majority vote of the Core. You set it up that way yourself, so that no one person would ever be able to control People Alert, not even you. Sorry, Art. Majority rule."

"I won't allow these murders to continue even if I have to go to the police!" Arthur announced, thereby pronouncing his own death sentence.

There was silence from the other end of the telephone line. Senator Glen Barnell collected his thoughts rapidly. If by chance his office phone was tapped, unlikely, yet possible, Arthur had already hung them both. At this point, there was nothing to lose.

"To hell with your new-found self-righteousness, Arthur! Michael was my sister's only son and his death devastated her! And to think that his own government betrayed and murdered him!" The Senator took a deep breath and tried to compose himself. "I'm sorry you feel that way, Arthur, but I urge you to consider your course before you continue. There are people who could be hurt. . ." The Senator smoothly inserted just enough inflection in his voice to carry the threat.

Arthur Rossford clenched the phone in his fist and snarled into the handset. "I have made my decision. Either the Core is completely disbanded and all People Alert funds turned over to the control of the national board of directors or I will go to the authorities. The choice is yours, Senator."

"Again, I am sorry you feel that way. I suppose you leave me no other choice but to call the other members. I'm truly sorry it has come to this," he lied. "I have an appointment across town in ten minutes. I'll be in touch."

Arthur heard the click, then the dial tone began buzzing in his ear. It was done. The secret inner circle of People Alert would never meet again and the killing would stop. He hung up the phone. Once again, he began massaging his temples in a vain attempt to relieve the throbbing pain in his head.

Weakly he pushed himself away from his desk and stood. On shaky legs, he walked to the door he had entered less than ten minutes earlier.

"Mr. Rossford, are you alright?" his secretary asked, her concern etched in the soft features of her full face.

"Actually, I'm not feeling very well at the moment. I think I am going to go home to North Hampton for a few days. Would you please arrange to have my chauffeur meet me in front of the building?" he asked weakly.

"Yes, of course...is there anything else I can do for you?"

He returned a warm, weak smile. "No, I'll be alright, Marge. But thank you. . . thank you," he said as he turned to make his way through the maze of work stations.

April 2, 2004   Chicago, Illinois

The once clean and sanitized one-bedroom apartment in Elk Grove Village was virtually in shambles by the end of the current tenant's third week. Though there was no actual damage, the amount of trash scattered throughout the unit and the stench of rotting food would have convinced any visitor otherwise.

Taking a break from his endless vigil in front of the computer screen, Jed Michaelson looked out his second-story window at the Chicago suburb while inhaling deeply from his cigarette. He stared into the glare of the descending afternoon sun, ignoring his stinging, blood-shot eyes. Had he been the type to enjoy the outdoors, it would have been a perfect afternoon for a walk around the neighborhood or stomping through the freshly fallen spring snow at the nearby park. He had considered the thought, for a moment, but decided another cigarette and Twinkie would suffice.

For three weeks to the day he had remained in his hermitage, engaging the outside world only through the television and occasional trips to the corner convenience store. His current assignment was not nearly as challenging as he would have hoped. After all, breaking into the central computer system of a national church organization was child's play compared to some of the other jobs Harverson had given him. For a hacker like Jed, breaking the password locks on the church's computer files had taken an average of three minutes each. Prioritizing and sifting through the seemingly endless list of divisions and committees had been time-consuming but not particularly difficult or interesting for that matter.

By now he had studied the personnel records of every division, council, and committee of the Lutheran Evangelical Church in America (LECA). He had run a handful through the FBI on the remote chance of stumbling onto something useful, but as he expected, nothing came of it. For the past thirteen days, he had been studying the clergy roster, calling up confidential files on each individual pastor, again with the slim hope of discovering… what? He had been asking himself the question for days. An assassin was on the loose and Jed was convinced his research was accomplishing nothing.

As he stood by the window, he paused to reflect on what he had learned. He was within two days of completing his illegal research and it appeared that he would conclude his assignment without producing anything useful in the hunt for *Go-el*.

About the only thing he had learned was that nearly fifteen percent of the church personnel had committed some form or another of professional misconduct ranging from misuse of congregational funds to charges of sexual abuse. Eleven percent had been treated for some form of emotional disorder and as many as twenty-five percent were in therapy. Though he had no way of knowing that the statistics would be similar in any of the mainline Christian churches, the information Jed Michaelson had discovered struck his agnostic mind with near lethal impact to his soul.

Slowly exhaling the smoke from his lungs, he muttered under his breath. "Religion, what a crock!" He dabbed out the remains of his cigarette and made his way from the window back to his computer, dodging the half-eaten pizza on the floor. At least the food was good, he told himself as he stuffed the remains of his Twinkie into his mouth.

April 3, 2004   Santa Rosa, California

The trip home from Gloucester, Virginia, where he had been secretly stationed while serving with SEAL

DEVGRU, had taken over seven months and had carried Matthew Pierson around the world. There had been his "personal business" to attend to but the truth behind his delayed homecoming was something he carried deep within his heart. He knew he would receive the lectures and a good scolding for not writing and/or calling for the last nine months—he deserved nothing less. In truth, it was the shame, guilt, and anger he carried within—for what he had done and for what he had left undone—that had delayed his return. Though he had not always gotten along with his family, they were good people, clean people. How could he face them?

Having already seriously disappointed his father once by joining the Navy instead of entering seminary and becoming a pastor, the thought of coming home to announce the news, "Hey, Dad, I just got court-martialed and dishonorably discharged!" was something Matthew had dreaded even more than the sentence itself. He had run away from his family's hopes and expectations and was returning a failure, a disgrace. And worse, his conscience accused.

The fact that he had once been an officer in the United States Navy, a SEAL who had undergone torturous training that few men could endure, meant very little to him now. At the age of twenty-eight, he was returning empty. Even the self-assurance that had once convinced him that he could accomplish anything was all but gone.

Thirty-six hours of driving gave plenty of time to think, too much time. Would his family be able to see through him, somehow able to see or sense the sins he had committed? The radio provided little distraction. News reports and Talk Radio shows focused on the lack of progress in the war with Iraq. Amidst all the conflicting emotion cascading through his mind and heart, talk of war made him long for his days with the Teams. As much as he had grown to hate it, he realized that the warrior within was far from gone.

Pierson took the exit off California's Highway 101 just north of Santa Rosa. Five minutes later, he parked on the street in front of his parents' house. Slowly emerging from the small car, Matt stretched his stiff legs. The moment of truth had arrived. *I'd rather be in combat,* he thought to himself with an inner chuckle, admitting to himself that this home coming was one of the scariest things he had ever done.

He stood still for a moment by the car, surveying the house he had only read about in his mother's letters. The family house in the hills just north of Santa Rosa, where Matthew had spent his adolescence, had been sold while Matt was in his second year with the Teams. Though he had always been good at visualizing things that had been described to him—a skill that had served him well as a SEAL—he was still amazed at how closely the house resembled what he had pictured in his mind.

Matt had not made it more than halfway to the front door when it suddenly swung open. Though he hadn't called to warn them of his plans to visit, it was as though his mother was expecting him. Monica Pierson rushed toward her only son and engulfed him in her arms. It had been almost two years since she had seen him, (and nine months since she had heard from him) a fact that she was sure to bring to his attention eventually, but not now. Now was the time for reunion.

Behind her, Dr. Howard Pierson appeared in the doorway and slowly made his way toward his son. His face was tense with a hint of sadness. Matt read the look immediately. *The disappointment has come home,* was all he could think.

Howard stopped behind his wife and waited for her to release her son. As if picking up on a cue, Monica stepped aside, her right arm still tightly around her boy's waist.

Matt stared at his father's face, their eyes briefly meeting. He hadn't changed much and his father's expression hadn't changed either. Then suddenly, without warning, tears swelled in his father's eyes and the sixty-six-year-old man reached out and grabbed his son, pulling him into a bear hug that could have rivaled any SEAL's.

"It's good to see you, son. I've missed you so much," Dr. Howard Pierson managed to utter.

Without warning, Matthew found himself weeping on his father's shoulder as they embraced. The prodigal son had returned home to be welcomed by the open arms of his loving parents.

As if to carry on the imagery of the ancient parable, the Pierson family gathered that evening around the dining room table to feast on what had always been Matt's dinner—lasagna, followed by freshly baked brownies for dessert. The only way in which the parable's imagery didn't fit was that the two of Matt's three sisters who were at the table, along with their husbands and collective three children, were also overjoyed to see their long-lost brother. In every way, the evening was a happy reunion.

Later in the evening, after the sisters and their families had returned to their homes, Howard called his son into his small study. As Matt entered the converted bedroom, an ironic thought brought a small smile to his face. Though the study was in an entirely different house, it looked the same as in the old house. Some things never changed.

His father stepped behind the dark oak desk and opened the top, right-side drawer, retrieving a stack of envelops of assorted sizes which were held together by a wide rubber band.

"These came for you while you were traveling. Most of it is the usual junk, but I thought you should have the honor of trashing it yourself."

Matt accepted the pile and began leafing through it. It was junk, for the most part, but some of it would have to be read. "Yeah, you called it right, it's mostly junk but thanks for saving it for me."

Once again, Howard reached into the drawer, this time extracting a single envelope. Instantly Matt recognized the official Navy insignia on the envelope, as well as the fact that the envelope had been opened.

"This also came for you," Howard said as he handed the envelope to his son. "As you can see, I opened it. I thought it looked important and since we hadn't heard from you in so long..." He let the accusation hang for a moment, "I figured I'd see if it was something that needed a response. Sorry."

"Don't worry about it," Matt answered. He opened the envelope. Inside there was only a single Polaroid snapshot of a slightly obscene nature.

The photograph was a close up of a man's bare, freckle-scared buttocks. In the white strip at the bottom of the Polaroid was scribbled a short message. "Remember, you saved this once! Pepper."

Matt burst into laughter. "Pepper, you son of a..." He caught himself, looking up at his father. "Oops, sorry, Dad. It's from one of my buddies in the Teams."

"Do you mind explaining?"

"Our chopper was hit by an RPG—a shoulder-launched rocket—as we were extracting from a job in, well, somewhere. Pepper—the guy in the picture, broke some ribs on the landing and was in pretty bad shape," Matt answered, still chuckling at the photo.

"You pulled him out, didn't you? You saved his life?"

"I didn't do anything he wouldn't have done for me," he responded, his expression suddenly turning serious.

"Why the photo?"

"It has to do with something he told me after I was..." he couldn't bring himself to say the words, not in front of his father. Once again, he felt the shame of the word *dishonorable* fill his thoughts. He turned away, heading for the door.

"Matt, what happened?" his father asked kindly.

Matt paused at the door for a moment, then continued through it. He couldn't answer, not now and even later he wouldn't explain; it wasn't allowed. "I'm sorry Dad, I can't explain," he said over his shoulder.

Chapter Seven

April 4, 2004   Washington, D.C. The Pentagon

"Admiral Mattison, I've got an update for you on that suspect in the Bartle assassination. It seems that the SEAL who assaulted the Admiral has just turned up after being invisible for the past six months," reported Commander Joshua Denzer.

"The SEAL, Matthew Donald Pierson, never returned to his job or apartment in New Jersey. For the last sixth months, we haven't been able to get a line on him. Last night our phone tap recorded a call between his mother and one of his sisters indicating that our suspect returned to his parents' home. I immediately dispatched a surveillance team to the house. As of an hour ago, he was still there."

As for the case at hand, as far as Admiral Mattison was concerned, it wasn't so much a matter of Pierson's guilt or innocence as much as risk. Having an ex-SEAL on the loose who had a record of uncontrolled acts of violence, in addition to information on the Navy's most secret unit, was simply too great a risk.

Mattison rubbed his chin thoughtfully. Sifting through the files on his desk, he found the one titled, *Pierson, Matthew D*. Opening it, he quickly scanned the court martial records. Two Bronze Stars and a Purple Heart. "What would turn a sailor like that?"

Impatiently, Denzer shifted his weight from one foot to the other, waiting for his orders. From the moment news had crossed his desk announcing the assassination of Admiral Bartle, Denzer had been certain that Pierson was the killer. Pleased that justice in the shadow world was often swift and lethal, he looked forward to the chance to bring the alleged killer to justice. After almost seven months of hunting, now all he needed was the order and he would administer that justice.

"It doesn't seem we have any choice. Put together a team and handle it. Remember who you're dealing with. No mess, understood?" Mattison ordered.

"Understood. I'll report back when it's done."

The conversation over, Mattison again rubbed his chin. Though he had only been following the existing procedures for "special circumstances," still he knew that he had just tried, convicted, and potentially sentenced a man to death. Slowly, almost reverently, he closed the file of Lieutenant Matthew Pierson. Within the next forty-eight hours, the file would be closed forever. But it would never be forgotten, at least not by the man who had condemned him.

April 4, 2004   Seattle, Washington

Blending into the community of the Seattle Lutheran Bible College had been much easier than Tim Parnel had expected. Though most the student body was comprised of students between the ages of eighteen and twenty, Tim had been surprised by the broad age-span. He guessed that roughly thirty percent of the students were somewhere in their mid-twenties to mid-thirties. Some were even in their fifties. Though he was thirty years old himself, his boyish face easily allowed him to pass for twenty-four, the age that his alias was registered under.

Yet far more surprising to Tim was the atmosphere of the school. When he had been drafted by the Task Force to go undercover at a Bible School, Tim had envisioned uniformed students with short haircuts and ten-pound Bibles under their arms. What he had found, in fact, was everything from crew-cuts to ponytails, body piercings and tattoos to flannel shirts and blue jeans, sport coats to tie-dye tee-shirts.

Each student had his or her own story and reason for being there; some because their parents forced them, others to search for God, some to find grace. Of all the reasons for coming to the Bible School, Tim's was truly unique. In the midst of those who desired a closer walk with God, Tim had come searching for a killer.

Despite the news of Deshaw's assassination, deep inside Tim knew he was on the right track. The same morning he had checked in with headquarters, Tim had gone to one of his morning classes, a class shared with the student whose eyes had the look of death. Both had been sitting in the back row and Tim had been studying the man as the professor continued his lecture on the role of the Christian Church in society.

Sandy blonde hair; taut, tanned face; gray-blue eyes and thin lips. He was dressed, as usual, in casual clothes, comfortable enough to put people at ease, yet conservative enough so as not to draw attention. His six-foot frame supported the build of an athlete. Handsome, but not enough to turn heads; muscular, but not a body builder. When he spoke there was no trace of any accent. All in all, Tim concluded, there was nothing outstanding about him. It made him perfect.

Then it happened. The man who called himself Jeffery Atkins turned in his chair, as if instinctively knowing he was being watched. Their eyes locked. Though the exchanged glance in reality it had only lasted a couple seconds, it had seemed like an eternity for Tim Parnel. Again, it was the eyes. They seemed to see right through him, as though the mysterious Bible student could see into his very heart. Tim felt naked under the gaze, but stubbornly refused to turn his eyes away. Though unaware, he had made his first mistake.

Atkins slightly nodded his head and smiled before returning his attention to the professor, but his eyes were like ice. A shudder ran up Tim's spine as he interpreted the smile. The mysterious man had just said, "I know you."

The thin smile was still etched in his mind now as he sat studying in the campus snack bar and lounge known as The Running Cup. Since the conversation with his boss, he had been waiting for an opportunity to further investigate his prey which meant specifically breaking into and searching Jeffery Atkin's room. But if the truth were to be known, Tim was scared, though he would never admit it, not even to himself. Though his books were open, his mind was on his real assignment. When would he get the opportunity to get into the room?

"Hi, Tim!" a girl's voice called.

Tim looked up to see Angela Hotchner rapidly approaching the table where he was seated. Without being invited, she slid into the chair across from him. He didn't mind. Suddenly his mind was on something other than his investigation. The young lady sitting across from him was twenty-one years old and under other circumstances, and in a different setting, he would have considered her fair game. But Tim had become completely disarmed by the beautiful girl's charm. Her heart was warm and her faith was sincere, a combination of qualities Tim had never encountered before.

"What can I do for you, young lady?" he asked as properly as he could. He was rewarded with the shy little smile that could buckle his knees.

"I was wondering if you could help me study for tomorrow's Church History test?"

"That's what I've been working on myself. Where do you want to start?"

"Well, I think I'm okay up to Constantine but that's where I start getting a little weak. How are you doing with it?"

"Oh, I think I'm a little weak on all of it so it's probably me who needs to ask your help," he replied with absolute honesty. The fact was, that he couldn't remember if he had ever picked up a Bible on his own before this assignment, much less studied Christian history. In fact, as he reflected upon his enrollment, he wasn't even sure if he had known who Jesus was, other than that he was born on Christmas.

"Hi, Tim. Hi, Angela!" another voice interjected. The two looked up to find that another student had appeared to join the study group that was forming. Tim had learned early in his stay at the Bible College that such impromptu study groups were one of the unofficial institutions of the school.

"Hey, there, Kyle! You want to study with us?" Angela asked. Of course, he wouldn't refuse. Kyle Eims was suffering from a severe crush on Angela, and it was painfully obvious to just about everyone, except Angela.

"Pull up a chair..." Tim broke off mid-sentence. Looking past his new study partner, who was pulling up a chair from another table, Tim saw Jeffery Atkins enter The Running Cup. Once again, their eyes locked, again the cold eyes bore into him. This time Tim nervously looked away. A second mistake.

"Boy, that sure wasn't a very friendly look he gave you, Tim. Is Jeff mad at you about something?" Angela inquired innocently.

"Not that I know of," Tim answered as if being called back from a trance.

"Maybe he got some bad news today," Kyle offered.

"Why do you say that?" Tim asked.

"Oh, I was by the front desk when a call came in for him. I think it was from his uncle."

"Oh, really? Was something wrong?" Angela asked before Tim could.

Tim looked across the room to where Jeff was now intensely engaged in conversation with another student.

Though too far to make out the individual words of the conversation, judging by the gestures, Tim concluded that the younger student was receiving a set of rather explicit instructions. *I wonder what that's all about?* Tim asked himself, half listening to the conversation of which he was a part.

"I don't know, but it sounded like he's going somewhere this weekend. He's leaving tonight."

"How do you know that?"

"Well, I took the message to Jeff on the dorm floor, and, well, I happened to overhear him when he returned the call," Kyle answered sheepishly.

"Why, Kyle! Are you telling us that you've been eavesdropping?" Angela teased playfully.

Though in Tim's eyes Angela was nearly perfect, he reluctantly had to admit that she had one fault—gossip. It seemed that she knew everybody at the school and more importantly, something about everybody.

Why he hadn't thought of it before, he would never admit. The truth was that when it came to Angela, his mind had not exactly been on his work. Young or not, Tim now admitted to himself that when she had been around, his mind had not been on finding *Go-el*. That had been a mistake but Tim was a man who learned from his mistakes. He could use her, in a manner of speaking.

Looking across the table, he gave her a smile. Then looking on beyond her, he noticed his suspect had abruptly broken off his conversation, storming toward the door, leaving the young student alone and looking very much as though he had just been scolded.

Tim wondered again what had transpired between the two. Suddenly aware that he was staring, he returned his attention to his companions. "I suppose we better stop yakking and get back to Constantine, don't you think?"

And so the three turned their attention to the study of Church history. For two hours, the trio paged through class notes and references, quizzing each other on the dates and controversies of the early Christian debates and decisions.

It had been another surprise to Tim that the studies were actually interesting. He had once assumed such things as theology and faith were abstract concepts that rarely related to everyday life. Yet here in this most unlikely place for a CIA agent, he was finding that in fact, theology had a great deal to say about everyday life. It was that thought which was once again troubling Tim as the study session began to wind down. It had been far more comfortable to assume that God was far off, abstract, or unconcerned with the daily lives of the human race. Now, as he became increasingly aware of God's presence in his life, he was becoming ever more uncomfortable with his current assignment, not to mention most his life. If God was real, then Tim Parnel would have to begin looking at his life and his heart. He would have to do some changing.

As the books were closed and pages of notes returned to their respective folders, Tim struggled to suppress the thoughts that were invading his soul. He had work to do.

First, he needed to talk to Angela, alone. That meant finding some subtle way of suggesting that the third member of the trio, Kyle, take a hike—figuratively speaking, of course. The problem was that Kyle seemed intent on walking Angela to her dorm floor. Yet while Tim struggled to find a non-offensive solution to his dilemma, it was Angela who provided the answer.

"Kyle," she said sweetly, "there is something I really need to talk to Tim about, so I won't be going back to the dorm right away, but I'd like to meet you for breakfast tomorrow. Is that alright?" she asked with disarming innocence. The poor boy was helpless.

"Sure, Angie, about seven-thirty in the cafeteria?" he responded, clinging to the promise of time with the object of his affection. With as much dignity as he could muster, he smiled and sprinted up the stairs to the main floor.

Tim looked at the young girl intently. "And what, may I ask, are you wishing to speak with me about, milady?" he asked, slipping into Shakespearean formality, a habit he had developed whenever slightly nervous.

Once, many years ago, in what seemed like another life, Tim had studied Shakespearean literature at Illinois State University, part of an education that had proven to be almost useless in his current career. His self-taught skill in lock picking and security systems had proven far more valuable. Still, quoting a few lines of Shakespeare now and then had softened the hearts of several young women, proving that there was at least one notable application for his formal education.

Angela Hotchner smiled bashfully and turned her soft brown eyes away from his. "To be honest, I just wanted to have a chance to talk to you. You know, to get to know you a little better."

Suddenly it became perfectly clear to Tim that the young woman before him was herself suffering from infatuation. Tim felt a surge of excitement rush through his body as his mind cursed his untimely birth and the lies he knew he would have to tell.

"What is it you want to know about me?" he countered, looking away as well, lest their eyes meet and he find himself unable to lie.

"Everything, I guess," she smiled, now raising her eyes to meet his.

"'Everything' is going to take some time. Could you narrow it down a bit?"

"You know what I mean. You showed up here three weeks into the quarter, and I don't know where you came from, what your family is like or even what you did before coming here. I just want to get to know you, that's all."

"Alright, I'll tell you a little about myself, but I need to ask you something, too."

"Okay, it's a deal. What do you want to know?"

104

"Well, what do you know about Jeff? I mean that look he gave me tonight, that was the second one like it today. I was just wondering if you knew anything about him. Maybe I did something to offend him and didn't realize it."

"Actually, I hardly know him myself. He's in his second year here but missed the first two quarters this year because he was on a trip in Europe with his uncle. Sounded like an incredible trip! He had one of those Eurail card-things and went everywhere. But really, now that I think about it, that's about all I know about him."

"You don't know where he's from, where his parents are, or anything like that?" Tim pressed.

She paused thoughtfully for a moment. "No, I don't think I've ever heard him talk about any of that kind of stuff. Maybe you should talk to some of the second-year students. They probably know more about him than I do." With a playful smile, the young beauty suddenly shifted the conversation back to her original objective. "Was that what you wanted to ask me?" she inquired with only the faintest hint of disappointment in her voice.

"Yeah, I guess that was it."

"Good! Now it's your turn. I want to know about you, so start talking."

Now the tight rope walk between truth and lies began. As the two began to walk along the maze of underground hallways which connected all the buildings of the campus, Tim began to share the story of his life with the young woman at his side. Though clearly a violation of standard operating procedures, Tim recounted the events of his life with an honesty and openness that surprised even him.

Raised in a low-income housing development in Denver, his father had been an alcoholic for the first twelve years of Tim's life, until one night, while driving home from a local bar, his father had driven straight into a retaining wall at a speed of over 80 mph. Since that time, he and his mother

105

had been left alone to face the cruelty and uncertainty of the world.

Without warning, a memory long forgotten sprang back to his consciousness. He remembered sitting on his mother's lap when he was only a boy and how she read him stories from the Bible. He remembered how as he grew he had so easily dismissed those stories and his mother's faith as myths for those who were too weak to face reality.

He told Angela of his college days, his love for Shakespeare and beer bashes, a disclosure which evoked a naughty giggle from the girl who had become his confessor.

Yet now, as they sat close to each other on the sofa of the recreation room, there was no more truth to tell. They had wandered the halls for fully an hour before Tim had suggested finding a comfortable place to sit. His cover made his age only twenty-four, which meant he would only have to account for two years after his graduation from ISU.

Had Angela not been so deeply touched by his story and blinded by her growing affection for him, she might have noticed the change. No longer did he look at her while speaking. With sweeping generalizations, he told her that he had worked for a construction company for the last two years, having been unable to employ his skills in Shakespearean studies.

After almost two hours, at approximately 01:00, Tim had finished all he could say. Inside his emotions seemed to churn from the strange combination of relief and guilt. Never before had he told his life story to anyone in such detail. Never had anyone listened as though they really cared.

"So, what brought you to here?" Angela asked. Her voice was tired, yet she showed no interest in retiring for the evening.

Of all the things for her to ask! How could he answer that? Again, he looked at her. Curled up on the coach, hugging her knees while resting her head against the back of the couch, Tim knew that he could not lie to her anymore, at least not about that.

"I came to search, that's all I can say."

She smiled. "I hope you find what you are looking for. I think you are in the right place."

They stared into each other's eyes without saying another word. Alone in the recreation room, the atmosphere had silently shifted from intimacy to romance. Desperately Tim wanted to reach out and hold the young woman beside him, but knew that such a move was wrong. In a moment of clarity, he realized how vulnerable she was at that moment, how easily he could take advantage of her and how horribly wrong it would be.

Gently he reached out and took her hands in his. "Thanks for listening. I think we better get some sleep, we've got that Church History test in the morning."

Somewhat reluctantly she agreed, allowing him to pull her to her feet. Ever the gentleman, he walked her to the entrance of her dorm floor. The walk had been quiet in contrast to the flowing conversation earlier in the evening. Angela had wrapped her arms around his, leaning towards him and resting her head on his shoulder. Again, Tim's emotions pulled in conflicting directions—his mind knowing better but his heart melting at her touch.

There, by the door to the second floor of the women's dormitory, their stroll came to an end. Before Tim could even think of an appropriate way to end the evening, Angela stepped toward him and gently kissed his lips.

Before Tim could even react, much less recover from the surprise, she pulled away with a smile that could only be interpreted as seductive. "Thank you, this was a special evening for me," she whispered before turning and then disappeared through the door.

Still trying to recompose himself, Tim smiled. Flattered of course by her attention, the real satisfaction he felt was that he had done the right thing. Though he could have made advances, and God knew he had preyed on his share of young ladies, he had chosen not to, and for all the right reasons. With a heavy sigh, Tim tried to clear his mind once again. Now he had work to do. Pivoting on his heels, he spun and headed for the hall leading to the men's dormitory. Now it was time to get to know Jeffery Atkins a little more personally, the man with the eyes of ice.

*   *   *   *   *   *   *

Lurking in the shadow of the soda machine just outside the entrance to the women's dormitory, Kyle Eims watched the older student disappear down the hall. Instead of returning to his dorm room following the study session he had shared with Angela and reluctantly with Tim, Kyle had decided that he would wait up for Angela—there was something he wanted to talk to her about. Yet now, for the life of him, he couldn't think of what that had been. He had waited for over two hours, long enough for suspicions to be born, long enough for suspicions to grow into resentment. But it was the kiss which he had witnessed that had turned his resentment into jealousy.

He had heard the sound of their approaching footsteps on the tile floor. Giving in to his jealous curiosity, Kyle had concealed himself in the shadows. His heart desperately hoped his suspicions were unfounded, yet the growing jealousy within longed for evidence to justify its existence.

Emerging from his vantage, he quietly followed Parnel from a distance.

*   *   *   *   *   *   *

Tim carefully surveyed the darkened hall of the men's first floor dormitory. He looked for light escaping from under each door, satisfying himself that all studying

108

and other nocturnal activities had ended. The sound of assorted heavy snoring, muffled only slightly by the thin walls, satisfied Tim that all was quiet. Silently, he slipped down the hall to Jeff Atkins undecorated door.

Before beginning his clandestine mission, Tim had stopped by his own dorm room, removing his shoes to reduce the noise of his footsteps. Then grabbing his penlight and a bath towel, he was ready to embark.

Now, positioned in the hallway alongside his suspect's door, he smoothly sank to his knees. Aiming the penlight under the door, Tim searched for trip wires or telltales which people in his field of work often set for unwelcome guests: the first used to inflict harm on the intruder, something Tim thought unlikely in this case, the second to alert the rightful occupant of the room that someone had entered without invitation—a far more likely prospect.

Sweeping the light left, then right, he didn't see it on his first pass. Fortunately, experience had taught him to check everything twice. On the second pass, he noticed a hair-like filament hanging from the bottom of the door on the hinge side. If the door were opened, the filament would be dislodged, and Atkins would know of the intrusion.

Instantly, his senses were at full alert. "Shit," he thought to himself. Despite all his suspicions, he had secretly hoped that he was wrong about Jeffery Atkins. The thought of a killer like *Go-el* in a holy place like this school caused his stomach to churn. But Aktins wasn't *Go-el*, he already knew that, so who the hell was he? Bible college students didn't use telltales on their doors.

Still kneeling, he studied the filament, memorizing its precise location and angle, committing the information to memory. The most difficult part of his mission would be to replace the filament in its exact location after searching the room. Satisfied that he could accurately recreate the image of the filament in his mind, he stood, returning the penlight to his pocket.

Removing a slim, flat piece of metal with irregularly notched edges from his back trouser pocket, he inserted it into the lock. With a straightened paper clip in his other hand, he slowly worked the two tools, simultaneously moving them slowly up and down, all the while applying clockwise pressure on the knob.

The whole procedure took less than ten seconds for the expert hands of the CIA operative. With the door unlocked, Tim silently slipped into the dark room. Taking the bath-towel which he had worn across his shoulders, he stooped and placed it at the foot of the door to keep the light from escaping into the hall when he flipped on the light switch. Before rising he removed the thin filament which was held in place by a tiny piece of tape. Last, he moved carefully to the window and drew the curtains.

Flipping on the light switch, Tim took three minutes to survey the room. It was imperative that he leave everything exactly as he found it, leaving no clue of his own making for Atkins to discover. Again, satisfied that he could visualize the room in its original condition, he began his search.

*   *   *   *   *   *   *

Hidden in the shadows, Kyle watched in fascination and wonder at the strange activities of the student who had stolen his love. What was he doing? Did it have something to do with the look Jeff had given him in The Running Cup earlier that evening? Why hadn't he turned on the light? With the rage of jealousy still brewing within, Kyle Eims waited for the mysterious man to re-emerge from the room.

*   *   *   *   *   *   *

110

After twenty minutes of silent searching, Tim had discovered nothing useful, yet it was precisely the things he didn't find that worried him. There were no pictures of family, no mementos from travels. There was absolutely nothing to reveal anything about the past of the strange Bible student. Again, it was perfect. He searched his mind for the words Stan Harverson had used to describe *Go-el*. Phantom, that was it. Jeffery Atkins was a phantom, of that he was now sure.

Almost satisfied with his search, Tim paused one last time to survey the room. There it was! Why he hadn't noticed it before he did not care. He was only thankful for his habitual double check. On the desk by the window was a pocket-sized note pad. The top sheet was blank, but the most junior investigator knew to hold the pad to the light to read the indentations left by the pressure of the pen strokes made on the previous sheet.

Barely legible, Tim strained his eyes to make out the colorless figures. "JFK...231...13:30," he read and committed to memory. Now having his first clue, Tim was satisfied with his evening's work and began the meticulous task of replacing every object he had moved or even touched.

Another fifteen minutes passed while Parnel finished his work. Now came the dangerous part of the mission. With no way of knowing who might be wandering the halls for a late-night bathroom trip, Tim now had to escape the room without anyone noticing. For all his skills, this part always came down to chance.

Quietly, smoothly, he swung the door open and swiftly stepped out, instantly looking up and down the hall. There was movement. At the far end of the hall, something had moved. Instinct told him to crouch and he obeyed, pulling the door closed behind him. He watched the north end of the hall intently, but there was no further movement. Had his eyes been playing tricks on him? It was possible, he surmised. After all, it was after 03:00.

Carefully he withdrew the filament from his shirt pocket. Using the penlight, he looked under the door. With the tape lightly attached to the end of the straightened paper clip, he slid the filament under the door, turned the wire up and gently pulled back, causing the tape to make contact with the inside of the door. Withdrawing the paper clip, Tim surveyed his work again. It was perfect. There was no way Jeffery Atkins would know his room had ever been entered.

Standing again, Tim began walking away from the scene of the crime, feeling the tension in his body relaxing with every step. Mission accomplished. Immediately he made his way to the closet-like phone booth downstairs from reception desk and reported in to headquarters, relieved that for once he actually had something to report.

*   *   *   *   *   *   *

Kyle laid in bed, his mind and emotions racing and warring in his head. What had he just witnessed? What should he do about it? Why had this new-comer stolen the heart of his love? These questions whirled through Kyle's young mind as he eventually drifted into a restless sleep.

April 5, 2004   **Santa Rosa, California**

For the second night in a row, Matt tried to sleep on the hide-a-bed sofa in his parents' living room. Though the faces that haunted his sleep were there every night, this night they were particularly fierce. After a near sleepless night, Matt rose at 05:00 and quietly put on his sweatpants, tank top, and running shoes.

Not wanting to wake his parents, he carefully opened the front door and stepped out into the cold, foggy morning. Though the temperature only dipped to 53 degrees that night,

112

the damp fog made the air feel much colder. For a moment, Matt considered putting on a sweatshirt but decided he would be warm soon enough. After the ritual five minutes of stretching, he set out for his daily five-mile run.

Reaching the street seconds later, Matt turned right to head toward the hills. As his eyes surveyed the foggy street, his senses were suddenly alert. Without breaking pace, he scanned the street. There was movement. In a gray sedan parked two doors up and across the street from his parents' house, something had moved. Did someone duck their head? There was no other movement.

Matt picked up his pace, resisting the urge to look back. If it were someone keeping an eye on him, it would be better not to let him know he'd been noticed. If they tried to put a hit on him, they'd blown their surprise and he would make them pay for that mistake. He continued running. No one followed him.

Thirty-three minutes later Matthew finished his five-mile run three blocks south of his parents' house. Cutting through an alley that would bring him within a block from the house, the ex-SEAL disappeared into the shadows and fog, now stalking, now the hunter.

Arriving at his parents' street, Pierson concealed himself behind the trash cans which would be collected later that morning. Searching for his prey, the hunter saw that the car was gone. Crouching low, he slid back down the alley the way he came. It wouldn't do to reveal his approach. He might need it again. He began to wonder if he was just being paranoid.

It was just after 06:00 when the former SEAL returned to the house. His mother was already up, wearing her pajamas and bath robe while starting to make breakfast. "Morning, Mom."

Startled, she turned and gave him a hug. "Good morning, Matt," she said, pushing him back while holding his shoulders, wanting to get another good look at her son as if to make sure he was really there. It was then that she noticed the star shaped, pink scar on her son's left shoulder.

"Oh, Matthew!" she gasped. "What happened to you?" Her eyes conveyed her motherly concern.

"I got careless once, Mom, that's all. It's really nothing," he evaded, cursing himself for not wearing the sweatshirt. He would have to remember the lesson. Scars raised questions.

His mother gently touched the scar with her fingers. "How long ago?" she asked, her voice revealing that she knew the nature of the wound and demanding an answer.

"About a year and a half."

"You didn't even...!" she stopped as the tears began to well up in her eyes.

"Mom, I'm sorry! The mission we were on was...," he stopped himself. "I didn't want you to worry."

It was obvious that there was no way to explain away the fact that he had been seriously wounded and had not told his own mother. "I'm sorry, Mom." He turned and walked toward the living room where his duffle bag contained his few belongings. As he turned, Monica saw the scar of the exit wound on the back of his shoulder.

Suddenly she rushed at him and grabbed him, turning him to face her again. "You listen to me! From now on, if you are in trouble, if you are hurt, I want to know about it! Do you hear me?"

Matt couldn't look at her. "Okay, Mom, I'll tell you," he answered, not at all sure if it was a promise he would be able to keep.

Once again, she pulled him into her arms and squeezed him. "Do you have any idea how much I love you?" she asked, not wanting or expecting an answer. "Now get some clothes on, you're going to get chilled!"

Matt grinned meekly. "Yes, Mom."

After a quick shower and shave, Matt took his place at the breakfast table, instinctively adjusting his chair to improve his view out the kitchen window toward the street. His father was now up as well and was reading the morning paper with one hand while holding his coffee mug in the other. At the stove, his mother was putting the final ingredients into her near-famous omelet. Matt had witnessed the scene perhaps a thousand times before but never had it evoked such emotion. He was home and it was good. A smile was spreading across his face when his father lowered his newspaper.

"What's got you so smiley?" he grunted in his croaky morning voice.

The question caught Matthew slightly off guard. "It's just that, seeing the two of you. . . it's just good to be home again, that's all."

Even Howard's morning grumps could not withstand the joy and pride he felt as he stared at his son. The disappointment he had felt when his only son had joined the Navy rather than enrolling in seminary had never changed the love he had for him. It was a fact that he had neglected to communicate enough at that time, however. "Matt, I can't tell you how good it is to have you here."

An awkward moment passed as the two men, father and son, stared across the table into each other's eyes. It was Mrs. Pierson who rescued them from the uncomfortable feelings of affection.

"Breakfast's on!" she announced as she began dishing out the omelet.

"Thanks, honey. Oh, Matt, that reminds me. I saw Pastor Steve last night at our council meeting and I told him you were home. He said he'd like to see you when you have time," Howard said tentatively, trying to the best of his abilities to avoid being pushy. He had been serving on the council of Immanuel Lutheran Church for the past two years. He knew that Matt and Pastor Steve had been close before Matt had joined the Navy and now secretly hoped that the pastor might offer Matt some guidance.

"Yeah, I'd like to see him sometime, too."

"He mentioned he didn't have any plans for lunch today. Why don't you give him a call?" he suggested innocently, but saw immediately that he had pushed too hard. Matt's expression had changed instantly. It wasn't anger, Howard recognized that immediately, but what was it? Sadness to be sure, but more. Then as quickly as the expression had come it was gone.

"I don't think I can make it today but I'll get together with him sometime. By the way, when you moved, did you hang on to my old scuba gear?"

"Yeah, it's up in the rafters in the garage. You want me to get it down for you?"

"No, Dad, that's alright, I can get it if you point me in the right direction."

Laying a plate full of toasted English muffins on the table, Monica slid into her seat and joined the conversation. "Are you planning to go diving?"

"Depends on whether my gear's still any good. I just thought I'd get it out and clean it up."

"I'll show you where it is after we eat. Oh, by the way, I was wondering if you'd help me out in the yard a little today?" Howard asked innocently.

For the second time in the still early morning, Matthew Pierson smiled, remembering how much he always hated yard work. Some things never changed.

Chapter Eight

"Were you able to get anything useful from that list of the people who attended that Liberation Theology conference?" Bill Kampo asked as he entered the Task Force private office just before 09:00. He had returned from Columbus the night before having gathered as much information as he could on the Deshaw assassination from the local police investigation. The killing had taken place a week ago and the Columbus detectives had yet to stumble across their first clue—not that the FBI or the *Go-el* Task Force had been able to find anything either. Now, after delivering his report to Austin and Stan, he wondered if his trip to Columbus would provide anything useful for the investigation.

"Just that the German couple on our suspect list from Trinity Seminary were at the conference. That's why we're keeping Susan at the Seminary as a prospective student for a few more days. Other than that, Pat and Brenda ran background checks on the others, but they haven't turned up anything interesting," Austin answered with frustration evident in his voice.

"What do you want me working on next?" Kampo asked.

"We got a call from Parnel early this morning. He's been checking out a guy named Atkins, Jeffery Atkins. Says he left the school in a hurry yesterday. Tim searched his room and found the details of an airline flight to New York. Brenda and Pat are trying to put together a list of potential targets in the area. Why don't you give them a hand?"

"Austin called the Bureau office in New York to get an agent to tail Atkins as soon as he steps off the plane.

Maybe that will lead somewhere," Stan informed the young agent as a matter of record.

"I thought Parnel said this guy was in Seattle when Deshaw was hit. Why are we still going after him?"

Stan studied the young man before him. He was bright, promising even, but he still had a lot to learn. He hadn't been around long enough to understand what could be learned by looking into someone's eyes.

"Tim's been working on a hunch and he's started picking up some strange things about Atkins. I gave him the go-ahead to continue probing."

"What has he found?"

"Nothing solid, yet."

Bill gave a smirk. "So he could be chasing his tail and getting us to follow."

Stan remembered hearing the same expression in Berlin from the lips of Helmut Osterhagen. He liked hearing it even less from a wet-behind-the-ears FBI academy brat. "Tell me, Bill, in your vast years of experience, have you ever heard of a Bible College student who leaves telltales on his dorm room door when he's out?"

"Well, no, but. . ."

"Half of good investigating is following your instincts. I've worked with Tim on and off for the last seven years, and his instincts are good. This Atkins may not be involved with *Go-el* but he's into something and he's dangerous. We're going to stick on him like glue until we're absolutely sure he's not involved with this and you are going to help until otherwise ordered. Do you understand me?" Stan barked.

Receiving the rebuke, though not fully comprehending his crime, Bill shuffled his feet nervously. "Sorry, boss. I didn't mean to. . ."

"It's alright," Stan cut him off for the second time. "Now get out of here and see if you can help save a life."

Stan watched the young agent leave the office then turned to find Austin sitting behind his larger desk, grinning like a school boy. It wasn't the grin as much as the fact that Austin Torvick rarely smiled at all.

"What the hell are you grinning about?"

"You're getting pretty defensive, old boy. You got to admit, the kid's got a point. We're still working on pretty slim information."

Had he not known it to be true, Stan might have fired off a defensive salvo but instead, simply nodded. "I guess he didn't quite deserve that but the boy gets a little too sure of himself sometimes."

"True, but then again, which of us doesn't?"

"Point taken."

"Let's get back to the issue at hand. You seem to think this Atkins is connected to *Go-el* somehow, don't you?"

"It's a gut feeling, Austin, that's all. And believe me, I am fully aware that the facts indicate otherwise. We ran a background check on the guy and he seems clean—no criminal record, solid family background, both parents still living in, ah," he stepped over to the smaller desk which was his and shuffled through a scattered pile of papers. "Spokane, Washington."

"But you still think he's dirty? Alright, Stan, let's roll with your intuition. Suppose Atkins is connected with *Go-el*, what does that tell us?"

Slowly Stan began to perceive where Austin was heading. Then suddenly it came clear. As though a light had just flashed on in his head, he blurted out the conclusion Austin already had in mind. "*Go-el* isn't the cryptic name for one man, it's a group, an organization."

Austin smiled. "That would explain a lot of things, wouldn't it?"

"The conflicting descriptions of Christoph Spielmann, the frequency of his attacks in Europe. . . and if we're right about Atkins, that's how he could be in Seattle when *Go-el* popped Deshaw. All along we have assumed we were hunting one individual, a phantom, but if there was more than one..."

"The problem is that if *Go-el* is a terrorist organization, what is their cause? What is their motive? Why haven't they ever made any demands? And maybe the most important missing piece is their funding. Who is their benefactor?"

"That's been the mystery from the beginning. Ultimately who is behind *Go-el*? Back in Europe we checked and double-checked our sources in Afghanistan, Libya, Iran, Iraq—all over the whole bloody Middle East. We checked every known European terrorist group. The attacks and victims seem to have nothing in common— especially Deshaw. At least the first attacks had been on military personnel or people connected with national security but Deshaw was on the senate transportation committee and was as pacifist as doves come."

"I haven't got any answers for those questions—yet, but I suggest that the two of us focus our attention on finding those answers. Let's go back to every victim. Somewhere there's a thread that connects them."

"We've been working that angle all along. If there's a connection, we're not seeing it, but go back to go and start over." Austin ordered.

After three weeks of working with Austin, Stan had reached his conclusion about the man. He liked him. He turned to leave the office so that he could run the new idea past the team when Austin called one more time.

"Oh, Stan, by the way, you were right."

"Really?" Stan asked, surprised. "About what?"

"We are going to get these bastards!"

April 6, 2004   New York City, New York

It was just after 08:00 when Jeffery Atkins, or rather now Philip Jamison, finally disembarked from his red-eye flight on the aged DC-10 at John F. Kennedy International Airport in New York. With no baggage to claim, he fought his way through the crowds to the row of car rental agencies which were located near the terminal exits. Approaching the Avis counter, he was greeted with a pleasant smile from a customer-service agent with long, curly, sandy-blonde hair.

"Good morning, sir. What can I do for you?"

How could anyone be so cheerful to a total stranger? For all she knew she could be talking to a killer or something, Atkins thought, amused by his own dark humor. "Yes, I believe I have a car reserved. My name is Jamison, Philip Jamison," he answered, producing his passport for identification.

"Just one moment while I call your reservation up on the computer, Mr. Jamison." She smiled again, obviously impressed by the British accent. "Did you just fly in from England?" she asked to pass the time while waiting for the reservation to appear on the computer screen.

"No, actually I've been in your country for almost a month. I'm just in from Los Angeles. Dreadful place, really. Still winter and it's already unbearably hot and smoggy."

Though she had never been in Los Angeles herself, she smiled politely and nodded her head as though she knew exactly what he was talking about. Had she thought to check, she would have found that the weather in Los Angeles had been unusually cold for the past ten days.

"Okay, Mr. Jamison. I have a silver Dodge Intrepid waiting for you in section E, row 3, stall 7. Your reservation indicates that you will be returning the car here tomorrow, is that correct?"

"Yes, that is correct." After pressing several more keys on the computer, she reached across the counter and handed the Englishman a set of keys and the assorted papers that needed his signature. "There you are, sir. You can pay when you return the vehicle. Your credit card will cover the deposit. The shuttle van will pick you up right outside these doors to your right. It should be here any minute. Thank you for choosing Avis." She continued smiling until her customer had turned toward the exit doors. Quickly she returned her attention to the Harlequin Romance novel which was concealed behind the counter.

"Excuse me, I need some information," a voice suddenly demanded.

Startled, she looked to see a man standing at the counter directly in front of her. He was well dressed, wearing a business suit with an open trench coat over it. More importantly, he was holding a badge and identification card which had three large letters across the top which read FBI. Frustrated with herself for not having seen him approaching, she stared at him blankly. "How can I help you?" she asked, her voice betraying her confusion.

"I need to the know the name of the man who just rented a car from you," he said abruptly.

"I'm afraid I can't give that..."

Slapping his identification on the counter he stared firmly into her wondering eyes. "You can and you will tell me the name of the man who just rented a car from you," he demanded.

After a moment of hesitation, she punched a number of keys on her keyboard. Though the transaction had taken place less than three minutes ago, the shock of being confronted by an FBI agent had driven the man so far from her consciousness that she could scarcely remember what he looked like, let alone his name. She became even more nervous as the agent drummed his fingers impatiently on the counter. Finally, the information was in front of her.

"His name is Philip Jamison."

"That can't be right. Check again."

"I'm sorry, this is our most recent transaction. That was his name, I remember now."

"Did he say anything? Where he was going? Why he was here? Anything?"

Struggling to collect her thoughts, the pieces slowly began to fall into place again. "He said he had just arrived from Los Angeles. He's from England, said he's been in the States for about a month. He even showed me his British passport."

"Damn that traffic!" the agent cursed. The call had come into New York's FBI office only twenty-five minutes ago with orders that an agent locate and tail a man named Jeffery Atkins. A description was given which matched the man who had just rented the car to a tee. If only he had arrived in time to see him get off the plane! "What kind of car did he rent?"

The clerk looked down at the computer screen again. "He rented a silver Dodge Intrepid."

"Where is it parked?"

"Section E, row 3, stall 7."

"Thanks," the agent called over his shoulder, already heading for the doors.

Five minutes later the agent screeched his government owned brown sedan into the Avis lot. Weaving up and down the rows of cars waiting to be rented, Special Agent Duane Pewonka arrived at section E, row 3, stall 7. It was empty.

"Damn it!" he cursed again. Well it wasn't his fault, and after all that might not have even been the right guy. Still he would have to report that he had missed his target. And of course, he would be blamed. What a way to start a day!

123

It had taken Philip Jamison seven hours to drive the 211 miles from John F. Kennedy International Airport to North Hampton, New Hampshire. Though the trip could have easily been made in five hours, even allowing for traffic, Jamison's instructions had called for him to pick up the tools he would need for the job. This meant a side trip to the Boston suburb of Dedham, where he found his package waiting inside the rental locker # 103 in the bus terminal. As instructed, he found the key to the locker beneath the third sink in the men's bathroom, secured with a piece of duct tape. Returning to his rented car, he navigated his way to I-95 North and made his way to North Hampton, New Hampshire.

Arriving just after 15:00, Philip stopped at a local coffee shop for a bite of lunch. He had a lot of work to do and after a red-eye flight from Seattle, he needed a little time for nourishment and rest.

Jamison chose a booth in the rear of the quaint ocean-side establishment which provided him with a view of the dining area and front entrance, as well as a quick escape through the rear exit.

Though he held a local newspaper in his hands, in fact he was studying a map of the North Hampton area which he had purchased at a gas station on the edge of town. The estate of Arthur Rossford was located one and a half miles off Route One, just three miles north of the town. After lunch, he would take a short drive up the coast for reconnaissance. The actual killing he had already planned on the flight. Now all that remained was to plan the infiltration.

He had been briefed on the security systems surrounding the Rossford estate in the email containing his instructions. Though the perimeter of the estate was protected by several advanced security measures, including microwave fencing and an elaborate video surveillance system, the primary security measure was comprised of an around-the-clock, four-man security team. Sixteen security men, mostly former special forces soldiers, were on a continual rotation. Most had been with Rossford for years and each was fiercely loyal to his employer.

Jamison scratched the stubble on his chin which had grown during his overnight flight. The restrictions his associate had given him would make this a very difficult kill. Under normal circumstances, a job like this would take months to plan. But his orders were to make the hit by Sunday, absolutely no later.

Folding up the map within the newspaper, Jamison turned his attention to his half-eaten lunch, allowing his mind to wander for a few moments. Though he had two days to complete his assignment, if he made the hit later this same evening or in the morning at the latest, he would have almost a day and a half for some fun in New York City. Though his cover as a Bible school student was ingenious, it was confining to his personal appetites. Of course, those had to be disciplined, for without control they could jeopardize everything.

Finishing the last bites of his Reuben sandwich, Jamison reached into the back pocket of his linen slacks and removed his wallet. Taking out a ten, he laid it on the table and slipped smoothly out of the booth, heading quickly toward the main doors of the café.

*   *   *   *   *   *   *

One hour later he was in position on a hill which gave a partial view of the Rossford estate. Concealed by the wild shrubbery that covered the hillside, he now surveyed the complex. The main structure, the guesthouse, and the guardhouse that served as the entrance to the estate were clearly visible from his perch.

From his vantage on the hill, Jamison confirmed his information about the static security provisions of the estate. An eight-foot-high stone-and-mortar wall surrounded the three sides of the twenty-three acres, while the thirty to fifty foot vertical cliffs protected the ocean frontage. The wall itself, for all practical purposes, was decorative, but the staggered array of fence-like metal posts provided a much more serious obstacle to a would-be intruder. He followed the staggered line of posts around the southern perimeter to the coastal cliffs where the transformer emitted its invisible beams. The web of microwaves transmitted between the staggered posts formed an invisible and virtually impenetrable barrier. Along the coastal cliffs, he could see no sign of the metal posts that formed the invisible fence. Apparently, the designer of the system felt the cliffs and pounding surf provided sufficient security from any ocean-side intrusion. Surrounding the main mansion, Jamison counted six video cameras and was sure there were many more.

Had time allowed, Philip could probably have overcome the high-tech obstacles but such an approach had already been ruled out. His goal was to slip in and slip out as quickly as possible. That left only one approach—the ocean. Jamison turned his binoculars on the pounding surf. It was by far the most physically dangerous approach but it was quite obviously the least expected. It would not be easy, but he would do it. He knew he could.

The only problem was that he had no way of knowing the location of the ocean-side video cameras. Well, first he'd have to swim through the pounding surf, then free climb the near vertical cliffs. Then he would worry about the cameras.

Satisfied with his reconnaissance, Jamison withdrew further into the shrubs, making his way back to the car that he had parked two miles south along the highway. It was already dusk and light was fading fast. He would have to hurry to prepare for his swim.

April 6, 2004   **Minneapolis, Minnesota**

Austin Torvick slammed the phone into its cradle and stormed out of the office he shared with Harverson, entering the open room occupied by the rest of the members of the task force. "Those idiots in New York never picked him up!" He spit out the words as though they were a curse.

Taking his cue, Stan slammed his fist down on the table where he, LeToure, and Kampo had been pouring over information on potential political targets in the New York area. Even the young Bill Kampo had come to acknowledge his own gut instinct that someone was going to die unless the Task Force could stop the man known as Jeffery Atkins.

"What did they say?" Stan asked, almost groaning.

"First, they confirmed what we already knew—that no one named Jeffery Atkins had arrived at JFK on any flight, at any time of day. Second, one agent, who arrived at the airport late because of traffic, caught sight of someone matching the description of Atkins but rather than following him immediately, went to the car rental service and got his name—a Philip Jamison, complete with British passport. By the time he got the information about the rental car, he had already lost him."

"What about GPS?"

"The Avis system is reporting that it is unable to locate the vehicle. Our suspect probably disabled it. The agent assigned to follow him issued an All-Points Bulletin on the vehicle, but so far nothing has come up. If he's as smart as he seems, he's probably swapped the plates with stolen ones." Torvick answered.

"Was the car rented for one-way or round trip? We might be able to catch up to him when he turns it in. At least we can get the mileage put on the vehicle when it's returned and at least figure his travel radius," Bill offered, somewhat sheepishly after his earlier rebuke. It wasn't until he finished his suggestion that he realized, along with the rest of task force, what the suggestion implied.

"In other words, we give up and wait for someone to get killed," LeToure interpreted, her elbows resting on the table, her chin cradled in her hands.

A feeling of utter helplessness swept through the room. Though everyone knew that Bill had not meant to suggest giving up, each knew that his suggestion would be their next clue. That would be after the media revealed the identity of the victim.

April 6, 2004   Santa Rosa, California

It was just after 19:00 on the west coast. The sun had just dipped below the horizon, the glow of dusk silhouetting the coastal hills west of Santa Rosa in the heart of California's wine country. Sitting alone on the back deck of his parents' house, under the light of the deck's two flood lights, Matt Pierson carefully turned the small screwdriver, slightly tightening the screw in the second stage of his scuba regulator that adjusted the flow of air. Earlier in the afternoon, while testing all his ten-year-old diving gear he had noticed that air was hissing from the mouth piece, a condition known as free-flowing.

He put the regulator in his mouth, inhaling and exhaling several times to make sure he had not turned the screw too tight, thus overly restricting the flow of air. A properly tuned regulator requires virtually no extra effort to inhale or exhale than normal breathing.

Satisfied that the regulator would function properly for the next morning's dive, he turned his attention to his spear gun. Though its paint was chipped and scratched from many fishing expeditions, Matt knew it would still function properly. A pneumatic gun used air compressed by a piston

128

to propel the spear. It packed enough punch to equal the power of a more traditional gun using three bands of surgical tubing.

Placing the shaft of the spear into the barrel, while planting the butt of the gun on his hip, he placed the safety cap over the tip of the spear and shoved the spear down the barrel, compressing the internal piston and arming the gun. Checking to make sure the safety was on, he then coiled the tether cord that attached the spear to the gun on its posts.

It was at that moment that the telephone rang from inside the house. On the third ring, Matt remembered that his parents had gone to a dinner party for the evening and if he didn't answer the phone, no one would. Sprinting across the deck to the sliding glass door, he slid it open and dashed toward the kitchen phone, catching it on the sixth ring.

"Hello?" he answered.

"Matt? I was just about to hang up. I thought you might have gone out for the evening," his sister Kathy said.

"Nah, Mom and Dad had that dinner party and I decided to stay here and get my gear ready for tomorrow's dive."

"Who ya gonna dive with?"

"I couldn't get a hold of anybody, so I'm going out alone," he confessed.

"I thought you were always supposed to have a buddy along," she retorted accusingly.

Matt closed his eyes as memories came suddenly back to haunt him. In the Teams, everyone was paired off with a swim buddy. Matt's swim buddy had been killed on mission during the early months of the war in Afghanistan. A wave of grief and anger flared and he wanted to shout into the phone, "I can't because he's dead!" He knew his sister had no way of knowing. Instead, all he could respond was a simple "I know."

"Well, anyway, Mike's and my plans fell through for the evening and we were wondering if you wanted to come over and play some cards. The boys would love to see you," she added to sweeten the proposal, knowing that Matt loved being with his nephews.

"Gosh, Sis, I don't know, I was kind of settled on watching the sitcoms, but I suppose...," he teased.

"Just be here in ten minutes," she snapped back playfully.

"Alright, I'll be there. Actually it sounds great."

Ten minutes, he thought. Enough time for a beer. He had just opened the refrigerator door when he heard the sound of a car door close, then another. Assuming it to be the neighbors, he went back out on the deck and began collecting his dive gear, checking off each piece as he packed it into his dive-bag.

Suddenly he froze. Footsteps. Someone had stepped on the gravel path on the east side of the house. He listened carefully. Faintly, he could hear the steps still approaching but no longer on the gravel. Someone was trying to be quiet, but not doing a good enough job.

Reacting quickly, he positioned himself against the wall and moved toward the northeast corner of the house to intercept the uninvited guest.

Ready to strike, he waited. The intruder was no more than two steps around the corner when suddenly a second intruder spun around the northwest corner of the house. The second intruder saw Pierson and instantly raised a pistol. The weapon spit three times, peppering Pierson with splinters from the siding of the house as he spun around the corner to intercept the first intruder, before allowing himself to be caught in the middle of a cross fire.

Pierson almost collided with his would-be attacker, who was now raising his silenced pistol. The man had been startled, causing him a moment of hesitation. Pierson instantly made him pay for his delayed reflexes. In one flowing motion, Pierson grabbed the weapon with his left hand, while slashing a rigid hand strike to the intruder's throat with the blade of his right hand. Twisting sharply, breaking the man's trigger finger in the process, Pierson tore the pistol from his stunned and gasping victim's hand. Swiftly raising the pistol to the man's head, Pierson prepared to dispatch the unwelcome guest, but before he could pull the trigger, his eyes met those of the helpless man in his grasp. He couldn't do it. He couldn't pull the trigger.

Knowing the second attacker would be coming around the corner in seconds, Pierson lowered the weapon and fired twice, once into each of the man's thighs. The man collapsed, trying to cry out but the only sounds to escape his fractured larynx were little more than grunts and pain-filled groans.

Wasting a precious second, Pierson moved behind the man, grabbing and raising his head by the hair. "I could have killed you. Remember that," he whispered. Then letting the wounded man's head fall, he spun and ran along the east wall of the house, hearing the second attacker round the corner behind him. Two more spits. Pierson heard both bullets whistle by, one passing near his left ear. Diving around the corner into his parents' front yard, Pierson twisted his head like an owl, searching for more attackers.

The front door to the house was open. He would have to move quickly. Crouching, he sprinted toward the open door. As he reached the steps leading to the door, a figure appeared in the doorway. Still closing the distance between the two, Pierson raised the weapon and fired two shots, one striking the figure in the lower leg, the other missing. With his leg blown out from under him, the figure fell forward out of the dark entry of the house into the glow of the front porch light.

The man tried to roll and acquire his target to return fire, but Pierson was already upon him. Whipping the pistol across the back of the man's head, Pierson allowed his momentum to carry him on into the entry way of the house. Instantly bullets struck the walls and floor around him.

Rolling to his right, into the living room, still more bullets passed close by, ripping into his parents' antique sofa. "Mom's gonna be pissed!" he muttered to himself, not having time to enjoy his humor. Sliding in behind his father's favorite recliner, he ducked as low as he could, waiting for the bullets that should have followed him. But nothing struck the chair, or more importantly, him. They were reloading.

The bullets fired within the house had come from at least two directions, meaning at least two more attackers. The interior lights in the front of the house were out, thankfully, and Pierson could see light spilling into the dining room from the kitchen. A shadow whisked across the doorway between the two rooms. He would start there.

From his position behind the chair, Pierson lunged, rolling from behind the chair toward the dining room. Silhouetted by the light of the kitchen, with his night vision impaired by the bright kitchen lights, the attacker appeared in the doorway, firing wildly at his rolling target. "Amateur," Pierson thought thankfully. Bullets tore up the carpet behind Pierson as he continued to roll. Reaching the dining room table, he flipped it on its side. Three more bullets struck the table, easily passing through the one-inch oak table top. Now it was Pierson's turn to fire. From a prone position, he swung the pistol around the overturned table, near the floor, his head following instantly, his eyes immediately acquiring his target who at least had the sense to use the doorjamb for cover. Pierson fired into the wall. Two shots, the bullets passing easily through the sheet rock wall. The attacker fell to the floor and did not move.

Now everything in the house was silent. Pierson listened for sounds from his fourth and hopefully last attacker. He waited. Still nothing. He pressed the clip release on the pistol. Catching the magazine, he held it to the light. Three rounds in the clip, one chambered. They would have to be enough. The odds were good.

132

Suddenly the sound of screeching tires broke the tense silence. He could hear footsteps, people running.

"Parker's down!" a voice called.

"Cover the back!" another ordered.

Two more, at least. The odds just worsened. He had to get out of the house. Leaping to his feet he charged into the well-lit kitchen. A short, unmuffled burst of automatic gun fire shattered the silence. The odds were now totally unacceptable.

Clearing the kitchen, he charged for the sliding glass doors leading to the backyard deck. Prepared to crash through the closed glass door, the machine gun fire erupted again, the errant bullets shattering the glass in front of him. Stumbling on the aluminum door frame, Pierson sprawled onto the deck, the broken glass slicing into his left palm and forearm. Rolling, he dropped off the edge of the deck. Thinking only of fleeing the scene, Pierson got to his feet and ran into the bushes that formed the perimeter of his parents' backyard.

"There he is!" a new voice rang out.

Concealed within the bushes, Pierson paused for a moment. He needed to think. Whoever his attackers were, surely they wouldn't chase him on foot through the neighborhood and risk civilian casualties. They would search the bushes, though. He could hear them approaching even now. Then an idea came to him.

For a SEAL, stealth was essential and the former SEAL now put his skills to full use. Stepping slowly on the outside edge of his feet, Pierson began working his way along the shrub row, back toward the house. As he had hoped, he could hear whispering, behind him now. The few words he could understand indicated that they assumed he had gone over the fence and was somewhere out in the neighborhood. It wouldn't be long before they would give up their search and return to the house.

Reaching the edge of the house, Pierson silently belly crawled or rather walked in a prone position, using his finger tips and toes, to the edge of the backyard deck. Sliding himself underneath, he lay still, listening and waiting.

It wasn't two minutes later that the attackers who had followed him into the bushes gave up their search and returned to the house. Now standing on the deck, almost directly above their target, the two men were met by another who had come from inside the house. With his pistol pointed straight up, ready to fire, Pierson listened.

"He made it over the fence. He could be anywhere in the neighborhood," one reported.

"What the hell happened?" the other asked. "Who is this guy?"

"That's not your concern. Our target has a sister that lives only two miles away. He might go there for help. Take Swede and Ortega and get over there. If you get a shot, kill him. He killed McCormick and put the hurt on Parker and Hill. I want this son of a bitch dead, do you read me?" Commander Joshua Denzer barked.

"Yes, sir!" he man snapped back.

Pierson remembered Pepper Adler's words. Apparently, *they* weren't going to let him walk away.

Lying still on the cool earth, with the boards of the deck inches above his face, Matthew Pierson suddenly had the sensation that he was lying in a coffin and figuratively speaking, he was. Though his attackers had failed to kill him, they had taken away his life. He knew he could never again return to his family for in doing so he would place them all in danger, and he would never allow that.

There beneath the deck of his parents' house, while the men above scrambled to clean up and take away the wounded, Lieutenant Matthew Pierson, ex-SEAL, Religious Studies major, beloved son, breathed his last and died. Only his body didn't know.

The man whose name was presently Philip Jamison had now been swimming for almost two hours, yet he had only covered just over a mile and a half of shoreline. Actually, he was making better time than he had expected, given the conditions. Swimming through moderate-to-rough seas was slow and strenuous even for the advanced combat swimmer that he had once been. The eight-foot swells continued their unending pattern, thrusting the weary swimmer up, then plunging him again into the trough to wait for the next swell to pass.

He had parked his vehicle at Hampton Beach State Park and entered the frigid water on the north end of the park, aided by the soft glow of the setting sun. Among the equipment in the bag he had picked-up in Dedham was a full, 7mm neoprene wetsuit, mask and snorkel, weight belt, and fins—all of which he now utilized, including a water-resistant pack which was strapped to his back.

With the sun's light completely gone, the only illumination available to the swimmer was given by the rising half-moon. He had swum about a quarter mile from shore before turning north for his approach to the Rossford Estate. The estate lights had become visible, at least from the top of the waves, about fifteen minutes ago. Breathing heavily through his snorkel, he began the most dangerous part of the swim. His approach required swimming toward, between and around the nearly invisible tidal rocks and in doing so, avoiding being dashed against one by the powerful breaking waves.

Within fifty yards from shore, Jamison felt himself sinking as a large breaker began forming behind him. He had hoped to time his final approach so as to pass through the dead zone during the several seconds of slack between the crashing waves. In his mind he cursed, but to no avail. Jamison now pumped his fins furiously in a desperate

135

attempt to free himself from becoming a victim of the dead zone, the area in tidal waters where waves break, or crashed in this case, trapping a swimmer between the incoming thrust of the wave and the outgoing undertow, never allowing its victim a chance to recover.

He scarcely had time to feel himself rising again before the next eight-foot breaker hurled him forward, directly into the side of a tidal wash rock. Striking the jagged rock with his left shoulder and the side of his head, the swimmer's mask was dislodged, instantly filling with water. Still caught in the momentum of the wave, he was then plunged into the foaming white water. Instinctively his right-hand tore at the buckle of his weight belt and released it.

Dazed and disoriented, Jamison struggled to bring his head above water, not even conscious of the direction of the water's surface. Finally, aided by the buoyancy of his wet suit, the wave released him and he rolled his head above the surface, gasping for air. The next wave hit before he could finish the breath. Rather than life-giving air, his lungs filled with salt water.

Only his training and fierce will for survival allowed him to survive. With lungs desperate for air and burning from the salt water, Jamison again pumped his fins with all the strength he could muster. A third wave crashed, but this time it propelled him forward. His hand struck another rock and he grabbed onto it with both hands, clinging to it as the water began to withdraw to form yet another wave in the endless pattern. Coughing and gasping, he waited for the next wave, releasing his grip as the wave propelled him further toward the shore.

Finally, he reached the rocks which formed the base of the cliffs belonging to the Rossford Estate. Pulling himself to safety on a high rock, Jamison coughed uncontrollably, vomiting several times during the next ten minutes. Slowly the coughing began to subside enough for him to evaluate his condition.

His mask had thankfully been pushed down around his neck and not lost. He would need it for the return swim. He felt the left side of his head. He found a large and very tender lump. He tried to raise his left arm and winced at the pain. The fingers of his right hand traced along his left clavicle, relieved to find that the bone was intact. A deep bruise, perhaps a mild separation. That would hamper him in his climb up the cliffs. He laid back on the rock, allowing himself five more minutes of precious rest before beginning his preparations for the evening's next task.

Another half hour passed as he removed his wet suit and dressed in the partially dry black clothes he had packed in the backpack. Dressed again, he gingerly slipped his arms through the straps of the pack and shouldered it, the remaining tools to be used in the evening's third task packed within it.

With his eyes now adjusted to the dark, he made his way across the tidal rocks to the base of the actual cliff. Though painful, he was again relieved to discover that his shoulder seemed strong enough to help pull him along.

Compared with the swim, the climb was uneventful. Reaching the ridge, Jamison's lungs still burned from the salt water and exertion but he could not, would not allow himself to cough. He checked his watch; it was 22:03. Freeing himself from his pack and opening it, he withdrew a waterproof case. Contained within was a pair of Starlight night-vision goggles. Adjusting the straps to his head, he lowered the goggles to his eyes. The images seen through the goggles appeared in shades of green and slightly out of focus yet they provided enough light and detail for his purposes.

He counted six video surveillance cameras. They were well positioned, but after studying their angles and fields of vision, Jamison chose his approach. Clutching his backpack in his fist and stooping low, he sprinted from point to point, always keeping just outside the vision field of the surveillance cameras.

Arriving at the main house, Jamison disappeared into the shadows as one of the security guards suddenly appeared from around the corner. Jamison quickly determined by the man's steady, unhurried pace that he was on patrol, obviously not alarmed. Again Jamison's lungs burned while he desperately struggled to stifle the urge to cough. The guard continued his route, which took him around the other side of the huge house.

$$* \quad * \quad * \quad * \quad * \quad * \quad *$$

Arthur had retired to his bedroom earlier that evening, reading himself to sleep. Suddenly he was awake again. Had there been a noise? Had something moved through the room? Still half asleep, Arthur rubbed his eyes and looked at the mantle clock which stood above the bedroom fireplace, directly across the room from the fully adjustable king-sized bed. It was 11:15 p.m. With his eyes coming into focus, he looked around the room. Everything was in order, nothing had moved. There was no one with him.

Sure that he had been dreaming, Arthur swung his legs over the edge of the bed. Standing slowly, unsteadily, he staggered across the room toward his private bathroom.

The truth was that Arthur's health had slipped considerably just in the last few days, a fact noticed by his daughter and his domestic help that had evoked deep concern about his wellbeing. In fact, it was earlier that evening while dining with her father and family in the main house, that Rachel had insisted that her Daddy call his personal doctor first thing in the morning. Reluctantly, he had agreed and everyone except Arthur left the meal feeling quite relieved.

Arthur, however, knew that no doctor could help him with his condition. He had decided to medicate his condition himself that evening, reading from the Bible's First Letter of

138

John, specifically focusing his attention on chapter one, verse nine. "If we confess our sins, God is faithful and just and will forgive our sins and cleanse us from all unrighteousness."

Remembering the verse now as he walked toward the bathroom, he prayed that the words were true. Reaching the door to the bathroom, Arthur reached inside, sliding his hand up and down the wall until his fingers found the light switch.

Instantly the bathroom lights brightened the room, but Arthur's eyes never saw the light.

*　　*　　*　　*　　*　　*　　*

Using a nine-inch, plastic-covered lead rod, the assassin struck his victim on the left side of the forehead, hard enough to render the aged man unconscious, but not with enough force to fracture the skull. Assassinations such as this were an art. Jamison caught the man in his arms lest he fall and damage himself, thus ruining the masterpiece in the making. Gently lowering the unconscious man to the floor, he surveyed his workmanship.

A large lump had formed and was already turning slightly purple yet the blow had not split the skin. Perfect. The old man's eye lids were partially open, the eyes themselves rolled up and quivering. That meant the victim might regain consciousness soon. That would not do. The assassin would have to hurry.

Working quickly now, Jamison removed the man's pajamas and dragged him to the side to the bath tub, which he noticed was equipped with Jacuzzi jets and was easily large enough for two. Opening the faucet, he began filling the tub with hot water. As the tub filled, Jamison raised the man's legs over the side of the tub, allowing the blood to flow to the man's head. Gently turning the victim's head, he traced his fingers through the gray hair just above and behind the man's right ear. Locating the post auricular vein, the killer left one finger on the vein, while reaching with his other hand to the vanity where he had left his backpack.

Withdrawing a small, black plastic case, Jamison opened it with his free hand. Suddenly the old man groaned and shifted slightly, pulling the assassin's finger from the vein. Jamison held his breath. It just wouldn't do for his victim to regain consciousness, not now. The man's head raised slightly, his eyes trying to roll down from there upturned position, but unable. The old man's muscles relaxed again, his head falling back to the floor.

With both hands free, the assassin quickly withdrew a syringe and small glass vile from the plastic case. Plunging the needle into the rubber cap of the bottle, he depressed the plunger, then slowly drew it back, filling the syringe with the appropriate amount of potassium chloride, a drug commonly used for treating diabetic comas or for cardio-pulmonary resuscitation. Yet tonight, the drug had other purposes. If administered in a large enough dose, the drug could actually trigger cardiac arrest and be completely absorbed into the body, leaving virtually no trace in the victim's blood or organs.

With the syringe filled and ready, Jamison again searched for the vein. Finding it, he parted the old man's thick gray hair with his fingers, allowing him to see the vein that was his target. With a quick stab, Jamison plunged the needle into the vein and slowly depressed the plunger, pumping the deadly dosage into the man's body. Withdrawing the needle, he wiped away the tiny drop of blood. When he was satisfied that there would be no more bleeding, he smoothed down the hair to cover the wound. Unless the pathologist was extraordinarily thorough, the tiny wound would never be found.

The drug now only needed time to work through the old man's system for the assassination to be complete. Satisfied with his work, he reached under the body and rolled it over. Now it was time for the real artistry. With the body now on its stomach, Jamison left one leg propped up on the edge of the tub. The other leg he bent at the knee, leaving it lying on the floor.

Across from the tub, next to the vanity, a towel rack held two towels. Grabbing the nearest in his fist, Jamison pulled it down and toward himself, allowing it to fall to the floor near the dead man's head. Grabbing the man's limp left arm, he brought it over the corpse's head, then closing the man's fingers around the bath towel exactly where he had grabbed it moments ago.

The final touch was the water. Satisfied that the tub was full enough, he shut the faucet. Cupping the water in his hands, he carefully poured water over the naked corpse, then spreading it with his palms. He completely wet the man's hair, smoothing it back with his fingers as one might do after rinsing their hair in a bath, all the while making sure the tiny puncture wound from the needle had not bled any more.

Now finished, the assassin stood to survey his deadly art. There was just enough water on the floor for someone who had just stepped out of a tub, or in this case, slipped out while reaching for a towel he had forgotten to get prior to the bath. The head was strategically turned to make it appear as though the victim had stepped out of the tub with his left foot and had slipped on the wet marble floor. The unfortunate man had plunged head first to the floor. The trauma had triggered a massive heart attack and thus the scene was complete. It was morbidly perfect.

Now only two tasks remained before the assassin made his escape. The first simply required waiting. In case one of the late Arthur Rossford's servants had heard the water running, he would wait ten more minutes, allowing an appropriate amount of time for a nice, hot bath. While waiting, Jamison submerged the almost fresh bar of soap in the water several times to soften its surface as though it had recently been used. Then he poured a small amount of shampoo into the water, allowing the Jacuzzi jets to mix it throughout the tub.

At the end of the ten minutes, Jamison opened the drain of the tub, allowing the water to begin its escape. Certainly a man reaching for a towel would have already opened the drain.

All was complete and the assassin began his escape, exactly retracing his approach route, though he dreaded re-entering the water. It was strange—the farther he got from the scene, the more his head and shoulder began to ache. Funny, he thought. He had not noticed either wound while practicing his art.

Chapter Nine

April 7, 2004   **Santa Rosa, California**

Neighbors had reported a disturbance and the sound of gunfire. Four Sonoma County Sheriff's Department squad cars were sent speeding to 312 Wikiup Circle. Though it had only taken six minutes to respond to the call, apparently that had been too long.

They arrived to find the front of the house wide open. From the light of the porch they stepped into the dark house. With weapons drawn and ready, four officers searched the house, discovering evidence of the carnage that had taken place only minutes ago. The stench of cordite gun powder hung in the air, the smoke making the air inside the house hazy as the officer's flashlights swept through the rooms. Toward the back of the house, the kitchen lights were lit, along with the flood lights on the back porch. Two pools of blood were discovered on the initial search, one on the front porch, the other on the kitchen floor. Numerous bullet holes decorated the walls and furniture of the living room with two more holes through the dividing wall between the dining room and the kitchen. The sliding glass doors which led to the backyard deck had been shattered, the broken glass lying outside, revealing that the impact that had shattered the doors had come from inside the house. There were bloody streaks on the deck amid and on the broken glass.

Sonoma County Sheriff's Detective Shawn McCallister had been the first homicide detective to arrive at the crime scene, which was now seven hours old. For all the evidence of violence, not one person, dead or alive, had been found. One more pool of blood was discovered on the gravel walkway on the east side of the house.

It was just after 23:00 when the owners of the house arrived to find their home in shambles and crawling with police officials. Obviously in the first stages of shock, the frightened couple was bombarded with a seemingly endless stream of questions, few of which they were able to answer.

Apparently, their son, Matthew Donald Pierson, age 28, had returned home five days before, having finished his tour of duty in the Navy. Other than that morsel of information, the most useful thing they had provided was permission to search the house.

It was in the living room, next to the kitchen, that one of the deputies made the discovery that offered the first clue to the violence that had taken place earlier that evening. Beneath the cushions of the hide-a-bed sofa which the Piersons' son had been using for a bed was found a sealed plastic bag, containing what the officers estimated to be about 8 ounces of cocaine.

The discovery had confirmed McCallister's suspicion that drugs had to be the motive for such carnage. To the owners of the ravaged house, it was one more blow to an already shocked and beleaguered couple. With McCallister's permission, the owner of the house, Dr. Howard Pierson, had called his daughter, who arrived five minutes later to give comfort to her parents. Apparently, her brother was supposed to have come over to her house earlier in the evening but never showed up.

Satisfied that he had obtained enough information from the family, he dismissed them, allowing them to go to their daughter's house for some much-needed rest. It was 3:00 a.m., after all.

Now, McCallister strolled through the house one more time, working his way around the crime team and officers who were busily decorating the house with bright yellow plastic tape with black letters which read "Crime Scene—Do Not Cross." For a moment, he empathized with the couple, Howard and Monica Pierson, he recalled. They had innocently returned to their house to find it shot up and to discover that their only son was involved with drug trafficking. Then his thoughts turned to the son. Matthew was his name. What kind of scum would endanger his whole family by trafficking drugs through his parents' house? He would find some answers when the sun rose and could get his hands on a copy of the creep's service record. With his thoughts swirling and anger growing, he continued his stroll, trying, along with the rest of the investigators, to reconstruct what had taken place.

April 8, 2004   North Hampton, New Hampshire

It was just after 8:00 a.m. when Rachel Rossford-Phelps entered her father's bedroom, hoping to playfully wake him and start his day off with a smile. He had seemed so down lately, not himself at all yet he would not say a word to anyone about what was troubling him.

Quietly pressing down the door handle, she tip-toed into the room, disappointed to find that her father was not in bed. He was up already on his own, apparently in the bathroom. Walking to the closed door, she knocked gently.

"Daddy! I just came to wake you up and get your day off to a good start," she called, but received no reply. Hearing no water running, she called again, "Daddy?" her voice questioning, but not yet worried. Still not receiving answer, Rachel knocked again, much harder this time. "Daddy? Are you in there?"

Wondering if perhaps he had woken early and gone for a walk, she almost turned away to search for him elsewhere but decided in the last moment to check the bathroom door. It was unlocked. Peeking in, she called one more time "Daddy?" Then she screamed.

The ambulance arrived fifteen minutes later, its crew discovering immediately that their services would not be needed. The coroner arrived with the first squad car from the North Hampton Police Department. Photos were taken, the bathroom and bedroom carefully searched. The officers quickly reconstructed the accident in their minds, sketching notes and taking measurements. Within two hours, the body of Arthur Rossford was given to the custody of the coroner, who would perform an autopsy later that afternoon.

While the police investigated the scene of the accident, the Rossford security force reviewed the video tapes of the previous day's surveillance. Nothing was out of the ordinary. There had been no alarms tripped, no evidence whatsoever that there had been an intruder or any other abnormality.

Between the physical evidence of the accident and the lack of anything suspicious from the night's surveillance, it was quickly assumed that Arthur Rossford had tragically slipped on the wet floor while reaching for his towel, striking his head against the floor. The autopsy would later determine that a massive heart attack had ensued and the case would be closed.

Comforted by her husband, Rachel decided to delay releasing the news of her father's death to the press until the next morning. She knew that she wasn't strong enough at the moment to handle the questions of reporters.

April 8, 2004　　　　　**Boston, Massachusetts**

Exhausted, the man who called himself Philip Jamison collapsed on the queen-sized bed in one of Boston's downtown hotels. The room had been rented on his behalf the day before. The key to the room had been the last item in the tool bag which had been provided for him. Arriving at his room just after 09:00, he wasted no time before placing his confirmation call. Only one word was spoken. "Done." His mission completed, he now drifted easily into a deep sleep. The Do Not Disturb sign ensured that he would not be disturbed while his message was relayed.

April 8, 2004
Trinity Lutheran Seminary, Columbus, Ohio

Half a country away, Gabriele Zibermann-Fitzbaun picked up the phone on the second ring, only to hang up a moment later. Rolling over in bed, she gently laid her head on the chest of the man beside her. Her husband, Dieter, was awakened on first ring, but since the phone was on the night stand on his wife's side of the bed, he allowed her to answer.

Raising his hand to stroke her long blonde hair, he whispered to her. "*Vas dat* him?" he asked in his perfected German accent.

"*Jah*. It is done," Gabriele responded applying her own adopted accent.

"Then I suppose I must get dressed and make the next call," he sighed, trying to raise his torso with the added weight of his wife's head.

Playfully she pushed him back down. "There is no need to hurry, old man," she teased. Though she didn't know his exact age, she estimated that he was at least ten years her senior, a fact which she continually taunted him with. "You have things to attend to here as well," she added, removing the need for further explanation by allowing her hand to explore his body.

Firmly grabbing her hand and painfully jerking it away from himself, he rolled onto his side to stare into his wife's face. "Business first, then we can play," he said sternly, momentarily forgetting his accent. Instantly

147

recognizing the look of rejection and anger that flashed across Gabriele's eyes, Dieter decided to soften his refusal. "With one little phone call, we will add $300,000 to our retirement fund, my love. We can celebrate when I return," he whispered, now gently pulling her hand to his lips and kissing it.

Though she was still pouting, he saw immediately that his change of tactics had produced the desired effect. Suddenly playful again, she pulled her hand from his grip and rolled away, wrapping herself in the blankets in the process. "I'll be waiting for you," she said with mock passion.

*   *   *   *   *   *   *

"This is your FTD florist, calling to confirm delivery of your flowers," Dieter spoke into the answering machine 900 miles away. "Your account has been billed. Thank you for your patronage and contact us again if we can be of any service."

The cryptic message complete, he hung up the phone. Leaving the public phone outside the Sinclair service station on Morse Road in downtown Columbus, Dieter drove his rust-eaten Volkswagen bug to a small unfurnished apartment which he had rented immediately upon his arrival in Columbus. A telephone was the only object to decorate the shabby downtown dwelling.

He and his wife had arrived in the United States one year ago, choosing Trinity Lutheran Seminary as the base for his operations in the United States. Continuing his extremely functional cover as a student of theology, Dieter Zibermann, whose real name had not been used in the twenty years since he left his Pittsburgh home, had chosen Columbus for its central geographical location in the United States. As with all the places he had called home over the last twelve years, arrangements were already in place for him and his wife to abandon their current home at a moment's notice, establishing a new base within days. Such arrangements by their very nature made establishing roots impossible, but such hardships were simply a part of his chosen career and he would have it no other way.

The one emotional tie he clung to was his wife, who now called herself Gabriele. Fully twelve years younger than he, he had met her in England five years ago, while his relationship with his current benefactor was beginning to blossom. Initially, he admitted, his attraction to her had been merely physical. Slowly that had changed as he discovered that she shared with him the central passion and driving force in his life—vengeance.

Her father had once been an aspiring broker with the Benson and Iverson Investment Group, one of London's most successful brokerage firms. Yet, when the group was indicted on charges of investment fraud, her father had conveniently been handed over as the proverbial patsy. His career ruined and publicly disgraced, his eventual suicide was only a matter of time. At that time only a girl, Dieter's wife watched helplessly as her father slipped deeper and deeper into the depression that led to the taking of his own life.

Her hatred of the British financial and political establishment propelled her into the world of radical activism—protesting, at times violently, almost any facet of British society. It was at a protest against American nuclear missiles on English soil that Dieter had met her though he had not been there to protest but to kill. Who his target had been he could scarcely remember. An activist priest? Yes, that was it, though he could not remember his name.

Suddenly the telephone rang and called his thoughts back to the present. He let it ring again and again. On the fourth ring, the answering machine came on, informing the caller that the tenant was unavailable. Immediately recognizing the voice of the caller, he picked up the receiver.

"*Jah*, I am here," he declared.

"I received your message about the delivery of the flowers, but I have not been able to confirm the delivery. Until I verify the delivery, payment will be withheld," the voice said with finality.

Dieter felt a wave of anger wash through him. "The flowers have been delivered, your bill is due. Now," he said tensely, wanting desperately to drop the cryptic language and tell the son of a bitch on the other end of the line that he was screwing with the wrong person.

"You will be paid as soon as we verify the delivery. Remember, the customer is always right," the voice responded arrogantly.

"I will check the account Monday. Would you like to place any other orders today?"

"No, thank you, not today. The wife and I will be going on vacation for about a month, so don't expect any orders until we get back but then I'm sure we'll keep you busy."

"All right then. We will be waiting for your next order. Remember, your account is due Monday. Thank you for your business," Dieter concluded and hung up the phone.

Angrily he kicked the barren wall of the apartment. His American network had been in place for six months already and there had only been two assignments! Now, he would have to wait another month. He kicked the wall again. His benefactor had better not try anything with the payment for the Rossford hit. He would not tolerate any irregularity with the financial arrangements.

His morning's work completed, Dieter left the decrepit apartment, locking the door behind him. With his mind now free from his responsibilities, he remembered the offer Gabriele had made before he left their single bedroom apartment in the married student housing of Trinity Lutheran Seminary. He had been rather hard on her earlier. The idea of buying her flowers brought a grin to his face. He loved irony, after all.

April 8, 2004   **Santa Rosa, California**

It was after noon when Howard and Monica Pierson woke from their sedative-induced sleep in the guest room of their daughter's house. Emerging from the bedroom they were greeted by the warm smiles and hugs from two of their grandsons, a greeting that under normal circumstances could have brightened their tired eyes and brought smiles to their faces as well, but not this day.

Kathy, the second oldest of the Pierson's four children, also greeted them as they staggered into the kitchen, smiling tiredly and handing each a cup of coffee. She invited them to sit at the kitchen table while she began serving the late brunch. Recognizing that neither Mom, Grandma nor Grandpa seemed interested in playing, the two boys quickly returned to the playground they had made of the living room.

Once the food was served, Kathy took her place at the table. There was a moment of hesitation as each waited for someone else to say the table prayer. Assuming the responsibility, Howard cleared his throat.

"Dear Lord, our God, we thank you for your love. We thank you for your blessings," he said wearily, unable to hide the sorrow in his heart. "Bless this food to our bodies and strengthen us for your service..." He paused to swallow back his tears. "And Lord, take care of our son, and bring him home," he managed to mumble. "Amen."

He could hear his wife and daughter sniffling. He paused for several moments, leaving his head bowed, knowing with certainty he could not contain his emotions if he were to look into the eyes of his family.

151

"Mike had to go into the office to get some work done this morning but he should be home anytime," Kathy interjected into the emotional void. "He said he would call a friend he has in the Sheriff's Department to see if he can find out anything about Matt."

"I just can't believe that Matt is mixed up with drugs!" Howard suddenly exploded. "I just won't believe it!"

"Kathy, he spent some time over here with you the last few days. Did he say anything to you? Anything about some sort of trouble, or what happened with the Navy?" Monica asked with an air of desperation in her voice.

"No, Mom, nothing. I even asked him what had happened with his discharge but he really didn't tell me anything." She paused for a moment, trying to recall something. "He did say something funny about the discharge, though. He said, 'Your little brother's got a problem with his temper, but you probably remember that.' He said it like he was joking so I just passed it off."

The ringing of the chimes on the front door interrupted the conversation. From the living room there were screams of excitement as Kyle and Jason rushed to greet their father, who was barely through the door when they slammed into his legs. "Whoa, guys! Go easy on me. You almost knocked me out of my shoes!" he said playfully, inciting the boys to further rough-housing.

"Okay, okay, that's enough. You guys go play in the living room for a little bit longer while I talk to Grandma and Grandpa. Later on I'll take you to the park and we can play catch," he promised his sons, knowing that at the ages of five and three, playing catch was more like "Daddy, go fetch!" As the two squealed their way back to the living room, Mike Rosetti made his way to the kitchen with the day's mail in his hand.

Not sure how to greet the somber assembly, he decided to state the obvious. "I picked up the mail on the way in," he announced, quickly shuffling through the half-dozen

152

envelopes. Suddenly he stopped, pulling a postcard from the other mail which he had carelessly let fall to the floor.

The postcard pictured one of Santa Rosa's famous landmarks, the Round Barn. Flipping it over he immediately saw that it was from Matt and began to read out loud.

"I want you to know that I'm alright. I don't know what they've told you about me, but I had my reasons. I won't be coming home again, I can't put you in danger because of my mistakes. I love you all. I always have, I always will. —Matt"

Immediately, Mike noticed the rust colored smudge of blood on the upper left corner of the card and the post mark from the Larkfield post office, dated with the current date. He must have dropped it off right at the post office last night for it to have gone out with the rest of the day's mail. Without a word, he handed it to his father-in-law, who read it for himself then passed it across the table to Monica, who in turn handed it to Kathy. "At least we know he's alright. I guess that's a start," she offered.

"What has he gotten himself into?" Howard asked, knowing that no one present could give him an answer.

"I talked to my friend in the Sheriff's Department. He promised he'd snoop around and call me when his shift goes off at six this evening. He might be able to tell us something."

"I don't care how I have to do it but I'm going to find out what's going on and I'm going to set it right." Howard declared with finality but without any idea where to begin. For now, he would have to wait. He stabbed the sausage patty on his plate with his fork in frustration. Howard Pierson did not like waiting.

April 8, 2004   **Minneapolis, Minnesota**

Rising from the office chair, Stan stretched his arms toward the ceiling while exhaling a long, slow breath. It was a subconscious relaxation habit he had developed years ago. He had been staring at a computer screen for the past six hours without a break, hoping against hope that by some miracle he might prevent a death, but each passing moment only feeding his feeling of utter helplessness. Pulling himself from his desk, he rose and stretched further.

Quietly moving behind her chair, Stan reached down and gently began massaging Pat Knodell's neck. She, too, had been up all night and most of the day studying every piece of information she could call up on political events in the New York area. She sighed with pleasure at his touch, letting her hands fall from the keyboard into her lap.

Stan had sent the rest of the Task Force home to their hotel rooms two hours ago, knowing that there was really nothing any of them could do but wait. Even Austin Torvick, who had been working for twenty-three straight hours, reluctantly left headquarters for some desperately needed sleep.

Aside from the light of a desk lamp and two computer screens, the office complex was now dark. Neither had noticed that the sun had set an hour earlier.

"Oh, that feels wonderful!" she purred.

"You need some rest, too, Pat," he whispered. "Why don't you call it a day and get some sleep. I can hold down the fort and hit the alarm if any news comes in," he suggested, secretly hoping she would refuse.

"As tired as I am, I don't think I could sleep. Besides, the hotel doesn't offer masseur services."

"Thanks, Pat," he whispered. This was one night he didn't want to be alone. "Should I order up some Chinese?"

"Ugh, if I never see take-out Chinese food again it will be too soon!" she protested. "How 'bout trying something different. Brenda and I had lunch the other day at a Mediterranean restaurant a couple blocks away. The food was great and they deliver. . ." she teased.

Stan groaned. Experimenting with exotic foods was not something he enjoyed. There were enough uncertainties in life, especially in the CIA. Food was at least one thing he could choose and control. "Do we have to?" he whined.

"Oh, come on, you big baby. Where's your spirit of adventure?"

"Alright," he conceded reluctantly. "Just order me something greasy," he taunted. Pat had been hounding him about his eating habits for years.

April 8, 2004   Santa Rosa, California

It was just after 7:00 p.m., PST, when the doorbell rang at the Rosetti house. Kathy was upstairs, giving her boys their Saturday night bath. Her husband and parents were downstairs, briefing the youngest of the Pierson children on the mysterious and tragic events of the last twenty-four hours. Naomi, Howard and Monica's youngest child, had arrived with her husband Chad and six-month-old daughter just after dinner.

Hearing the doorbell, Mike excused himself from the rest of the family and answered the door, surprised to see his friend from the Sheriff's Department standing there, still in uniform.

"Steve!" he said with surprise and a smile. "Come on in."

"I can't, Mike. I need to talk to you," Deputy Steve Kalbach answered seriously, motioning for Mike to step outside. The two walked down the path to the driveway.

"Steve, what did you find out?" Mike asked impatiently.

Nervously, Steve looked up and down the street. "You owe me for this, Mike. I'm putting my ass on the line right now, you know that?"

"Thanks, Steve, I appreciate it. Now what did you find out?"

"Your brother-in-law is a bit of a mystery. I got a look at his service record. Most of the active duty section is classified. All we know is that he was a SEAL with two bronze stars and a purple heart. He was also court-martialed six months ago and dishonorably discharged for trying to kill an Admiral. After his court martial he moved to New Jersey, then dropped out of sight—closed his bank accounts, canceled his credit cards—I mean, he disappeared. Now, he shows up here home for three days and ends up in one hell of a shoot-out. The crime team counted fifty-seven bullet holes in your in-laws' house and recovered seventy-three spent casings. There were three pools of blood—one on the front porch, one on the kitchen floor, the third on the side of the house. There were also some streaks of blood on the deck in the middle of a bunch of broken glass. All that carnage and not one body, not one witness. The crime team also found twelve grams of coke. I tell you, Mike, your brother-in-law is into something bad. Every law enforcement agency is looking for him now. There's an All-Points Bulletin on him that lists him as armed and extremely dangerous. That's about all I was able to get, and I've got a hunch it's all anybody knows."

Mike Rosetti stood still, allowing the information to soak in. He had known that Matt was a SEAL but that was about all. As bad as he thought things were before, he knew now they were much worse.

"Mike, I've got to ask you. Have you heard from him?"

Not knowing why, Mike shook his head. "Not a thing."

"Do you know anything that could help? You do realize what happened last night, don't you? Someone tried to kill him, and may have. If you know anything or if he contacts any of your family, have him turn himself in for his own good." The deputy's eyes bore into his friend's. "Do you hear me Mike? I'm talking about his life."

"I hear you, Steve. And thanks, thanks for everything. I'll get in touch with you if I hear anything," he answered, lying for the second time. "Keep me posted, okay?"

"It's a two-way street, Mike," he answered, turning toward his car.

"Thanks again, Steve," Mike called.

The deputy waved his acknowledgement without turning. Mike returned to the house, once again the bearer of distressing news. As he feared, the news fell like a weight on shoulders already over-burdened with grief and concern. Inevitably, the conversation arrived at the bottom-line question—what do we do now?

"Mom, were you able to find the addresses of any of Matt's friends?" Kathy asked, leading the way to her suggestion. After bathing her boys, she had put them to bed and was now thankful that they had fallen asleep peacefully and quickly.

"Only one, the one who's the pastor now, Ken Holmquist," she answered weakly, her eyes swollen from crying.

"I think that should be where we start. Let's call him. Maybe Matt will contact him."

"Wait a minute, let's hold up for a minute," Mike interjected. "We're skipping something pretty significant here. This postcard we got from Matt is evidence that the police would want to know about. I didn't mention it to Steve but I probably should have."

"I know what you're saying, Mike, but if the police think Matt's dealing drugs, they're not going to go out of their way to see that he's brought in safely for questioning. Until we learn more about what's going on, any information we give to the police could lead him into more trouble," Howard countered.

"Withholding information is a pretty serious charge, Dad," Mike responded as a matter of fact.

"Losing a son is a pretty serious thing as well!" his father-in-law snapped.

Wisely, Mike backed down, knowing that this was not the time to lock horns. To be perfectly honest, he had a strange gut feeling that Howard was right. Maybe it was why he had instantly lied to his friend from the Sheriff's department. "Sorry, Dad, you're probably right."

"Hon, you probably remember Matt's pastor friend better than I do. Do you think you feel up to calling him?" Howard asked his wife.

"Of course," she answered, feeling somewhat patronized. "How much should I tell him?"

"Just that Matt's in trouble and that if Matt should happen to contact him, have Ken tell him to get in touch with us."

Monica walked over to the kitchen phone with her overflowing red address book, a possession which had come to symbolize her personal protestation against the modern world of computers. Finding the number, she rhythmically pressed the buttons and waited for the call to go through.

"Hello, you've reached the home of the Holmquist family. We're sorry we can't take your call right now. If you will leave your name, number, and a brief message, we will call you back as soon as possible."

Monica froze for a moment after the tone, unsure whether or not to leave a message. When she spoke, she found herself struggling for words. "Hello, this is Monica, ah, this is Matt Pierson's mother, Monica Pierson." She paused in frustration as she tried to decide what to say next. "I need to talk to you about Matt. . ."

158

"Hello? Don't hang up, I'm here," Sarah Holmquist answered, winded from her race from the bathroom, where she had been changing a diaper.

"Is this Sarah?" Monica asked.

"Yes, hello Mrs. Pierson! It's good to hear from you. Did Matt make it home yet?" she asked, instantly regretting the question.

Swallowing back her tears, Monica answered. "Sarah, Matt came home five days ago, and he's gone again." She heard Sarah's sigh. "He's in trouble, Sarah, and I was wondering if you or Ken might know anything about what's going on with him."

Ken and Sarah Holmquist had graduated from Northwest Lutheran University the same year as Matt, Ken with a degree in religious studies that matched Matt's and Sarah with a degree in elementary education. In the six years since their graduation, Ken had completed the Masters of Divinity program at Trinity Lutheran Seminary in Columbus, Ohio, and was busily settling in to his first call, a small rural congregation in Sunburst, Montana. After four years of classroom preparation, it was now in his second year in the parish that Ken was finally learning what it really meant to be a pastor. Sarah had taught second grade for three of Ken's years in seminary. Since their senior year, however, she had been hired to full-time employment by her now one-and-a-half-year old twin girls.

Sarah felt tears well up her in eyes as she remembered the conversations she and Ken had shared with Matt just a week ago when he had shown up at the parsonage unannounced. She had hoped he would go home and reconcile with his family. She had prayed that going home would help put his troubles behind him. From the few words his mother had spoken, Sarah realized that her prayers had yet to be answered or that for them to be answered, things would have to get worse for a while before they got better. "Mrs. Pierson, Matt was here visiting us just last week..."

159

The rest of the family waited in the living room unable to hear the conversation. Howard wrung his hands repeatedly, appearing nervous to his children. In fact, he was struggling with his thoughts, trying desperately to remember something, something very important. Just as Monica re-entered the room it came to him. "Pepper!" he blurted out without explanation. His mental breakthrough was rewarded by curious stares from his family.

Ignoring her husband's outburst, Monica reported her conversation with the Holmquists. "Ken said he hasn't heard from Matt since last week. Before Matt came home, he spent a week with them in Montana, but said Matt didn't mention any kind of trouble, though he said he could tell that Matt was really struggling with something. Searching for something, I think he said."

"Not much help," Naomi said.

"I guess that means that all we can do now is wait," Kathy concluded with a trace of fatalism in her voice.

"No," Howard said emphatically. "I just remembered something that I've been trying to remember ever since last night. 'Pepper!' That's the name, or at least the nickname of one of Matt's buddies from his SEAL Team." He proceeded to explain the mysterious photograph that Matt had received.

"Pepper? You don't know his real name?" Naomi's husband, Chad, asked with their six-month-old baby girl cradled comfortably in his arms.

"No, Pepper was the only way Matt referred to him."

"I guess that's another dead end, then," Chad concluded.

"No," Howard contradicted, "it means I'm going to Norfolk," he announced.

Across the continent, a telephone rang in a comfortable two-bedroom condominium in the bayside town of Yorktown, Virginia. Three times the phone rang without an answer.

Unknown to the caller, the owners of the condominium at that moment were deeply engaged in the ritual that husbands and wives around the world perform after a time of separation. In this case, the husband, an enlisted man in the Navy, had just returned from a two-week training exercise in some unnamed part of the world.

Though exhausted, Master Chief Warren Adler had managed without too much difficulty to muster the energy to properly greet the woman he loved.

The phone continued ringing as Adler debated his course of action. It was not his personal pager, that only rang when the Team was being activated. Still, it could be someone from the base...

"This better be something good!" he snarled into the receiver of the phone beside the bed. He heard his wife sigh and felt her roll away from him. "Couldn't they leave you alone for at least one night?" she muttered quietly.

"Pepper, this is Preacher."

In spite of his frustration, a thin smile spread across his face. "Preacher, you son of a bitch, your timing is absolutely unbelievable, if you get my meaning!" Hearing the name Preacher, Nancy Adler turned back to her husband, forgiving the interruption since it was not an official Navy call. "Is that Matt?" she mouthed. Warren nodded affirmative.

"Nice to hear your voice too, you old geezer!"

"Where the hell are you, you pencil-necked, never writing, never calling piece of pond scum?" Though he had deliberately tried to avoid obscenities for the sake of his wife, his poetry won him a punch in the shoulder.

"Hey, Pep, I'm in trouble."

161

Warren sat up in bed instantly as though an officer had just called him to attention. Nancy noticed he now wore his game face, which alerted her that something was wrong.

"What happened?" Pepper asked.

"You remember what you told me in the parking lot when I was leaving? You were right."

"Shit," Pepper said flatly. "How did it go down? Are you in one piece?"

"Yeah, I'm fine, but I need some help."

"Name it."

"I need a new life."

Chapter Ten

The morning sun struggled to spread its light through the misty skies over Seattle. Inside the cafeteria of the Seattle Lutheran Bible College, students gathered in various states of readiness to begin their day with breakfast, which this morning included French toast, a fact which signaled the students that tomorrow's lunch would be Monte Cristo sandwiches and the next day it would reappear in yet another manifestation: bread pudding. For veteran SLBC students this was not particularly welcome news.

Nevertheless, on its first time around, the French toast was actually quite good this morning, Tim Parnel admitted to himself. Though uneventful, Tim's weekend had been tense as he waited for two days to hear news of an assassination that apparently never took place. On Friday, he had been sure that his suspect was traveling to New York to kill someone but he had no idea whom. Now, as Monday began with a gloomy start, he was no longer sure of anything.

On the personal side, the weekend had also been one filled with frustration. Three times he had to make excuses to Angela why he couldn't leave the campus to join the traditional weekend activities. Had that not been enough, he was finding it increasingly difficult to resist her subtle advances. All in all, it had been an aggravating weekend.

Absentmindedly Tim mopped up the excess syrup on his plate with his last bite of French toast. Raising the fork to his mouth, he momentarily froze as he watched Jeffrey Atkins enter the cafeteria. So he was back and with him the same eerie chill that always seemed to accompany him. But where had he been, and more importantly, what had he done?

163

Gathering his dishes onto his tray, Tim rose and deposited his dirty dishes in the kitchen. As he made his way to the exit, he passed Kyle Eims, who was rushing to get his breakfast before the kitchen staff began putting the food away. A curious look was exchanged which Tim lightly dismissed as petty jealousy. He had, after all, unintentionally stolen the affection of the poor boy's desire. Tim continued on down the hall, hurrying now so as not to be late to his first class. Though the change was not complete, Tim Parnel was rapidly adapting to the life of a Bible school student.

Back inside the cafeteria, Kyle had finished assembling his breakfast tray and was searching for a breakfast companion when his eyes fell upon Jeffrey Atkins, who was sitting alone at a corner table, his back to the wall. Though Kyle scarcely knew Atkins, there was something urgent which needed to be discussed. Weaving his way around the tables, Kyle hurried to the lone man, only to be greeted with a cold and suspicious look.

"I'm not feeling very sociable this morning," Atkins coldly greeted the timid young man.

"I won't stay if you don't want me to but I need to talk to you about something," he answered sheepishly.

"Have a seat, then," Atkins said with a forced smile, wondering what, if anything, the little busy-body knew that would interest him. Watching the boy take his seat, Atkins stared coldly at him, waiting for him to speak.

"I wanted to talk to you about something that happened the other night. Something I saw..." he blurted out nervously.

"Go on."

"Well, it happened on Friday night, after you left to see your uncle."

"How did you know I was visiting my uncle this weekend?" Atkins asked without betraying his sudden interest in the conversation.

164

Caught, Kyle squirmed uneasily in his chair. "Well, I was kind of by the front desk when your message came in the other day, and I...I guess I must have overheard the message..." he confessed.

"You would do well to stay out of my business," Atkins rebuked, allowing just enough anger to escape to sufficiently frighten the boy. "Now, what is it that you need to tell me?"

"Well, it was Friday night, and I was...oh, I got up late, you know, to go to the bathroom, and I noticed something strange."

"Get on with it!" Atkins snapped.

"There was somebody standing by your door. I knew you were gone so I decided to watch and see what was going on. It was strange. He knelt down, and it looked like he shined a flashlight under the door. Then he stood up again and unlocked the door and went inside. He must have been in there twenty minutes, but I never saw the lights go on. Finally he came out, knelt down again, then got up and left. That's all. I just thought you would want to know..."

"Who was it?" Atkins asked flatly, though his instincts were now fully alarmed.

"I don't want to get anyone in trouble..."

"Let me worry about that. Who was it?" he demanded.

As if betraying a sacred trust, Kyle looked down at his lap and mumbled, "It was Tim."

"Tim who?" he demanded again, already knowing the answer.

"Tim Parnel," Kyle answered softly. "You're not going to get him into trouble, are you?" he asked, sensing that he had done something terribly wrong.

"No... Not unless he stole something or did something really bad. No, I'll just talk to him and find out what he was doing."

Somewhat relieved, Kyle offered a sheepish smile. "I just thought you would want to know."

"I appreciate that," Atkins answered honestly, how much so young Kyle Eims would never know.

With his message delivered, Kyle sensed correctly that he should find another place to sit and eat his breakfast. Looking over his shoulder, he noticed two more students race into the cafeteria, trying to catch the food before it was put away. "Oh, there's Barry and Karla, I was hoping to see them before class," Kyle lied, excusing himself from the awkward silence that had followed his brief conversation with Jeffrey Atkins.

Atkins watched as the boy hurried away. So his instincts were right about Parnel. He would have to learn more about his new adversary, he thought. Finishing his own breakfast, Atkins hurried to the pay phone in the narthex, just in front of the chapel. Dialing a memorized number, he waited for the tone to sound on the answering machine.

"The cats are getting curious. Call me at 01:00, my time."

The cryptic message complete, he hung up, checked his watch, and rushed off to class. As he trotted down the hall, he recalled that his first Monday morning class was Church History, a class which he shared with Tim Parnel. *This should be interesting*, he thought as he rounded a corner and jogged toward the classroom.

April 9, 2004   Minneapolis, Minnesota

It was just after 09:00, CST, on a cold and rainy Monday morning at the *Go-el* Task Force headquarters in Minneapolis. Apart from Michaelson and Parnel, who were still deployed in the field, the Task Force was assembled for the Monday morning briefing. Susan Belcourt had returned

166

from Columbus late Sunday night after an unproductive investigation of the suspects at Trinity Lutheran Seminary and was just beginning to give her report.

"After four days of posing as a prospective student, I had a chance to do quite a bit of snooping around. From what I was able to pick up, most of our suspects at Trinity are nothing more than political activists. There's the German couple, Dieter and Gabriel Zibermann-Fitzbaun. I didn't find anything solid on them but either of them could fit the profile. I didn't get a chance to see them myself but I got some general descriptions of them. The community there at the Seminary is fairly tight and it seems like everybody knows something about everybody. Anyway, I was talking to this student and asked a couple innocent questions about the Germans. The student I was talking to happened to mention that the couple travels a lot, sometimes together, sometimes separately. It's interesting, but both of them were at the Liberation Theology lectures the day Deshaw was hit. At least two other students I talked to saw them there. From what else I could gather, they're pretty regular students. I got a look at their transcripts and their grades are good. He's working on a Doctorate of Theology and she's enrolled in the MDiv program—that's a Masters of Divinity" she explained.

"What the hell is that?" Bill Kampo interrupted.

"It's the degree program for students who want to become pastors," she explained tersely. *He should have known that from his prep work for this investigation, not to mention he was a pastor's kid*, she thought without saying.

"So the bottom line is we can rule out everyone from our Trinity list," Austin Torvick concluded.

"I don't know if I'd go that far, Austin. I'd drop everyone except the German couple," Susan amended the proposal.

"Why keep them on if they've got alibis?" The question came from the usually quiet Brenda LeToure.

167

"It's not that hard to slip out of a conference for a half hour or so without being noticed. Besides, they fit our suspect profile better than anyone on our suspect list. I'm just saying we shouldn't forget about them. Do some more digging, find out a little more about them."

"Alright, let's keep that in mind. Stan, Pat, did you come up with any activity in New York that could be linked to *Go-el* or this fellow from the Bible School in Seattle?" Torvick asked, already knowing the answer. With a Task Force as small as theirs, formal briefings such as this were merely formalities, since most of the time everyone already knew about anything someone else on the team dug up. Still, formal briefings gave assurance that informal lines of communication didn't accidentally leave someone in the dark.

"You already know the answer to that, Austin," Stan snapped, his frustration more with the situation than his superior.

"The only thing noteworthy that happened anywhere in the northeast is that Arthur Rossford died of a heart attack this weekend," Pat Knodell said while holding up the front page article from the morning newspaper. "It's amazing what you can learn by reading the paper."

"Anything unusual about the death? Anything that might tie it to our Seattle traveler?" Torvick pressed.

"It seems pretty cut and dried. An autopsy was done—massive heart attack, that's about it. Besides, how in the world would Arthur Rossford be involved with *Go-el*?" Pat concluded.

"Bill, what have you heard about the rented car in New York?"

Bill Kampo cleared his throat. "I just called the Bureau office in New York. As of 08:15 this morning, the car had not been returned; still no GPS signal. Not much we can do with that."

There were nods of agreement on that point. The mood of the room was somber, even for Monday morning standards. It seemed once again that even after more than a month, they were no closer to *Go-el* than when they had started. The briefings continued, with each team member reporting on his or her work which for all their combined efforts, changed the bottom line very little. Suddenly the telephone rang, interrupting LeToure's report. Being nearest the phone, she answered with the appropriate greeting.

"Emil and Brown Insurance. How may I help you?"

"Hi Brenda, this is Tim," Parnel said, forgetting the assigned response. "I can't talk, but tell Stan that Atkins is back."

"Right, I'll pass it on. Are you alright?"

"Yeah, I'm fine, I just have to get to my next class. Were there any hits over the weekend? I listened to the news but didn't hear anything."

"No, nothing happened."

"Alright, got to go," Parnel said, his voice conveying his disappointment.

Turning back to the assembled Task Force, Brenda relayed the message.

"I think that should close the case on this Jeffrey Atkins character," Kampo announced smugly.

"Which leaves us absolutely nowhere," Brenda agreed. It was perhaps the first time the two had agreed on anything.

"Where do we go from here, Boss?" Susan asked, directing the question to Torvick who slowly shook his head.

"Stan, I may be in charge, but this is your baby. What do you think?" Austin asked.

Stan began slowly pacing, rubbing his chin thoughtfully. The team waited. Suddenly he stopped and turned to once again face his colleagues. "Okay, I'll admit it. Without Atkins, we have nothing. So I say we stay on him.

Tim's cover is solid at the Bible school and he can keep an eye on Atkins."

"But he's not connected with *Go-el*! We know that!" Bill blurted out.

"We know that? What we know is that we have a Bible school student who leaves telltales on his dorm room and takes sudden unexplained trips to New York, but arrives using a different name and speaking with a heavy English accent. Doesn't sound like your average Bible school student to me."

"But you're forgetting he's got an alibi and Tim gave it to him!" Kampo protested.

"What professional assassin wouldn't have an alibi?" Stan snapped back. "Austin, I've been thinking about what you said the other day. What if we're not hunting one man? What if *Go-el* is a hit team? One does the hit, the other has a built-in alibi. Next time it's reversed. They cover each other. Susan, what was your impression of that German couple?"

"I'm not sure what you're getting at. I've already told you what I found out about them."

"I know, but those were facts. What I want to know is what you felt. What's your gut feeling about them?"

Belcourt sat thoughtfully, trying to find words to express her feelings, a task which she was not trained to do. "Stan, if you are expecting me to say that I've got some kind of sixth sense that the two Germans are somehow involved with *Go-el*, I don't. There are a few things that are suspicious but I don't feel anything one way or the other."

"Do you think we should drop them?" Stan persisted.

Again she sat thoughtfully. "Well, no."

"Why?"

"I don't really know."

"That's exactly what I was getting at. Let's not burn our bridges just yet. Austin, what are the chances of getting

170

the Bureau office in Columbus to put the Germans under surveillance?"

"I'd have to give them a reason and if we tell them it's connected with *Go-el*, we run the risk of tipping our hand if there is a leak somewhere in the system," he answered.

"I didn't say we had to be honest. If the Germans are clean, surveillance will clear them, but if by chance they are connected to *Go-el*, we've got 'em."

Now it was Austin's turn to pace. Obeying the call of his addiction, he reached into the liner pocket of his sport coat to retrieve a cigarette. He was in the process of lighting when he heard Susan Belcourt distinctly clear her throat, reminding him that there was no smoking in working areas in the new FBI. He glared momentarily at her and returned the cigarette to the pack. At last he turned again to face Stan.

"Seeing as how we've got nothing else to go on, I'll go with you on this, for now," he finally answered with an obvious lack of enthusiasm. "If nobody else has anything to offer, I suggest we all get back to our projects."

The briefing was concluded and the members returned to their computers or stacks of files, though without much excitement. On Friday, they collectively had sensed that they were closing in on their target. Today, it seemed as though they were no further along than when they had begun. They were still chasing a phantom, or now maybe more than one.

April 9, 2004
C.I.A. Headquarters, Langley, Virginia

The phone call had come as a surprise and now had Russell Seabrook's mind working in high gear, churning over what he had learned from the conversation he had just ended with a former Secretary of State who still wielded

171

considerable influence in the political arena of the nation's capital. More interesting than what was said were the things unsaid, comments made and left hanging, innuendos and omissions.

As the Director of Operations for the Central Intelligence Agency, Seabrook did his best to avoid the limelight of media and political attention, content to let others grasp at the attention and the fleeting glory. So on those recently rare occasions when the CIA actually had a moment of glory, a successful operation or an intelligence coup, no one sought him to share the congratulations. Yet when operations went bad or an intelligence lapse cost lives on the ground, he was the first to hear about it. It was a cross he didn't mind bearing.

The assassin *Go-el* had struck on American soil and so it was inevitable that the powers that be would turn to him to explain how this could happen and what was being done to assure that the assassin would not strike again. He imagined similar calls would be made to the FBI as well. The calls from the White House, the Pentagon, and the Chair of the Congressional Intelligence Committee had been expected and had come in due order throughout the day following Deshaw's assassination. But the former Secretary of State? Why was she so concerned about the hunt for *Go-el*? He thought about *Go-el's* victims so far, trying to recall if the former Secretary had been close to any of them. Was she afraid for her own safety?

It was that question that really intrigued him. There was only a select group of people who needed to fear *Go-el*, and Seabrook knew them all or so he had thought. If the former Secretary of State had been involved, did the conspiracy go all the way to the top? That would present him and his associates with an interesting dilemma.

He'd check in with his counterpart at the FBI to learn where they were in their investigation of the Deshaw hit. Seabrook was reasonably sure that his people hadn't drawn any closer to *Go-el*, which was just fine. He didn't want them too.

April 9, 2004   Issaquah, Washington

Jeffrey Atkins had received the cryptic reply to the message he had placed that morning about half an hour ago. Now he was again placing a call, this time from a small apartment in the sprawling town of Issaquah. Like the apartment on the other end of the telephone line his, too, was unfurnished with the exception of a small card table, one chair, and a large cargo trunk. Withdrawing an object from the trunk, he waited for an answer on the other end of the line. It kept ringing. Reflexively, the assassin began disassembling the pistol he had extracted from his toy chest. Finally his call was answered by an answering machine 2,200 mile away. He listened to the recorded message, then waited for the beep. "It's me. Pick up the damn phone," he said impatiently.

"What's the problem?" the voice of Dieter Zibermann demanded.

"There's a player at the school who has developed an unhealthy interest in my affairs."

"Who is he?"

"Parnel, Timothy Robert Parnel," Atkins answered.

"What do you know about him? Is he a cop? FBI?"

"That's what you're supposed to find out. He doesn't act like a cop, though. Apparently he broke into my room while I was on that business trip over the weekend. You find out who he is and I'll take care of him."

"You sit tight," Zibermann ordered. "If it becomes necessary, I'll take care of your new acquaintance. If you take him out, whoever he's working for will know you did it and then you'll be of no use to me, if you understand what I mean. We cover each other, remember? That's why we need each other."

Enraged, Atkins drew in a deep breath, intentionally attempting to restrain his temper. "You just find out who he is," he snapped, slamming the phone down, abruptly ending the conversation.

Half way across the country, Zibermann too, hung up the phone, though calmly. He no longer allowed himself to display anger. It was far too dangerous in his business. The less emotion expressed, or even felt, the better. He pressed the buttons of the phone, entering a memorized number that would connect him with the other side of the nation. Another answering machine, another cryptic recorded message, another given in response. Now again he would have to wait.

Where had they slipped? There was no way that anyone should be on to Atkins. Mentally he retraced his movements over the past year. The Germans had gotten close in Berlin, far too close, but he had lost them there, hadn't he? No, he could find no mistakes in his escape from Europe. Had the mistake been made here in the States? Possible, he thought, but so far they had only attacked once, well twice really, but only once publicly as *Go-el*. If there had been a mistake with the Deshaw hit, how could they possibly be on to Atkins? After all, he was in Issaquah when the trigger was pulled.

He was so entrenched in his thoughts that when the phone rang next to him, the sound startled the aging assassin enough to cause him to reach for his pistol. Relaxing, he let the phone ring until the answering machine clicked on. He waited to hear the voice of the caller.

"This had better be important. Your orders were to lay low for a month and wait for me to contact you!" Russell Seabrook barked.

"We've got a problem. Someone seems to be overly curious about a colleague of mine, someone named Timothy Robert Parnel. Find out who he works for and what they

174

know about our operation. Call me at this number when you learn something. That's all. Out."

April 9, 2004   San Bernardino, California

It had been an unusually cold and rainy spring thus far in southern California, yet still the smog camouflaged the mountains which surrounded the city of San Bernardino. With a map of the city and a torn-out page from a telephone book on the seat next to him, Matthew Pierson, whose current driver's license identified him as Matthew Craige, slowly fought his way through the morning traffic which daily congested San Bernardino's main arteries. Before making his escape from the Santa Rosa area, he had purchased a 1995 Dodge Dakota, paying in cash from a bank account he had opened under an assumed name following his discharge. In spite of its age, the mid-sized pickup had only 38,000 miles on it. The camper shell over the pickup bed provided both storage and lodging for the homeless owner of the vehicle.

With the radio tuned to a local classic rock station, Matthew Craige finally arrived at his destination, making a darting left turn across two lanes of traffic into the parking lot of Our Savior's Lutheran Church. Noticing the street-side church sign, Matthew was pleased that his memory had once again served him well. Beneath the Sunday Service and Sunday School schedules, the sign read, "James Olafson, Pastor." He had found the right church.

Parking beside a bright red Toyota Celica which was parked in the spot reserved for the pastor, Matt stepped out of the pickup, chuckling to himself as he did. Again the thought struck him, *some things never change.* Pastor Jim still loved his sports cars. Straightening his tie and smoothing his shirt, he headed toward the entrance to the church office.

"May I help you?" the church secretary asked politely.

"Yes, I'm here to see Pastor Olafson."

"He's in his office but I will call him on the intercom. May I ask your name?"

"Matt, Matt Craige. I'm an old friend," he explained.

"Just one minute," she smiled. "Pastor Jim, there is a man named Matt Craige here to see you," she spoke into the intercom.

A minute later, the Pastor who had once confirmed a young boy named Matty Pierson emerged from his office. His Scandinavian sandy blonde hair was beginning to show streaks of white, but in every other way the sixty-seven-year-old pastor looked just like Matthew remembered him.

"Hello, I'm Pastor Olafson, may I..." He paused mid-sentence as he slowly began to recognize someone he had not seen in years. "Matty? Is that you?" he exclaimed warmly, instantly grabbing his former student's right hand, shaking it vigorously, not noticing the bandage wrapping Matty's hand. His grip had grown stronger in the years that had passed which only added to the pain. "Oh, I am so sorry!" he exclaimed as he realized what he had done. "What happened to your hand?" he asked with genuine concern.

"I cut myself shaving," 'Matty' answered with a grin, though his hand ached. "It's good to see you, Pastor Jim."

"Well I'll be..." the pastor said, appraising his former Confirmand. "I almost didn't recognize you! This is going to sound foolish, but I thought you had dark brown hair when you were younger," the pastor commented.

"I've been in the sun a lot lately and that always seems to bleach it out a bit," Matt replied with a mixture of embarrassment and nervousness. "Hey, Pastor Jim, I know you're probably pretty busy, but could I pull you away for a cup of coffee?"

176

Pastor Olafson studied him again briefly, his instincts after years of caring for people alerting him that this was something important. "Sure, I can stand another cup. Give me a minute to finish something up and we'll be on our way."

Fifteen minutes later the two were sitting in a booth by a window in the rear of the nearest Winchell's Donut House, each with a donut in one hand and coffee in the other. As with police officers, it seemed that donuts and pastors just belonged together.

"Well, Matty, I think it must be at least twelve years since I last saw you. What are you doing these days? With that tie you look like you could be a pastor!" he teased. One of the lessons Matthew had learned during his work in counter-terrorism was that the best way to avoid suspicion was not to act like you were hiding. Thus he was now dressed as any other professional might be on a Monday morning, wearing pleated slacks, a shirt, and a very conservative tie.

"Not quite," Matt countered, covering the fact that the well-intentioned joke had struck a very sensitive nerve. "That's one of the things I wanted to talk with you about, actually. But first I have to ask you something," he added, instinctively passing a subtle glance around the donut shop. "Has anyone come by asking questions about me?"

Instantly Pastor Olafson was concerned. "No, Matty, what kind of trouble are you in? You didn't use your family name back at the church and my memory isn't that bad— your hair is naturally dark brown. You want to tell me what's going on?"

"You're right, I am in trouble," he answered, too ashamed to look his former pastor in the eyes. He cleared his throat and shifted nervously on the hard-plastic seat. "I... I don't even know where to begin..." he stammered.

"Last I heard you had just graduated from PLU with a major in religious studies and though everyone—myself included—expected you to go to seminary, instead you went and joined the Navy. Why don't you start there?"

"Alright. You probably remember that I had always thought about becoming a pastor," he began, looking up long enough to see his one-time mentor nod. "Well, I don't know if you can understand or not, but when I graduated, everybody expected me to go to seminary. Hell, I even thought I would go to seminary. But when it came time to enroll, something in me just, I don't know, rebelled? I made up my mind that I was going to do something totally different with my life, at least for a time. So I joined the Navy, hoping I could make it into the Dive and Salvage Command. You know I've always loved diving. I guess I thought I could get some training for professional dive work. I don't know, maybe I was just running away." He paused as much to contain his emotions as to collect his thoughts.

He hadn't intended for this to become a confession, but he realized that was what was happening. Maybe that was what he really needed anyway. He brushed the thought aside. Pastor Olafson sat silently, intently.

"Anyway, in Officer Candidate School some officers must have thought I had some potential 'cause I was recommended for BUD/S." He noticed the questioning look on his pastor's face. "Oh, I'm sorry. BUD/S stands for Basic Underwater Demolition/SEAL training, basically the beginning of the Navy SEAL selection process. You have to understand that SEALs are among the best warriors in the world. I don't know if I started out wanting to be a SEAL as much as I just wanted to know if I could make it. Well, I did. I made it through SEAL school, hell week and all, on my first try." Again, he paused and scanned the donut shop, the parking lot, the street beyond.

"Pastor Jim, maybe I don't need to say this, but what I'm about to tell you, well, nobody is supposed to know, you understand?" Again the veteran pastor nodded without a word.

178

"It turns out I did pretty well on my first deployment. I got recommended for a chance to get into a special group. Again, I was curious. Could I make the next step? I made it through more training and was selected to be on the SEALs counter-terrorist unit. They call it the Naval Special Warfare Development Group. Some people still call it SEAL Team Six. The stuff we do..., the stuff I did, will never make the papers."

Pastor Olafson raised his hand to interrupt. "Matt, I think I need to tell you, you don't have to tell me anything you shouldn't and I'll try not to ask any question that could compromise you. But tell me what you want me to hear. Everything you say is between you, me, and God. Okay?"

This time it was Matt who nodded before continuing his confession. "Pastor Jim, I've got to admit, it was exciting and there's a part of me that loved being in the Teams. SEAL Six was activated eleven times in the first two years I was with them. You know the slogan, 'Join the Navy, see the world?' Well, we got around," he admitted with a flicker of pride. "After 9/11, we did two six-month tours in Afghanistan. We ran Ops almost the whole time we were there. We saw some action. You understand what I'm saying?" he asked, making direct eye contact for the first time since he began.

"Are you saying you killed people?" Pastor Olafson asked pointedly.

Matt winced as if a bright light had just flashed in a dark room. "Yeah, that's what I'm saying," he confessed.

"I'm sorry, go on," the pastor said kindly.

"Anyway, I was dealing with things alright until one day, about eight months ago, our Team was activated. My unit was doing some joint ops with SEAL Team Three off the coast of Colombia. This Admiral shows to brief us on our mission. That should have been our first clue something wasn't right. No one with that rank had ever personally briefed us for a mission. He told us were to do a preemptive strike on a Colombian drug lord who was supposedly planning to launch some kind of terrorist campaign against U.S. targets throughout the Caribbean."

Again, Matt paused, this time rubbing his temples as if to drive away the phantom faces which suddenly appeared once again to haunt his mind. "This Admiral gave us all the intel we needed for the hit. It was supposed to be real simple – take down the druggie's yacht and eliminate our three targets. We had satellite and drone surveillance, details on the druggie's security, everything.

"I should have known from the get-go that something wasn't right. We had no trouble swimming in or boarding. We snuffed the two guards on the main deck and got inside without a sound. There were eight of us—deployed just like on a drill, one of us covering every doorway and the staircase.

"Then it hit the fan. One of the servants, at least that's what we figured, must have gotten up for a late-night snack or something. Anyway, this guy suddenly appears in the kitchen doorway. Pepper dropped him instantly with a double tap in the head.

From across the table, Pastor James Olafson watched and listened intently, aware that his one-time Confirmand was now reliving a nightmare even as he was speaking.

"The guy went down, but he dropped the plate he was carrying as he fell. We heard rustling from the yacht's guest rooms and we reverted back to training—strike fast, strike hard. I was on point and three of us charged down the hall toward the yacht's master suite. I could hear a woman's frightened voice and a man's voice trying to quiet her—but they were speaking English! I motioned for the other two to continue to the master suite while Deano and I stopped to clear the room where I heard the voices. Deano breached the door and I instantly recognized our third target." Pierson was sweating now, his mind's eye seeing things far away, long ago.

180

"You know, when you train at the levels we do, you get to the point where you don't think, you just react. I double tapped him in the head without hesitating," the ex-SEAL confessed, pausing to sip his coffee and again survey the donut shop, the parking lot, the street.

"Then his wife starts screaming at me and crying and tries to grab at me. I put my HK in her face and made my first operational mistake. 'Back off!' I yelled at her. I tell you, I was so pumped I swear I would have popped her if she came any closer. But I'll never forget the way her face changed. She stepped back, staring at me. 'You're Americans!' she said. You killed him! He works for you! We're Americans! You killed him!'" His hands were trembling and an inadvertent tear rolled down his cheek as he repeated out loud the words that he heard in his sleep for eight months. It was the first time he had told anyone what had happened in the room on the yacht.

Pastor Olafson saw the tears. "Oh, sweet Jesus," he prayed silently.

"I don't think I can explain it, but I just froze. Miguel Sanchez—that was supposed to be his name—an Intelligence officer for a Colombian drug lord, not an American!" Pierson said, his voice low, his eyes angry.

"We don't know where it came from, but one of the druggie's speed boats pulled alongside the yacht and opened fire on Bingo and Digger, our guys covering the deck. Then things went nuts. Pepper and Hawkins came back from the master suite— they had waxed the druggie— and said we were pulling out, but I just stood there and all the while the guy's wife is screaming, "You killed him! He was on your side!" Deano gagged her and zip-tied her wrists, but she kept staring at me, as though she could see right through my hood. Deano grabbed my arm and tried to push me toward the door. 'We're pulling out, now!' he shouted in my face. I pulled away and saw the guy's wallet on the nightstand by the bed. I grabbed it and ran to catch up to Deano and Hawkins. Just as we reached the main deck Deano caught a bullet in his spine. He was dead before he hit the deck. It was my fault." He finished, his voice trembling.

He suddenly realized that other patrons of the donut shop were watching him and he came back to the present. Across the table the pastor was silently praying—for the young man across from him and for the victims.

"They lied to us. I killed an innocent man," he concluded.

The pastor noticed the sudden change in the mood of the young man across from him. The anguish he had seen in the young man's eyes shifted to anger. Was he angry at himself? At the mission? The pastor wondered silently.

"When we got back to the carrier, the Admiral who gave us our orders met us on the deck. I was pretty pissed and demanded some answers. He tried to tell me that I had just done my job, followed orders and all that crap! I didn't have to understand, just obey. That's when I lost it, man. I just blew!"

Matthew stopped, silently shaking his head. Suddenly he scanned the donut shop again, then the street and parking lot. Again, he noticed that several customers had been watching him. Abruptly he stood. "It's not safe here. You mind going for a walk?"

"Sure," Pastor Olafson replied. The young man seemed paranoid and the pastor began to suspect that his former student might be suffering from Post-Traumatic Stress Disorder. He filed the thought in his memory. It was obvious the young man had more to tell.

Two blocks away was a small city park toward which the two men headed.

"Matt, you said you 'lost it'. What did you mean?"

"That about says it. I lost control; I blew up."

"What happened?"

"Admiral James Bartle was the one who briefed us on the mission. He was the one who showed us the photos of our targets. He knew who my target really was and why my team was sent to take him out. I threw the bastard to the floor and tried to get some answers. I swear I would have killed him if someone hadn't whacked me upside the head."

"You attacked a superior officer? I've never been in the military but don't they usually throw you in prison for something like that?" the pastor questioned, trying to subtly test the young man's story.

"Under normal circumstances, yes. But Bartle didn't want a trial or an investigation. So the lawyers settled it out of court—I didn't have much to say about it at that point. Because of my service record they waved time in the brig and settled on a dishonorable discharge on the charge of assault with intent to kill." Matthew chuckled. "Well, at least I couldn't argue with them about that. I might have killed him!"

Not sure what or how much of the story to believe, Pastor Olafson pressed on, listening carefully for discrepancies, watching closely for physical signs of a mental disorder. "So you were dishonorably discharged. How long ago did this happen?"

"Last year, July 13, to be specific," he answered without hesitation. "You know, Pastor Jim, you're the only person I've talked about this with since I left the Teams. I really appreciate you letting me unload."

"Any time, Matt. I mean that. But if you don't mind my asking, why did you come to me? I mean it's been seven months since your discharge. Haven't you talked with your family? Have you sought out any help—counseling or something like that?"

Matt began to recognize his former pastor's suspicions and felt his anger flare. "You don't believe me, do you? Think I'm a little nuts, huh? I shouldn't have ever come," he said in a controlled tone. "We're done here. Thanks for the time," he concluded, turning away.

183

Suddenly a hand gripped his left upper arm. Instinctively Matt spun, grabbing the pastor's hand and twisting it free from his own arm.

"Matt, I'm. . . it's just that. . ."

"It's fine. Don't worry about it."

Pressing his luck, Pastor Olafson again grabbed the young man's arm as he turned away. Again, Matt seized the hand like a vise, roughly breaking its grip on his arm. This time he almost struck the pastor.

"Matt, please. I want to listen to you, I want to help in any way I can. But the story you just told me is about a world I know nothing about. I'm trying to understand, really!" he pleaded.

Their eyes locked on each other's, Matt finally released his grip on the pastor's hand. "Okay...I'm sorry, too." Their eyes still locked, Matt continued. "Pastor Jim, it may sound crazy, but it's true. If you don't believe me, why don't you call my parents and ask what happened to their house last Friday night!"

Still looking into the young man's eyes, Pastor Olafson knew that he wouldn't need to make any such call. The eyes he saw were pleading, even desperate, but they were not crazy. Of that he was suddenly, inexplicably sure. "That won't be necessary. I'm sorry, Matt, really. What happened at your parents' house—are they okay?"

"Yeah, they're fine, I suppose. They weren't home when it happened. It took me seven months to find my way home after my discharge. I pulled into Santa Rosa about a week ago. Things were going great and I was finally starting to think about the future, but then Friday night rolled around and changed everything. I was getting ready to go to Kathy's house when someone tried to put a hit on me."

"You mean someone tried to kill you?"

"Not just someone. There were at least seven of them. I put the hurt on two and killed one, I think," he said with a lack of emotion that frightened the pastor.

"Thankfully, they were amateurs—either that or they were awfully sloppy. The short of it is that I got away and came down here." He offered a slight grin.

"But why would anyone try to kill you after eight months?"

"After my discharge, I couldn't just walk away from it. I had to know why I was sent to kill that guy." The ex-SEAL retrieved his wallet and withdrew the State Department Identity card that had belonged to Michael Claypool. He handed it to the pastor. "So, I spent the next three months trying to put the pieces together and the last three months trying to decide what to do with what I learned."

The two had been strolling around the perimeter of the park and slowly found their way to one of the benches in the center of the park. Taking a seat, the young man continued.

"So, what did you decide to do?"

Pierson kicked at the dirt and shook his head. "Bad things, pastor. Bad things."

Suddenly Pastor Olafson made a connection that made his blood run cold. "Wait a minute, Matt. Admiral Bartle, isn't he the one who was assassinated in London earlier this year? Oh, Matt, you..."

The Confirmand shook his head and gave a dark smile. "Someone beat me to it."

Pastor Olafson looked at him, "Is that supposed to be funny?"

"No, I guess not. By the time Bartle was hit I had already decided to walk away from it all. Problem was, I didn't know where to go. When I finally went home, they came after me. I guess I'm back in the same place."

The two sat quietly for a moment, one deep in thought, the other deep in memories still fresh enough to hurt. Around them, the sounds of the city played their erratic melody; the hum of automobile engines; the occasional blare of a car horn; a distant siren wailing. Then, ringing out above sounds of the city, the bells of nearby Saint Francis Cathedral announced that the noon hour had arrived. Hearing the bells, Pastor Olafson suddenly looked at his watch, as if to challenge the accuracy of the church bells.

"Criminy!" he exclaimed, "I can't believe it's already noon! Matt, I hate to do this to you, but I'm afraid I have a lunch appointment that I just can't miss. Looks like I'm already late."

"No problem, I understand."

"Tell you what, why don't you come over for dinner tonight? Johanna will love to see you," he invited hopefully. Matt looked away with a pained look on his face. "Matt," the pastor said gently "what's the matter?"

"Pastor Jim, the kid you knew as Matty Pierson is dead. He has to be. You have to understand, if you tell anyone that you've seen me, or mention our conversation, you'll be putting both of us in danger."

The pastor stared at the young man with intent but unbelieving eyes. He was truly trying to understand and accept his former student's revelations but to do so would involve acknowledging the existence of a world that he subconsciously preferred didn't exist. The young man who now used the last name of Craige stared at the face of his one-time mentor.

"Listen to me, Pastor Jim. The world I am in is a world without grace – there's no forgiveness, no second chances. You cross the wrong people and you're dead. Period. You can't tell your wife you saw me. You can't tell anyone."

Still wrestling with his own conflicting emotions, the pastor slowly nodded. "Alright, Matt. I can't say I understand, but I promise you that no one will know that I've seen you. Can we get together again? Maybe I can help you somehow."

"I don't know, I shouldn't have come in the first place. I've already placed you in danger if anyone finds out."

"Now listen to me, Matthew. You told me that you haven't spoken of these things to anyone until today. For better or worse, now I do know and maybe I can help you. We'll meet at the church this evening at, oh, about eight o'clock. Any further objections?" the pastor announced with authority.

Matt grinned. "No. I'll be there. Now you better get to your meeting. And thanks, thanks a lot."

Chapter Eleven

Evening, April 9, 2004
C.I.A. Headquarters, Langley, Virginia

It was just before five o'clock and Russell Seabrook was still fuming about the phone call he received earlier that afternoon. His face again flushed at the thought of being given orders by someone who worked for him, not to mention that an operation was going on right under his nose and he was unaware! Angrily, Seabrook depressed the intercom button which connected his voice with the office of the Deputy Director of Operations of the CIA. "Morganson, I need to talk to you right away. I'm in my office."

Three minutes later, Henry Morganson entered the office of his direct superior. "What do you want?" he asked as he entered the office.

"Hank, I just got off the phone with the President and he's breathing down my neck to know what progress is being made on tracking down this *Go-el*, terrorist. A while back you told me you were working on some leads. Have you come up with anything?"

Hank Morganson, shuffled his feet nervously. It was time to give a report to his superior. He had managed to keep *his* operation, the *Go-el* Task Force, off the radar of the Director of Operations for five weeks but now it was time to come clean. If he didn't think quickly, it would be more of a confession.

Following his meeting with Stan Harverson and the FBI Director Frank Rucker over a month and a half ago, Hank had neglected to obtain authorization from the Director of Operations, his direct superior. Even as it was still being discussed, Hank had seen that the joint FBI/CIA Task Force was his chance—his last chance—to redeem his doomed career. He had decided that very day that the Task Force would be his responsibility. If it succeeded, the credit would be his; if it failed, well, that really didn't matter.

But now his game had been called. It was time to let his superior in on his scheme.

"Russ, just over a month ago, Stan Harverson, our CT chief in Western Europe, flew in from Berlin for an urgent and unorthodox meeting. He wanted to meet with you and Rucker from FBI, but you were briefing the President that morning and you sent me, remember?"

"Of course," Seabrook answered curtly, though in fact he had no recollection of it. "Go on."

"Anyway, Harverson had stumbled onto a tip back in Germany that *Go-el* was planning to close up shop in Europe and start hitting targets here in the States."

Seabrook gasped. "That was over six weeks ago! Are you saying we knew *Go-el* was here over a month before the Deshaw hit?"

"Yes, but Harverson had no idea of his identity, targets, or benefactor. All he had was a tip that *Go-el* was coming to America. He didn't have much information, but he had an idea. His idea was to set up a joint CIA/FBI Task Force—combining the information available to us through Interpol and our overseas connections with the FBI's domestic network. The goal was to get a head start on *Go-el*, hopefully intercepting him before he struck. Obviously, that didn't happen."

"Obviously. Why wasn't I informed?" Seabrook said coldly, now consciously restraining his anger and growing concern.

"Harverson is sure that there is a high-level leak on our side. Where the leak is we have no idea. Rucker demanded that the Task Force be under direct FBI control since the investigation would be on U.S. soil and ordered that no one else know—no one else. He made that clear. Sorry, boss, I took it as an order."

189

Russell Seabrook grunted disapprovingly. "Who's on the team?"

"From our side, we've got Stan Harverson, Pat Knodell, Tim Parnel, and Jed Michaelson. FBI's got Austin Torvick heading it up, an agent named Susan Belcourt, and two rookies, a guy named Bill Kampo and a gal named Brenda LeToure."

"Austin's a good man. What have they learned?"

"I'm not entirely sure. Stan's reported in a few times but again, they're trying to keep the information loop as small as possible. Last I heard they put Parnel undercover at some college near Seattle. Personally, other than a few suspicions, I think they're still chasing shadows."

Russell sat still, thoughtfully biting the ear piece of his glasses while processing the information he had just received. At least finding out who was interfering with *Goel's* operation had been easy enough. The difficult job would be deciding how to respond to it. Well, he would have time to consider his next move.

"Alright, I'll brief the President. He shouldn't be kept out of the loop. From now on, Hank, I want full briefings from the Task Force. If there's any flack about it from Rucker, I'll deal with him. You just keep me fully posted from now on! Do you understand me?"

Silently, Hank let a sigh of relief escape. He had managed to keep his job, at least for another day.

Evening, April 9, 2004   San Bernardino, California

Pastor Olafson returned to the church, which was in fact his second home, just minutes before 8:00 p.m. that evening to meet the mysterious young man who had once been his student. By 8:30 p.m., he began to wonder whether his pupil would keep the appointment. At 9:00 p.m., the pastor decided reluctantly to return home. Perhaps something had come up which prevented Matthew from coming. The thought suddenly sent a chill down his spine as he remembered the troubled young man's story. Closing the magazine he had been reading to pass the time, he rose from his chair. As if procrastinating to give his pupil just a few more moments, he wandered around his office, straightening piles of papers, returning a few books to their proper place on the shelves. Finally, with a sigh of disappointment, the pastor turned out the lights, closing the office door behind him. Walking through the quiet and empty narthex, he exited the building, locking the door behind him.

Pastor Olafson noted with relief that the air was cooling off nicely and it promised to be a pleasant evening. Under normal circumstances, the cool air would have given the pastor the assurance of a good night's sleep. But tonight his mind was already warning him that sleep would not come easily. "Where was he?" he asked no one in frustration.

He was just unlocking the door to his Toyota Celica when a voice called out, startling him enough that he dropped his keys to the ground. Turning to the direction from which the voice had come, he saw his pupil emerge from the shadows of the hedge row that surrounded the church parking lot.

"About to give up on me, huh?" he spoke softly, grinning as he closed the distance between the them.

"Where have you been? I've been worried sick about you, young man," the pastor scolded.

"I'm sorry Pastor Jim. I had to make sure that you weren't the only one waiting for me."

"Matthew, I gave you my word I would not speak to anyone and I didn't. I am disappointed that you doubted me."

"It wasn't you I was worried about. I'm sure by now they've researched my background enough to know that we're acquainted. They may have sent someone to keep an eye on you."

Pastor Olafson gave the young warrior a disbelieving look. "Matt, I..."

"I don't expect you to understand, just believe me. The people who tried to kill me have access to any information about me they need and if they think you've talked to me... you could be in danger, too. I was checking things out for both our sakes," he offered as a defense. Slowly, a devious grin appeared on the young man's face. "We live in a world of sin and darkness, Pastor. A long time ago you taught me about the Light, now I'll teach you about some of the darkness, if you're still willing to listen."

The pastor stared incredulously at his former pupil. "Obviously, I didn't teach you enough about the Light!" he chided. "Do you want to go inside or do you want to stand out here all night?" he asked, slightly annoyed.

Pleased that even after all these years he could still get under his pastor's skin, Matt answered with an impertinent grin. "You mind going for a drive?"

Fifteen minutes later, the two parked the pastor's sports car at the scenic viewpoint half-way into the San Bernardino Mountains, unofficially known as "Inspiration Point." Now overlooking the city of San Bernardino two thousand feet below, the one who now called himself Matthew Craige had finished briefing the veteran pastor on the attack that had happened three nights ago, in Santa Rosa.

"Oh, Matthew, can you imagine the grief your parents are going through?" the pastor sighed. "They don't even know if you're alive!"

"Actually, they do, or they should anyway. Later that night, after the attack, I bought a postcard and put it in the mail saying I was alright but I wouldn't be able to come back."

"But Matthew, you have to explain to them! You have to let them know! Maybe they could even help you!" Pastor Olafson exclaimed. He and his wife had been close friends of the Pierson family for years and could not imagine the anguish he knew they must feel.

"I would like nothing else than to do just that but you still don't understand, do you? The people who are after me tried to kill me in Mom and Dad's own home! Do you really think it would mean that much to them if someone in my family got hurt while they tried to get me? I can't go back without putting them in danger. Believe me Pastor Jim, I've done some awful things and made some pretty big mistakes in my life, but I am not going to let anyone hurt my family because of the choices I made," he said with finality.

The pastor leaned back in the leather bucket seat of the Celica, silently struggling with his emotions as he tried to understand events of a world totally foreign to him, praying desperately that God would grant him some words of counsel, some insight that might help his young friend. No words came. Uncomfortable with the silence, the pastor finally blurted out the only words he could find. "Matt, you mentioned this morning that after your discharge, you did some bad things. What did you do during those months?"

Matt grimaced, the memories becoming fresh again in his mind. "After the court martial, I set up a place for myself in New Jersey. I knew they'd be tracking me for a while, so I set myself up with a job at a night club owned by one of my old friends from BUD/S. But I had no intention of settling down. I had to know. After a month of planning, I disappeared from the States for a while and went back to Colombia, where this whole mess started. I did some digging and found out a guy from our embassy in Bogotá was into drug trafficking in a big, I mean huge way." Matt suddenly stopped, squirming in the seat of the sport car, the all too familiar feeling of darkness, guilt, shame, and anger overshadowing him.

Sensing that the warrior was about to share something important – not for his own sake but for his Confirmand's – Pastor Olafson urged him to continue. "Matt,

193

you can't keep this all inside your heart. It will eat you alive. Talk to me," he said with a practiced kindness and firmness.

Matt let out a long sigh. "I made an arrangement with a Colombian drug heiress and did a 'snatch and grab' on the guy from the embassy, a guy named Richard Maier. They beat the crap out of him and cut him up really bad but he was tougher than they thought. He wouldn't talk no matter how bad they hurt him." His voice trembled. "In the Teams, we learned how to make people talk. If you do it right, you don't even have to hurt 'em much. Just make them believe they're drowning."

Pastor Olafson involuntarily turned his head away, breaking eye contact, grieved that one of his students had done this to another human being. "What did you do to him after he talked?"

Pierson looked away and shook his head. "You don't want to know."

Insightfully the pastor pressed. "Try me, I'm a good listener."

Pierson turned his head back to his pastor. "Well, if you really want to know, that's when everything went to hell. Helena – the heiress I told you about—decided that she had learned what she needed to know and didn't have any further use for Maier or me. She tried to kill us. I told you, Pastor, I did some bad things. I guess it's not a good idea to get on my bad side 'cause I killed her and every thug she had working for her. No loose ends."

Pastor Olafson looked in disbelief at the man seated next to him. The grief that had been in his eyes moments ago was replaced by burning anger. "What did you do with Maier?"

"I bandaged him up as best as I could and dropped him off near the embassy. I'm sure he's living comfortably on his government disability, supplemented, I'm sure, by his drug-dealing revenues."

Pastor Olafson sat still for several moments, processing the things he had heard and praying for God to grant him wisdom to help the young man. "So, what did you learn from him?"

Matt shook his head, "That, Pastor, you don't need to know. If they even thought you knew, you'd be dead," he said as a matter of fact.

"Then what did you do with what you learned?" he countered, not sure he could bear the answer.

"You want the truth? First, I got the hell out Colombia. Then I got 'out of my mind' drunk for about a month. Then I decided it was time to walk away and never look back – exactly what one of my buddies in the Teams had told me to do. I guess I'm a slow learner."

Again, silence filled the car. Finally, Pastor Olafson knew it was time to deal with the present. "So where do you go from here?" he asked awkwardly.

Matt gave a slight smile. "To be perfectly honest, I haven't got the faintest idea. It's kind of funny. In a very real way I could do anything I want, be anyone I want. Like it or not—and believe me I don't—I have a new life ahead of me," he answered without hope, knowing that there was nothing he wouldn't give to have his old life back.

Suddenly, as though a light had just been switched on in his head, Pastor Olafson found the words he had been searching and praying for. "Matthew," he said with authority, "I want you to listen to me. I can only take your word that going home would endanger your family and I respect your desire to protect them. So, I'll accept your conclusion. You've got a new life ahead of you. What kind of life do you want it to be?"

"What are you getting at?"

Filled with conviction, inspired, the pastor turned in his seat so that he could look directly into the eyes of his onetime Confirmand. "Matt, several times in our conversations this morning and tonight you referred to the mistakes you have made in your life. It may sound like a cliché, but God loves and is more concerned about where your heart is right now and where you go from here then what's in your past. What do you think God wants you to do?"

"Probably stop killing people," he answered sarcastically.

Pastor Olafson actually broke a smile. "Right, I suppose that would be a good first step, but what about the next? I'm serious, Matt!"

"Pastor Jim, you've got to understand. God and I haven't exactly been on speaking terms for quite a while." Matt looked at his former Pastor, suddenly suspicious that the veteran spiritual warrior had some ideas for his future.

"Matt, from the time you were a boy you knew that God was calling you to serve him. I remember talking with you about becoming a pastor many times. You will have to make the decision for yourself, but I want you to consider going to seminary," the pastor said enthusiastically.

His enthusiasm was rewarded with a distasteful grunt as Matt turned in his seat away from his former mentor. "A lot has changed since I was a kid," he said flatly.

"What has changed, Matthew?"

Suddenly the former SEAL spun back to face the man sitting next to him. "I wasn't a killer then! Haven't you listened to anything I've told you? I shot a man dead in front of his wife! I helped torture a guy! Are you saying I should just forget that, pretend it never happened? I don't think so, Pastor!" he snarled the words he had been unable to voice for almost eight months.

The old pastor was still praying, as he always did when counseling, asking God to give him words to minister to his former student. Suddenly, an idea formed in his mind. "Matthew," the pastor said calmly, finally back to dealing with a world he knew very well, "I want you to tell me what

196

Martin Luther said was necessary for a person to do before receiving Holy Communion."

"Ah, come on! I'm really not in the mood for your confirmation pop quizzes!"

"Answer the question," he demanded.

Amazed at the seeming irrelevance of the question, Matt shook his head in disbelief. But he knew that tone of voice. He knew that if he didn't answer the question, the answer would be shoved down his throat. Vague images of the little pamphlet he had memorized so many years ago returned to his mind. It was the little book Martin Luther had written to teach the basics of the Christian faith. He remembered how he dreaded sitting in front of Pastor Olafson to recite its contents, section by section, for his confirmation class. But he could not recall the words he had learned in what seemed like another life.

"I can't remember..."

"Then let me remind you. It says that, 'a person is well prepared and worthy to receive Holy Communion who believes these words: given and shed for you for the forgiveness of sins. But anyone who does not believe these words, or doubts them, is neither prepared nor worthy, for the words for you require simply a believing heart'."

The words came drifting back as if returning from a distant land. "Okay, I remember. But what does that have to do with anything now?"

"It means just this. You said things had changed in your life from the time you were confirmed, when you were a kid, but these words have not changed. Jesus gave his life for you, to forgive your sins. It means he paid the price for your sins and for mine. These words have not changed and never will because they come from God himself. The only thing that has changed is that, if anything, is that you probably now realize more than ever how desperately you need the grace and forgiveness that only Jesus can give you."

"But I killed an innocent man!"

Pastor Olafson nodded sadly. "Yes, yes you did, and much more, but that is not your problem." Matt looked at his spiritual mentor inquisitively, not understanding. "You think that you've committed sins too great for God to forgive, but that is not your problem. The problem is you no longer believe." Sadness filled the pastor's eyes because he had witnessed it happen to so many. "Somewhere along the way you stopped trusting in God and put all your faith in yourself. Now you discover that you are not as virtuous as you once thought, not as smart," he paused, "And, no offense, not as strong as you thought. And now you find yourself very alone."

The words were like a sharp sword and they cut deeply, but rather than a warrior's blade they came like a surgeon's scalpel, cutting to heal and not to destroy. Pierson hung his head.

"My young friend, the love God has for you has not changed, and the blood Jesus' shed for you is more than sufficient to wash every sin of yours— and mine, too, for that matter— as white a snow. The question is, do you... can you believe this?"

Matthew's head was swirling. More than his sins, his college years of critical study and analysis of the Christian faith had caused him to question, to doubt. It was part of the reason he had fled to the Navy rather than seminary. He shook his head. "Pastor Jim, the things I learned in college... the questions and challenges... I don't know if I can believe."

Pastor Olafson gave him an understanding smile. "You're not being asked if you have all the answer to the questions of the universe. Jesus simply asks, 'Do you trust me? Will you accept what I have done for you?' He invites you to let him forgive you, to let him help you now."

Matthew Pierson turned away, staring out the window at the lights of San Bernardino two thousand feet below them. Tears filled the warrior's eyes and he fought to hold them back. He could not answer, knowing something deep within him desperately wanted to believe, but something else warred against it.

Sensing the inner struggle, Pastor Olafson asked his young friend if he could pray for him. Pierson again lowered his head and nodded, hoping that the pastor's faith might give word to the cries of his own heart. The pastor reached over and gently laid his hand on Matt's head and began to pray.

Though he would never remember the specific words of the prayer spoken by his childhood pastor, he would never forget their effect on him. Pastor Jim kept his hand on the warrior's head, feeling him tremble beneath the touch as Matt tried to hold back the flood of emotions coursing through him. How much time passed neither knew, but when their eyes met again, Matthew Pierson was on his way to becoming a new man.

Looking straight into his confirmand's eyes, he spoke the Church's words of absolution.

"God is merciful and blesses you. By the command of our Lord Jesus Christ and for his sake, I declare to you that your sins are forgiven in the name of the Father, and of the Son, and of the Holy Spirit." Then reaching across and making the sign of the cross on the penitent's forehead, he said, *"Blessed are those whose sins have been forgiven, whose evil deeds have been forgotten. Rejoice in the Lord, and go in peace."*

The power of the words had a physical effect on him. The chills that ran throughout his body seemed to proclaim the truth that God had honored the confession and given the promises proclaimed. A lone tear fell from his eye, but was no longer a sign of pain but relief, a tear of thanksgiving from a man reborn, a man who had been given hope. For the first time in as long as he could remember, he felt peace.

Few words were spoken as the two returned to the church and prepared to go their separate ways. Habitually parking the car in the spot reserved for the pastor, Olafson again turned in his seat to address his Confirmand. Though it was after midnight and he knew his wife was probably frantic, he also knew that his work was not yet done.

"So how do you feel about seminary?"

This time Matt almost laughed. "I don't know if I'm ready to be a pastor just yet. I think I better first just learn how to be a Christian."

"I didn't ask if you felt ready to be a pastor," Olafson retorted. "I asked if you felt ready to go to seminary, perhaps a step in the direction of becoming a pastor, but not the same." He corrected. "Matt, go to seminary. You don't have to decide about your calling. Enroll as an unclassified student. There you can study and learn for yourself what it means to be a Christian. Believe me, Matt, I've been doing some thinking. There's no place you could be safer. Whoever your enemies are, they'll never think to search for you there. Matt, anyway you look at it, it makes sense."

It was worth thinking about, Matt admitted to himself. And praying about, too, he reminded himself.

Chapter Twelve

The office of Admiral Lewis Mattison, Commanding Officer of Naval Intelligence, was in its usual state of disarray, reflecting the lack of organizational skills belonging to its current resident. Yet organizational skills had not won Lewis Mattison his rank or the title that accompanied the office. Throughout his career in the Navy, the Admiral had displayed a unique ability to clean up other people's problems and mistakes, not to mention his own.

True to his character, Mattison was always a pleasant man to work with—that is when things were going his way. Today, things were not going his way. In fact, things hadn't been going his way since Friday night. Again, true to his character, when things didn't go his way, Lewis Mattison was a tyrant as anyone in his department could testify. Today his secretary cringed each time he emerged from his office, as he had just done.

"Where the hell is he?" he demanded, knowing full well that the young woman could not answer.

"There hasn't been any word from him yet, sir," she responded nervously. "I called the airport and his plane landed on time, over an hour ago. He could be caught in traffic though," she added timidly.

"I suppose," he grunted, returning to his office, leaving his secretary to breathe a quiet sigh of relief as he disappeared.

Dropping his twenty-pound overweight body into his desk chair, he again picked up the file of Lieutenant Matthew Pierson. He really no longer needed it, for over the weekend he had read it so many times, he now had it virtually memorized. Flipping through the pages again, he pondered the man whose life he studied. Indeed, there was plenty of circumstantial evidence that could link him to Admiral Bartle's assassination. He did commit a serious breach of conduct and from the classified section of his service record, he certainly had the potential of becoming a major threat to his government, not to mention society at large.

Yet there was something unsettling about the case. Maybe it was just that he empathized with a fellow Special OPS soldier who at one time was apparently a hell of a good SEAL. But there was more. In the week since he had given the order for the former Lieutenant Pierson's termination, Mattison had made a few phone calls and pieced together a little more information on the actual assassination of Admiral Bartle and the other hits attributed to *Go-el*. Something inside told him that the pieces just didn't fit.

In his years of working with Naval Intelligence, Admiral Mattison had carried out and given orders which involved the unpleasantness of murder, the disposal of bodies and other such activities of the shadow world. Though in reality such activities were very rare, occasionally such actions were necessary. But in all his previous cases, the targets were all clearly guilty or at least clearly a threat to national security. But there was nothing clear about this case.

"Admiral Mattison? Commander Denzer is here. Would you like to see him now?" the secretary interrupted his thoughts through the intercom.

"Of course I would," he muttered to himself, but not loud enough for his overly sensitive secretary to hear. "Yes, send him in."

Seconds later, Joshua Denzer entered the office. Mattison motioned for him to take a seat in one of the two chairs on the other side of the desk.

"Alright, Josh, where do we stand?"

Denzer shook his head. "I can't tell you much more than I did the other night. He got away clean."

202

Angry and frustrated, Mattison now exploded. "Just who the hell did you think you were going after? Gandhi or some damn pacifist that would simply let you walk in and capture or kill him? This guy's an ex-SEAL for cryin' out loud!"

Ashamed and angered, Denzer tried to mount a defense. "I thought we had it covered. I had two four-man teams, one for the assault, the second for back up. Eight men should have been enough. I debriefed with the team all night Friday. It sounds like he must have heard Parker coming around the side of the house."

"And what the hell did you think you were doing trying the hit at his parents' house? I told you, no messes!"

"Admiral, his parents were gone. He was alone. We had the opportunity. I made the decision to send them. Believe me, if I had it to do over, I'd do a lot of things differently. I'm sorry. Next time I'm going to get him. You've got my word on it."

"I don't need it. You're off the case."

"You can't pull me off this case!" Denzer exploded. "Lew, he killed one of my men! Geez, Parker's probably going to lose his leg. I want this guy! You can't pull me! Not now! I want that son of a bitch!" He was on his feet now, leaning across his superior officer's desk.

"Sit down, son, or I'll climb over this desk and knock your ass into that chair!" Mattison barked, half rising from his own chair. Slowly, Denzer returned to his seat.

"Now you listen to me. You tell me one more time what I can or can't do and I'll not only pull you off this case, I'll run your butt right out of here! Do you read me?" he snarled.

"Alright, I'm sorry, sir," Denzer answered through clenched teeth. "But that son of a bitch killed one of my men!"

The Admiral leaned back in his chair, assuming a less threatening posture, allowing himself a moment to check his own emotions. "You know Josh, if I was Pierson's lawyer, I'd say what he did was self-defense, pure and simple. He's at his parents' home, minding his own business and suddenly four thugs start shooting at him. What's he supposed to do?"

Denzer just glared at the man on the other side of the desk. Now he was defending the bastard! He had never liked his boss, but now he fully hated him.

"What did you do after your so-called hit?" Mattison asked in a demanding voice, anxious to return to the matter at hand.

"I told you on the phone Saturday morning," Denzer answered like an insolent teenager.

"You'll tell me again, right now."

"I ordered some of the team to get McCormick's body and help the wounded into the cars. We didn't have time to cleanup. Later that night I procured a sheriff's uniform and blended in with the uniforms at the scene. When I had the chance, I stashed a bag with 8 ounces of cocaine under the cushion of a hide-a-bed and slipped away."

"What do the local cops have?"

"They found the coke and have an armed and dangerous APB out on him. Other than that, they don't know anything. I talked to one of the detectives and it sounds like they're betting it's all drug-related. No way it will ever get back to us."

Mattison rocked back in his desk chair, stretching his arms in front of him while cracking his knuckles. "Okay, Commander. What do you suggest we do now?"

It was the question he had been waiting for and dreading. "Well, if there was any question before, there isn't now. When we find him, we kill him, I don't care if we have to use a sniper or a bomb or what. He's dead."

"And how do you propose we find him? He evaded surveillance for six months when he had no idea anyone was looking for him! You can bet your butt he ain't gonna make it easy for us again."

204

"He can't hide forever! Keep me on this case and I'll find him!"

Mattison withdrew a cigarette from his shirt pocket, lit it and pulled a long drag from it, disregarding the no smoking policy of the Pentagon. "Okay, Josh. Tell you what I'll do. You're still on the case but you aren't going to find him."

Denzer was puzzled. "What do you mean?"

"I mean you aren't going to hunt for him, you're going to let someone else hunt for you," Mattison said with finality.

"Admiral, I don't understand," Denzer said, not appreciating being toyed with. "What do you have in mind?"

"The local cops think Pierson's somehow connected with drugs—thanks to you. Who was this McCormick character who got waxed?"

"He was an independent contractor who did work for us from time to time," Denzer shrugged.

"Any family?"

"No, his records list no relatives or dependents," Denzer answered, still unsure where his superior was heading.

"Perfect. Alright Commander, here's your job. McCormick is now a DEA agent, killed in the line of duty by Matthew Pierson. Make it so and release it to every law enforcement agency."

It was beginning to dawn on Denzer what Mattison had in mind. "So we let everybody else find him for us," he concluded. "Then we intercept him and take him out, right?"

"Wrong. If, and I mean if, they catch him and bring him in alive, we step in and do some interrogation of our own. It's what I should have done in the first place."

"You can't seriously..."

"You have your orders. They should keep you plenty busy for a while. Report to me when you're ready to release the news," Mattison cut him short. "If you have any ideas about trying another hit on Pierson without my permission...let's just say I won't just fire you. Do you read me?"

Joshua Denzer nodded as he rose and turned for the door. Once outside the office, the nervous secretary gave him a sympathetic look. Though she could not hear the specific words that were spoken inside the office, she had heard raised voices. Secretly she was thankful that she had not been involved. She offered a consoling smile at the flushed man as he hurried past her desk.

April 10, 2004   Washington, D.C.

Edith Deen arrived fifteen minutes late for the lunch appointment she had scheduled. Though she had arrived ten minutes early to the Ristorante i Ricchi, Washington's finest Italian restaurant, she had used the extra minutes for her security detail to confirm that her meeting would remain completely private as well as to send a message to her guest that she was the one who was in control. She would wait for no one.

Russell Seabrook had arrived promptly at the agreed time and had been escorted by the hostess to the reserved table. When she arrived, he knew the former Secretary of State had sent him a subtle message by her tardiness. Such trivial displays of power annoyed him, yet his curiosity about the meeting remained unabated. Ever since her call inquiring about the CIA's efforts to locate *Go-el*, he had pondered her interest in the case. Inquiries and superficial investigations had revealed no obvious connections between Deen and the *Go-el* victims. He had, however, learned enough to know that this woman was both cunning and ruthless. From what he had learned so far, she was not above destroying reputations, careers, or even families in the pursuit of her agendas. Like a game of chess with a master, Seabrook looked forward to their lunch and the game of who-would-play-whom.

"Have you been waiting long?" she asked without hint of apology.

"Does it matter?" he answered with a forced smile.

Answering with a similar half smile, she answered. "No, not in the least."

"Since our time is limited, I suggest we commence with our orders," Seabrook interjected, asserting control of the meeting.

Their food ordered, he began the conversation before she could. "I must admit, I am curious why the former Secretary of State would be interested in talking to a middle management worker from the Farm." He was rewarded by catching the annoyed flash from her eyes.

"Mr. Seabrook, I did not invite you here to play cat and mouse but to discuss with you the security of our nation and how someone with your abilities and current position could help ensure that security." Her eyes boring into his, she continued. "Now is that something you are interested in discussing or do you simply want to play?"

Unintimidated, Seabrook folded his hands on the table in front of him. "My attention is yours."

Unamused, she began her presentation. "A person in your position understands very well that there are times and circumstances that require those of us entrusted with the leadership of this country to make decisions on behalf of this nation that the public simply would not understand. If you study American history, you can clearly see examples of that in every presidency, under every congress. As the Deputy Director of Operations at the CIA, I am sure you have had to make such decisions yourself." She paused to read his reaction so far. Expressionless, Seabrook waited for her to continue. Breaking from his gaze, she inadvertently glanced down at her water glass. "Without going into detail at this time, decisions were made during our administration that have had tremendous positive impact on our national security and foreign policy. Yet they were of a nature that some would not approve and required regrettable sacrifices that some refuse to forgive."

Seabrook studied her as she spoke. Her reputation on the hill was unflappable, a rock, never displaying emotion, always in control. Her eyes betrayed her, or was this a performance? He thought he saw fear. "Let's cut to the chase, Ms. Deen. The real issue here is *Go-el*, is it not?"

Again her eyes gave more than she intended. "My earlier call to you revealed that much. There are people like myself with a great deal of power who are very threatened by this *Go-el* or whomever he represents. These are people who are loyal to this country and have acted in its best interest, whether or not the public would agree. *Go-el* must be stopped and I am asking for your assistance."

"As I told you over the phone, there already is an active investigation underway," Seabrook said, feigning surprise, naiveté. "I really don't know what more I can do. We have good people working on it. They'll catch him, I'm sure... They're just trying to find the thread that ties the assassinations together." He let the statement hang, dangling it in front of her like bait. She had already said enough for him to know what she was involved in, what "actions" she and the others had taken "for the good of the country." She was a master manipulator but she had no idea that he already knew it all; all she was doing now was confessing her own involvement in the crimes.

"Trust me, Mr. Seabrook. I believe there is a way for you to help. You see, the Task Force you have assembled... In their hunt for *Go-el*, it is very likely they could uncover information that would cause great harm to our country. On behalf of your country, I am asking you to disband the Task Force. Say you are dissatisfied with their progress – it has been almost four months with very little to show for their efforts."

Seabrook stared at her, hatred rising up within. But he, too, had mastered the game of deception. He would not let her see even a hint of what he felt inside. "It is not my operation to disband. The FBI insisted that since the investigation was now on U.S. soil, they would be in control. I am afraid I cannot help you."

"Then I would ask three things from you. First, I want all information about the Task Force– staff, deployment, activities. Second, communicate with me directly any information learned from their investigation." She paused, again looking down to the water glass. "Third, pass on information to the Task Force that will not interfere with their hunt for *Go-el* but will steer them away from certain information and individuals I need to protect." He gave her a disapproving look. "Assume what you will, Mr. Seabrook, but what I am asking is in the best interest of our country. If you don't believe that, this conversation is over."

Conveniently, the waitress arrived with their food. After the waitress departed, Seabrook took control or so Deen led him to believe. "Ms. Deen, in the interest of our country I believe I can be of service. However, there are some things I will ask of you. If you agree, you can count on my support. They are not, on the other hand, open for negotiation." She stared at him coldly, knowing that he was enjoying the power he seemed to believe he had over her.

"Go on," she said.

"First, I need the details. What actions were taken in our country's interest? Who is involved? What steps have already been taken to protect these secrets? Second, what was or is your role in this and… how have you benefited from these actions?" She began to protest but he cut her off. "I will not negotiate and let us be clear, I've been around Washington long enough to know that no one does anything for the good of the country if it is not also very good for themselves as well. Should I continue or have you already rejected my terms?" With an exaggerated wave of her hand she motioned for him to continue. Seabrook nodded. "And third, as I just suggested, what are you offering me? What you are asking requires significant risk on my part. Now, let's enjoy our food while you consider my terms."

They began to eat, the heart of the conversation on hold, the eating interrupted by awkward attempts at casual conversations that neither were interested in. As they finished their hastily eaten meal, Deen dabbed her lips with her napkin. "Mr. Seabrook, I am afraid the time has escaped us. I will make some inquiries about your requests and you will be contacted." She pushed her chair from the table and rose, moving behind him and placing her hands on his shoulders, leaning close to his ear. "Do not underestimate me, Mr. Seabrook. We both know things about each other now that could prove very, very dangerous if this trust is broken."

With that she strode away toward the entrance, where her escorts met her and ushered her out of the restaurant. Seabrook leaned back in his chair. He had enjoyed his meal very, very much.

April 10, 2004   Norfolk, Virginia

Spring rains were falling over much of Virginia. Accompanied by his son-in-law, Chad Olsen, the husband of his youngest daughter Naomi, Howard Pierson had flown into Norfolk late Monday night, to be greeted by an unceasing downpour of cold rain that had continued throughout the day.

Howard had insisted that he should make the trip alone, but he was unable to withstand the combined pressure of his wife and children, who unanimously demanded that he take someone with him. Chad's work schedule was the most flexible so he volunteered for the mission. Arriving in Norfolk too late to begin their search, the two found a hotel and spent a restless night, anxious to begin their work.

Driving a rented car, armed only with maps obtained in Santa Rosa through the American Automobile Association, Howard and Chad had spent the day trying to locate a man known to them only as Pepper.

Using their maps, they first found their way to the Norfolk Naval Base 3 and Naval Air Station. Careful not to reveal their identities or the identity of the person they were searching for, the two casually questioned the guards at the main entrance to the base. Hinting that Chad was interested in enlisting and trying out for the Navy diver program, the two, posing as father and son, asked where they might find some Navy divers to talk to. They were advised to go to the Little Creek Naval Amphibious Base. Accepting the humiliation of being seen as a SEAL wannabe, Chad ignored the smirks of the sentries, satisfied that they had earned at least one clue.

From Naval Base 3, the pair of amateur investigators found their way to the Little Creek Naval Amphibious Base on the shores of Chesapeake Bay. Here, information was more difficult to come by. Home of the Navy's SEAL Team Two, the demeanor of the sentries was much more severe, more suspicious. Still posing as father and son, holding to the same cover story, they soon discovered that there was no way they were going to get onto the base. In a last effort, Howard made one more plea for information.

"Look, all we really want is to find a frogman or two and talk to them for a while so my boy can find out a little more about what it takes to be a frogman," Howard pleaded, deliberately using the antiquated reference to frogmen to enhance their innocence. Chad had stood quietly by, resigning himself again to the roll of the pathetic wannabe.

211

Obviously amused, the sentries chuckled openly. "Well if you want to meet a real frogman," one sentry said sarcastically, "you could try going to The Red Sea Dog bar up on Ocean View Avenue," he said, pointing north. "But if I were you, I'd think twice about going there. It's a pretty rough crowd and they're not overly friendly to strangers," the first sentry added as a somewhat friendlier warning.

Realizing they had received all the information they were likely to get, Howard and Bill turned to walk back to their car. As they walked away, the two heard the second sentry call out, "They especially don't like wannabes!"

Chad cringed, now angry, tired of his role as "the goofy kid who wanted to be a SEAL when he grew up." They could hear laughter from behind them. Chad started to turn but Howard's hand grabbed his shoulder. "Let it go, Chad. We got what we came for," he said.

Now it was 8:00 p.m. and the two sat in their rented car, waiting for the clientele of the bar to begin to appear. Slowly, vehicles began to pull into the parking area of the bar. Deciding that there were enough people gathered within, they decided it was time to take their chances.

Cautiously, they entered the bar and were greeted by suspicious glances from customers who were obviously regulars. The majority of the clientele appeared to be young men and judging from their physiques, were probably active duty SEALs. There were several men who were older. Howard estimated their ages ranged from late thirties to a few probably close to his own age of sixty-six. Then there were the women. A few seemed to be attached to particular sailors but the majority seemed to be at The Red Sea Dog to flirt with the strong young warriors. Two women in their forties sat at the bar next to a couple of older men, who Howard assumed to be their husbands.

Satisfied that the newcomers were of no particular threat or of any particular interest, the attention of the locals soon returned to their own conversations or drinks. Satisfied

212

as well that he had adequately surveyed the customers at the bar, Howard took a moment to survey the decor. He was surprised at the absence of military mementos, decorations, or insignia, since the bar was obviously a hangout for enlisted Navy personnel. Then he noticed something over the bar, above the mirror. It was a cartoon-like figure of a red seal with a devilish grin on its face. That confirmed it. This was without a doubt it a SEAL bar. Other than that, it seemed like a very normal seaside bar.

Together, Howard and Chad made their way toward the bar while the music of Credence Clearwater Revival reached their ears above the sounds of blended conversations and laughter. Arriving at the bar, the two took their seats at the nearest available bar stools, soon to be greeted by a medium height, burly, barrel-chested man.

"What can I get you tonight, strangers?" he asked with a surprisingly warm smile while wiping the counter with a towel. Chad noticed that the man had a tattoo on his left forearm that was identical to the laughing red seal that hung over the bar mirror.

"We'll each have a beer," Howard answered for both of them.

"I'll need to see his I.D." The muscular man motioned toward Chad. Though already twenty-three, Chad could easily have passed for a high school student with his innocent, boyish face. Once again feeling belittled, Chad took out his wallet and handed the bartender his California Driver's license.

"So, you boys are from California, huh? Whatever would bring you to a place like this?" he asked in the same friendly tone, yet his eyes revealed his suspicions.

Deciding on the spot to drop any pretense, Howard laid his cards on the table. "We're looking for a man called Pepper. He's a SEAL."

"Don't know anyone that goes by Pepper," the bartender lied. "Tell me, why would you be interested in finding him anyway?" he asked with all traces of friendliness gone.

"If you don't know him, it shouldn't matter to you, should it?" Howard responded slowly. The bartender was visibly angered by Howard's refusal to give him information.

"Look, whoever the hell you are, this is a SEAL bar. Now unless you tell me you're either both SEALs, which I doubt, or you tell me what the hell you're doing here, I'll call a couple of my mates over here and have them throw you the hell out of here! Do you understand what I'm saying?" he snarled.

Instantly, two of the younger men who were at the bar took up positions behind the strangers. Angered by a day of humiliation, Chad turned to face the two who had just joined the conversation.

"These two beauties from California just came prancing in here asking about some guy called 'Pepper'," he announced sarcastically. "Now have either of you ever heard of any fool with a name like that?" The two young SEALs exchanged a smirk and shook their heads.

"Well then," the bartender continued, "it seems like you've stumbled into the wrong place. Why don't you boys escort our guests to the door."

One of the young SEALs roughly took hold of Chad's shoulder. It was the last straw. Chad threw a quick jab to the man's mouth with his right fist, while raising his left for a hook that would never find its target. Smoothly blocking the second punch, the SEAL countered with one well-placed shot to Chad's nose, breaking it and creating a fountain of blood.

Howard stepped between the two before more damage could be done, holding his hands up in a gesture of peace, if not surrender.

"Alright, stop it! Hold on!" he shouted with a fair amount of authority in his voice. "We're looking for a man who goes by the nickname Pepper. He's a SEAL and we were

214

told this was a SEAL bar. We were hoping someone could help us find him," he concluded, surprised to see that he now had the undivided attention of the entire clientele of the bar.

"Alright then, Mr. California," the bartender said with heavy sarcasm, "I'll ask you one more time. If someone here were to know this 'Pepper' you're looking for, what would be your reason for wanting to find him?"

Himself now angry, Howard turned to face the burly bartender, staring him straight in the eyes. "The man we're looking for is a friend of my son." Howard spit the words out.

"And who might your son be?" the bartender pressed.

"You don't need to know."

The two stared at each other, locked in a stand-off. With blood flowing from his broken nose, Chad strained to launch another attack at the SEAL, whose lower lip was bleeding from Chad's jab. This time, however, Howard restrained him, pushing him back onto a bar stool. "That won't solve anything," he spoke softly but firmly to his livid son-in-law.

"The two of you've got a lot of nerve coming into my bar and taking a swing at one of my customers. You've got guts though and I respect that. But you're in the wrong place if you're looking for Pepper Adler. He's with another outfit now and thinks he's just a little too cool for our sort now. He and his buddies hang out at the Bay Side Tavern up near Yorktown. But if you two start trouble up there, there might not be someone as nice as me to keep them from rippin' your hearts out."

Beating a cautious but hasty retreat, Howard and Chad backed their way out of the bar while the eyes of all were on them. Once back within the safety of the car, Dr. Pierson tended to Chad's aching nose, all the while lecturing him on the foolishness of allowing himself to be baited by bullies, not to mention the utter futility of throwing punches at guys who had bar room fights for fun. After setting his

215

son-in-law's swollen, definitely broken nose, he concluded his lecture. Howard then withdrew again his only weapon, the map. Locating Yorktown, he traced the route with his finger on the map. It would take at least half an hour to get there.

After getting directions to the Bay Side Tavern from a local Yorktown bus driver, the two arrived at the small, run-down bar just after 10:00 p.m.. Exhausted, Howard parked the car. After insisting that Chad wait in the car, Howard entered the bar alone.

Moving quickly, he approached the bar, only glancing briefly at the handful of customers. Met at the bar by yet another burly bartender, Howard decided on a still more direct approach.

"Excuse me, I need your help."

The bartender gave the stranger an appraising look. "What can I do for you?" he asked, his voice neither friendly nor hostile.

"I'm looking for a man who goes by the name Pepper, Pepper Adler."

From a table in a dark corner of the small tavern, Warren Adler turned his head at the mention of his name. His wife, Nancy, also turned to see who was asking about her husband. Several other heads around the room also looked up, first turning toward the bar, then looking back at their comrade's table. Warren shook his head slightly, telling his friends that he did not know the man who was asking about him.

"Why are you looking for him?" the bartender asked flatly.

"He was a friend of my son," Howard answered, having learned that honesty brought better, safer results.

As if reading from the same script as the bartender of The Red Sea Dog, the bartender of the Bay Side Bar followed with another question. "And who's your son?"

216

Howard looked around the room, then leaned forward speaking softly. "My son was a SEAL until about eight months ago. His name is Matt, Matt Pierson."

The bartender stared in disbelief. "You're Preacher Pierson's father?"

"Preacher?"

"Yeah, that's what everybody called him. My name's Bob Watkins," the man announced enthusiastically, offering his hand with a warm smile.

Taking the big man's hand, Howard gave a firm shake. "I'm Howard Pierson."

Before Howard could stop him, the suddenly friendly bartender began ringing a ship's bell. When he had the whole bar's attention, he made his announcement.

"Listen up you bunch of maggots! We've got a special guest with us tonight! I'd like you to meet Howard Pierson, Preacher Pierson's father!"

A few cheers and hoots went up and several men gathered around at the bar.

"Well, how's the Preacher doing?" one asked.

Awkwardly and unsuccessfully, Howard tried to minimize the attention. Suddenly he felt a hand, a huge hand, clamp down on his shoulder. He immediately turned to the face the man.

"Alright, back off, you animals. I believe the gentleman is looking for me," Warren Adler announced. One look at Howard Pierson's face and Adler knew the stranger wasn't lying. The resemblance between father and son was profound.

"So you're Pepper," Howard said.

"Master Chief Warren Adler, at your service," the big man grinned, "but my friends call me Pepper."

Nervously looking around again, Howard lowered his voice. "I need to talk to you, but I think it needs to be a little more private. Can we go outside? My son-in-law is out in the car."

"Sure, let me introduce you to my wife and I'll ask her if she minds waiting for a while."

After a brief introduction to Nancy Adler, the two stepped out into the cold rain. Climbing into the rented Chrysler LeBaron, it was Howard's turn to perform the introductions.

"Chad, I'd like you to meet Master Chief Warren Adler."

The two shook hands. "What the hell happened to you?" Adler asked bluntly.

"He had a little run in with some SEALs over at The Red Sea Dog. The one who hit him doesn't look too pretty, either."

Pepper gave Chad an approving look. Though not advisable, taking a swing at a SEAL took guts.

"I don't know whether to call you Warren or Pepper," Howard began awkwardly.

"Call me Pepper. Everybody does," he grinned.

"Pepper, we've got to talk to you about Matt."

"You don't have to tell me. Matt's in trouble, I know. He called me a couple nights ago."

"He called you? Is he alright?" Howard cut in.

"Yeah, he's fine, I suppose. He didn't give me any details, but he said he was ambushed at your house in Santa Rosa," the veteran counter-terrorist confessed. "But I've got to tell you, he's not coming home again, he made that clear to me. He said it would be too dangerous for your family and for him. Frankly, I think he's right."

"I know this is a sensitive question, but I want an honest answer. Is Matt involved in any way with drugs?" Howard asked forcefully.

"Drugs? Preacher? Are you kidding me? That kid's as straight as an arrow! Hell, by SEAL standards he hardly even drank!" Suddenly Pepper's face turned deadly serious. "Why are you asking about drugs?" he demanded.

218

"After the ambush or whatever happened last Friday, the police found a bag of cocaine among Matt's things," Chad answered, sparing his father-in-law the pain of having to voice the words.

"Bullshit!" Pepper exploded. "No way! The sons of bitches planted it! Oh, this is bad, man. This is bad."

"What are you saying?" Howard asked with a growing sense of hopelessness.

"I... I don't know a delicate way of saying this but someone wants your son dead, and they've got the power to see to it, one way or another. Planting the drugs was just a way to get the local cops and the Feds hunting for him. But don't kid yourself. If the cops get a hold of him, he'll be dead. He'll be a sitting duck."

"But who are 'they'? Who's after him, and why?"

The Master Chief looked around the parking lot nervously, instinctively checking for any sign of danger. He now was clearly worried. "Look, we're getting into some pretty sensitive stuff here. From this point on, everything I tell you is stuff that never happened, do you understand what I'm saying?" Pepper asked with a severity that needed no further emphasis. The other two in the car nodded to indicate that they understood.

"Matt was a member of DEVGRU, what some people still call SEAL Team Six. It's the Navy's counter-terrorist unit; similar to the Army's Delta Force. Secret stuff, man. About nine months ago, Admiral James Bartle, then working for Naval Intelligence, briefed us personally for a preemptive strike on a drug dealer who was making threats about hitting U.S. targets. Our job was simply to hit the druggie before he could hit us. We had three individuals to hit.

"Some things went bad, and Matt ended up drilling one of our targets, right in front of the guy's wife. But that's not the only thing that shook him. She was yelling at him in English. That she was an American. Matt grabbed the guy's

219

wallet and found out the guy he killed was also an American—one worked for the State Department. Then one of our guys bought it while we were extracting.

"We got to the carrier and I tell you, none of us were in very good moods. Preacher – Matt – is madder than hell and gets right in that son of a bitch Bartle's face, wanting to know why we were sent to kill an American. Bartle is, or was," he corrected himself, "a prick. He told Matt he was paid to kill, not ask questions. In short, that's when Matt lost it. He tried to rip the Admiral's head off with his bare hands."

"Wait a minute, Admiral Bartle? Isn't he the one who was assassinated in England a couple months ago?"

"The same." Adler answered. "Listen. I've been out on forty-three real life missions—twenty-three of them with Matt. I don't know if I understand why we were sent in on half those missions, I just did what I was told—which is exactly what Matt did. But that job, that was different. It wasn't right from the beginning.

"After Matt's court martial, he dropped out. He told me he was going to find out what really happened. I think he also needed some time to put things back together. That night wasn't good for any of us, but Matt took it hardest. He was the one who pulled the trigger."

Pepper paused, seeing the pain in the eyes of his friend's father. Letting out a deep breath, Warren Adler realized he, too, had some emotions to deal with from that night. Though the air was cool, he was sweating. "Look, Mr. Pierson, I want you to know something about your son. We were in the Philippines and our chopper got hit by an RPG. I was busted up and Matt pulled me out, knowing full well the bird could blow any second. He earned his first bronze star on that mission. You remember a little over a year ago hearing in the news about that al-Qaida cell that seized a school for girls in Afghanistan—right after we went and kicked out the Taliban? Your son took a round in the shoulder to save a little girl they were about to execute. It

220

won him his second bronze star and a purple heart. He's a good man, Mr. Pierson, don't ever doubt that."

Tears were in Howard's eyes now, tears of love, tears of pride, tears mingled with determination. "What can we do to help him?" he asked the warrior, clearing his throat.

"To be honest, I don't know. He knew something like this could happen so he took some precautions." Suddenly he paused, again scanning the parking lot. "Remember, what I'm saying doesn't get repeated, anywhere or to anyone, okay?" Once again the two nodded their agreement.

"In our unit, we often do things that are unorthodox according to military standards. We use false IDs, smuggle weapons on commercial airliners—basically we operate the same way as the guys we're trained to hunt. Anyway, right after the court martial, Matt gave me an envelope with two complete sets of IDs, including passports, and $15,000 that he had saved. When he called the other night, he asked me to send the envelope to a post office box in Los Angeles. If you were really careful and covered your tracks, I suppose you could get in touch with him through the P.O. Box. One thing a guy always needs when he's underground is money, cash. $15,000 doesn't go very far these days. I threw in a couple thousand extra to help but still it won't last long."

"We can get money to him, but how will he know we sent it? Does he check the box periodically or something?" Howard asked, relieved that there seemed to be something he could do to help his son.

"He said he'd be checking the box once every week or two in case I needed to get in touch with him. Other than that, he said he'd call me if he got into more trouble or needed anything. That reminds me, I'll give you my address and phone number. You got something to write with?" Chad handed the warrior a pad of note paper and a pen.

"If you want to get a message to Matt, it's probably safest if you do it through me. If you have to call, don't call from any of your homes—your phones are probably tapped, mine might be too, for that matter. When you call, use a pay phone. Say your representing, umm... 'Venus Marketing, prize division'. Say something like 'if you want more information about your prize, call...' and give the number where I can reach you. Give a time, like maybe four hours later for me to get the message and return the call. Sound alright?"

"Sounds good," Howard answered. "Pepper, you know I can't thank you enough for helping my son, I..."

Pepper cut him off. "Your boy saved my life and he's one of the finest men I've ever served with. You don't need to thank me for anything."

"Still, thanks for what you did," Howard brushed the protest aside. An awkward moment of silence passed as the new friends watched the rain dance on the windows of the car.

"Well, under ordinary circumstances, I'd invite you guys to stay the night at our place, but given the way things are, it's probably better not. Nancy's probably getting pretty anxious to get home," the big sailor said, opening the car door.

"If this ever blows over, we'll all get together under better circumstances," he said with a sad smile. "You two take care of yourselves, and you," he pointed at Chad, "keep your guard up." With that, he pulled himself from the car and jogged back toward the bar.

With a satisfied look, Howard met eyes with his facially deformed son-in-law. Chad saw immediately that something had changed in his father-in-law. No longer did his eyes betray the hopelessness he had seen since the attack on his son. Now they were intense, determined.

"Well, we got what we came for. Let's get back to the hotel and get some rest. It's been a long day."

Chapter Thirteen

April 10, 2004
Trinity Lutheran Seminary, Columbus, Ohio

Dieter Zibermann and his wife had just returned to their apartment after their morning classes for a quick bite of lunch before scurrying off again to their one o'clock Systematic Theology course. Upon entering their apartment and tossing their book bags on the kitchen table, Gabriele noticed the red message-indicator light of the answering machine was flashing. The two exchanged a serious look. Gabriele depressed the play back button.

"Hello, this is John from the library. I found the information you requested. You can reach me on our toll free line. Thank you."

Again the two exchanged a troubled look. "I guess I won't be making it to Systematic Theology today," Dieter said flatly.

"I'll take notes for you, dear," Gabriele said playfully, trying to break the tension.

"Thank you, my love," he smiled in return, rewarding her efforts. "I'll be back as soon as I can."

It took a little less than half an hour for Dieter to reach the shabby unfurnished apartment in downtown Columbus. Entering, he immediately went to the telephone and dialed the memorized number.

"Yes?" the voice of Russell Seabrook answered.

"This is your best friend calling. I understand you have some information for me."

"Yes. It seems my troublesome deputy director has organized a joint CIA/FBI Task Force to search for the notorious *Go-el*. The one whose name you gave me is one of our field agents. He's there to keep an eye on a suspect, but they don't have anything solid, yet."

There was silence from the other end of the line after Seabrook finished his abbreviated report. Dieter closed his eyes, cursing. They had been setting up their covers and their American network for over a year and the one who was supposed to offer them high level coverage was now saying that an investigation had been going on right under his nose! Not only that, somehow, they had gotten close enough to put an agent onto one of them! Silently he cursed his benefactor.

"Well, it seems we have a fairly significant problem, doesn't it? Now what do you propose we do about it?"

"The undercover agent is watching a guy named Atkins, Jeffrey Atkins. Is he part of your organization?"

"You know I can't answer that."

"Cut the crap, Lyson. If he is not one of yours then they're just chasing air but if he is, then you said it yourself, we've got a big problem."

"You'll have a bigger problem if you ever use that name again!" the man who called himself Zibermann snapped. Stephen Lyson was a name which he had not used in years and the handful of living people who knew it also knew better than to ever use it.

"Yes or no. Is Atkins part of your network? Like it or not, we need each other."

Though the conversation lapsed into a tense silence, the rage radiated through the phone lines. After several long seconds, one word was communicated. "Yes."

"Okay then, your orders stand. We need a month to make adjustments on our end. You tell your boy to lay low for now and keep his nose clean. The longer he stays clean, the less suspicious they'll become. They've got nothing solid on him yet."

"He's too close. They are too close. I'm going to pull him out."

"No! Let's not panic. Pulling him out will only confirm their suspicions. You're a professional and I'm assuming Atkins is, too. You have your orders. Tell him to sit tight for now. I'll call you in one month and you'd better be ready for action."

With that the secured line of fiber optic communication was severed as Dieter heard the clicking sound of a phone being hung up. Rage seemed to flow through his body, triggered by the hearing of the name that had once been his. Long repressed childhood memories drifted into his consciousness, as if to fan the flames of his anger. He turned to see a crying child, only to face an empty room. The crying continued to ring in his ears, only now he could hear the distant crack of leather striking skin, the dull thud of fists pounding flesh again, again, again. With a sudden shake of his head he called himself back to attention. He had another call to make.

Getting a phone call through to a student at the Seattle Lutheran Bible College was often quite a challenge. Cell phones had proven to be impractical, given the thick concrete walls of buildings and mountainous setting of the college campus that blocked most cell phone service. So for the most part they relied on land lines which were actually a little safer for confidential calls anyway. First, the call was answered by the receptionist at the front desk. Then, after giving the name and dorm floor number of the person the caller wished to speak to, the call would be transferred to the dorm floor. There, the hall phone would ring repeatedly. If the caller was lucky enough to find someone on the floor to answer the phone, they would then check to see if the desired student was in his or her room or somewhere else on the floor. More often than not, however, no one would answer the hall phone in the dorm, so the call would eventually be transferred back to the front desk, where the caller would have the opportunity to leave a message.

Such was the case and frustration for Dieter Zibermann as he tried to reach his associate at the Bible school. After no one answered the phone on the dorm floor, the receptionist finally answered the call for the second time. "I'm sorry, there doesn't seem to be anyone on that floor at this time. May I take a message?" the young voice asked sweetly.

"Yes. Tell Jeffrey that his uncle called and that I need to speak with him as soon as possible."

"Okay, I'll make sure that he gets the message. Thank you and have a nice day."

Dieter was already lowering the phone as the receptionist concluded her rehearsed closure. It was the second time he had been forced to contact Jeffery through the Bible school's ridiculous system. He cursed himself for not checking out all such details more carefully. The Bible school had seemed like the perfect cover for the third party of the *Go-el* triad. Communal living provided the assurance of witnesses to collaborate the various prearranged alibis that Atkins would employ when his services were needed. As they had done from the beginning, the presumed innocence of church workers or in the present case students of the Bible or theology, allowed an almost unparalleled freedom of mobility. But he hadn't considered the potential difficulties involved in something as simple as placing a phone call. Next time he would be more thorough. Dieter never repeated his mistakes.

He leaned back against the wall, nestling his shoulders into a comfortable position to rest and wait for the return call. He grinned to himself as he thought of his present alias. A theological student, training for a life of service in the Lutheran Church. At one time he had genuinely desired to pursue ordination, to proclaim the God of love to all the poor sinners of the world.

All that had been before his father's death, before the man who became his stepfather entered the young life of

226

Stephen Lyson. The beatings began on a beautiful spring Saturday morning, April 23, 1973, when young Stephen was only thirteen years old.

Even now, 31 years later, the memories of that first beating haunted him. They continued off and on for the next two years, varying in severity, once leaving him hospitalized for two days. His mother had made excuses to the doctors.

The day that had shaped the course of the rest of his life had finally come on a cold winter's night in late December, 1975. It was Christmas Eve, to be exact. Young Stephen and his mother and stepfather had attended the early Christmas Eve service at a neighborhood Lutheran church where Stephen's mother had occasionally brought him to Sunday School years ago, before the marks of the beatings began raising uncomfortable questions from the well-meaning Sunday School teachers.

Now 44 years old, Stephen Lyson's pulse quickened as the memories of that fateful evening played through his mind as though recorded on video. His stepfather began drinking as soon as they walked through door. Within an hour, he was clearly drunk, his mood angry, his words harsh and rude. In a vain attempt to spare her son the abuse she knew would come, his mother tried to send the fifteen-year-old to bed, anything to get him out of the room, out of range of his stepfather's drunken wrath. Her efforts, however noble, led her irrational husband to direct and unleash his anger on her.

Watching from the top of the stairs, he saw his mother being beaten, his stepfather's rage seeming to grow with every blow. Stephen began to pray that the horror would end but suddenly stopped. In a moment of clarity that changed his life forever, young Stephen Lyson knew what he had to do.

He remembered hearing once in Sunday School that God used people to be his hands and feet on earth. It was in that moment that he realized God needed his hands and his feet to put an end to the evil taking place before his eyes. With the confidence of one who believed he was acting on behalf of God, Stephen Lyson calmly walked down the stairs, past the violent struggle taking place in the living room and into the kitchen.

A moment later he returned to the living room, clutching a large kitchen knife in his hand. Unseen, he approached his stepfather from behind and plunged the knife into his back, again, again, again.

The coroner who testified at the boy's trial said that he could identify eight puncture wounds in the dead man's back that exactly matched the blade of the kitchen knife. There was never any real question of the boy's guilt and Stephen was swiftly sentenced to the State Youth Facility where he served his term until he was eighteen. In an effort to be lenient in light of the abuse the boy had endured, the judge had left open the door that the young murderer might be released at his coming of age, provided that he behaved well in the youth prison.

Well-behaved he was not, however. Frequent violent behavior led to extended periods of time in isolation, time which Lyson used to contemplate his future and to prepare himself in body, mind, and spirit.

If there was ever a case of a young man being misunderstood, Stephen Lyson was the one. His violent behavior was attributed to a social disorder stemming from his years of abuse. His interest in the Bible and religion were brushed off as byproducts of his personality disorder. But those who had jumped to such conclusions were wrong on both counts.

Six months before his eighteenth birthday and the chance for freedom, there was a remarkable change in the young man. There were no more fights in the yard (largely because few dared challenge him—he had earned a fierce reputation) and even his attitude toward the guards and authorities changed. Lyson had realized that if he were to fulfill his destiny, he would first have to free himself from his incarceration.

When the parole board met shortly after his birthday, they were clearly impressed by his dramatic turn-around. The parole board released him on the condition that he immediately enlist in the United States Marine Corps, a condition which the young man found quite acceptable.

In the Marines, Lyson's crude fighting and survival skills learned during his incarceration were honed to lethal perfection. Trained as a sniper, qualified as a small weapons specialist, Lyson's confidence in his abilities and his special calling blossomed. Despite the widespread disillusionment and distrust of the establishment and the anti-military attitudes which swept the nation during the late 1970's, Lyson committed himself completely to the cause of God and country, as he understood each. Willingly he embraced the anti-communist agenda of the military, dedicating himself—body and soul—to the defense against and ultimate destruction of the godless ideology. For six years Stephen Lyson was a model Marine—seemingly fearless, skilled, resourceful, and deadly. Steadily he advanced in rank, achieving the rank of Gunnery Sergeant in January of 1987. Yet what should have been another step toward a promising career turned out to be another turning point in the young warrior's life.

With his new rank, Lyson was removed from field work and training, which had fit him so perfectly, and for the first time in his military career, was plunged directly into the bowels of the military bureaucracy. At a time when the war machine of the United States of America was grasping for new release of Federal funding, Gunnery Sergeant Lyson saw a side of the military he had not directly encountered before. Political games, corruption, abuse of authority, and negligence began to tear at the idealistic view of the Corps that Lyson had so fully trusted. Disillusioned and disgusted,

Lyson resigned from the Marine Corps only four months after his promotion.

Bitter, Lyson spent the better part of the next seven years offering his skills to various governments and individuals as a mercenary. As his reputation spread, the fees paid for his services rose proportionately. His range of activity sent him around the world, participating in conflicts in Angola, Zimbabwe, the Philippines, as well as several uniquely sensitive operations in Europe, including one mission in Romania.

Should one have read his resume, if such a document existed, one might have been tempted to assume that the disillusioned Lyson had simply sold out his ideals to the highest bidder, becoming a mercenary in the worst sense of the word. Such an assumption, however, would be very wrong.

Stephen Lyson never fought or killed merely for money. From the killing of his stepfather to his current arrangement with Russell Seabrook, every action in which Lyson had involved himself was always motivated by a belief in the cause. Killing was his calling, not just an avenue for wealth. Whereas Saint Francis of Assisi once prayed, "Lord, make me an instrument of thy peace," the prayer that defined Stephen Lyson was, "Lord, make me an instrument of thy wrath."

It was in October of 2003 that Lyson believed his prayer had finally been answered in its ultimate sense. On a deserted fishing pier in the town of Ztele, on the North Sea coast of Germany, he had met a mysterious man who gave him a vision; a man who opened the doors to his personal destiny. His was the task of executing judgment on the corruption of his nation.

Though he trusted no one, least of all his current employer, they both agreed that those on the Claypool list needed to be terminated. As long as they shared this goal, he would work with Russell Seabrook, the deadly marriage

230

between the two would remain. *But if Seabrook is unfaithful, there will be a divorce, a permanent one*, Zibermann vowed to himself.

As if somehow sensing that the time of reflection was complete, the phone on the floor beside him began ringing. It took three rings for the sound to reach the assassin in his trance-like state. Shaking his head as if to wake himself, he answered the phone.

"Hello?"

"Uncle Dieter? It's Jeff. I got your message."

"Ah Jeff, how is the weather in Seattle?"

The code completed, Jeffery Atkins cut to the point. "What did you find out?"

"It's bad. Your friend is part of a Task Force set up between the FBI and CIA to hunt for *Go-el*."

"*Scheisse!*" Atkins cursed, inadvertently slipping into his native German tongue. "I'll take care of him."

"No, you will not. You will not do anything as a matter of fact. Your orders are to sit tight. Do nothing to attract attention. Do you understand me?"

"No! I do not understand you!" Atkins exploded, his voice echoing in the closet-like phone both. It was too loud. "My 'friend' has searched my room! My 'friend' is going to die," he announced trying to control his voice.

"Listen to me, Jeffery. They have nothing solid on you, they're just suspicious. If we make any move, it will only confirm their suspicions. Back off and lay low." He was answered with silence from the other end of the line. "Those are your orders. If something changes, I'll be in touch. You don't have to like it, just do it."

The line went dead. Zibermann shook his head. His associate was young and hot-tempered and could well become a liability. But for now, he was needed. He just hoped the orders would be obeyed. They did not need more complications.

Two thousand miles away, Atkins slammed his fist into the wall of the small, closet-like phone booth outside the chapel of the Bible college. Rage was flowing through his veins and he wanted to kill—not just anyone—but a student named Timothy Parnel, the one who was watching him, the one who had invaded his room. Again, he slammed his fist into the wall. Rising swiftly, he stormed out of the booth and hurried down the hall, consciously trying to control himself lest some inquisitive student become curious about his behavior.

Reaching the nearest exit, he stormed through the door. Outside a heavy mist was falling, but Atkins paid it no mind as he walked swiftly along the tree-lined road that circled the campus.

The fresh air helped clear his mind and calm his body. Collecting himself, Atkins reached a firm decision. From this moment on, Parnel was on trial—if he got any closer, he would die. As for himself, he would watch, wait, and obey his orders—for now.

April 11, 2004   **Santa Rosa, California**

Sheriff's Detective Shawn McCallister was busy filling out yet another criminal report, part of an endless task that occupied fully one third of his time. Though no less horrible, the report at hand was more or less routine— another case of domestic violence. This particular case had resulted in the hospitalization of the wife and one child. It was the third time the Sonoma County Sheriff's department had been called to the residence and this time, the husband was sure to spend time in jail. Finishing one page of the report, he flipped to the next.

Suddenly a file was thrown on his desk, falling half across the report he was working on. "Watch it!" he snapped irritably without looking up.

"You'll be interested in that," the Chief of Detectives answered coldly.

McCallister looked up somewhat apologetically. "Sorry, boss. What is it?"

"Some information about that Pierson guy from the shooting the other night. It was just faxed to us a few minutes ago."

McCallister opened the file and quickly scanned through it, searching for its conclusion about the suspect, Matthew Pierson. He was wanted for drug trafficking and suspected in the murder of a DEA agent. McCallister shook his head. "I knew it." He thought of the suspect's parents he had met on the night of the shooting. They had seemed like a nice couple—a nice family, he corrected himself after remembering the daughter and son-in-law who had come to the crime scene. It wasn't their fault their son turned out to be scum. "Boss, I'm gonna get this son of a bitch," he promised.

"You're not the only one who wants him. Check in with the FBI and DEA. Work with them as much as you can. You understand me?" the Chief Detective ordered.

"Yeah, boss. I understand," McCallister muttered. He hated working with Feds.

*   *   *   *   *   *   *

The phone of the Law Offices of Jacobson and Rosetti rang just after three o'clock. The secretary of the small, two-lawyer firm answered and immediately put the call through to one of her two bosses.

"Mike Rosetti. How can I help you?"

"Mike, it's Steve," Deputy Kalbach announced. "Something just came in on your brother-in-law I thought you should know about. But first I need to ask you something. Have you or anyone in your family had any contact from Matt? Have you learned anything about him?"

Rosetti paused uncomfortably for just a moment before answering. It was too long. "No, as far as I know no one has heard anything yet."

Interpreting the pause correctly, Kalbach challenged the answer. "Mike, we had an agreement. If you know anything, you had better tell me now."

"Look Steve, when I can tell you anything, I will. Now what did you find out?"

"No way, Mike. We had an agreement. A two-way street, remember? Do you have any idea how much trouble I'd be in if anyone found out what I've told you? And you haven't given me anything. I know you're holding back. You come clean with me or I'm through telling you anything— and believe me, if you really think your brother-in-law is innocent, you need me on your side, because they're out to get him, big time. Now what's it going to be?"

Mike took the phone from his ear in frustration. He hated lying to a friend, and he knew it wouldn't work anymore. He had to think, he had to decide.

"I haven't got all day, Mike. What's it going to be?"

Returning the phone to his ear, Rosetti made his decision. "Look Steve, I don't have the right to say anything. Can you come over to my place tonight?"

"No way. I'm not sure, but I wouldn't be surprised if your place was under surveillance. If I show up..."

"Okay, can we meet somewhere? I think you should talk to my father-in-law."

"I'll be at the downtown mall at seven o'clock tonight. Meet me in the food court."

"Alright, we'll be there. Now what did you find out?"

"Not so fast. We'll see each other tonight. I'll tell you then."

"Fair enough—and thanks, Steve, for everything."

"Yeah, yeah, save it. Just be there tonight and be ready to spill your guts."

The line went dead. Rosetti scratched his chin with the receiver. Meeting with Steve and coming clean would be a good thing. Whether he could convince his father-in-law of that would be another matter.

It was another matter, indeed. Mike Rosetti had left work as soon as he could get away after the phone call. Driving straight to his in-laws' house, he found Howard Pierson hard at work, patching more of the bullet holes that decorated his living room. Though the shooting occurred almost a week ago, the distinctive stench of cordite still lingered in the house. The repairs were only just beginning.

Rosetti pled his case, three times. Each time Howard exploded, exclaiming that Mike had no right to say anything to anyone. Mike had tried to explain, tried to defend himself, but to no avail. In the end it was Monica who interceded on behalf of her son-in-law. Eventually, Howard yielded to the combined influence of his wife and the father of two of his grandsons.

It was just before 7:00 p.m. when Dr. Pierson and Rosetti arrived at the mall. Casually scanning the tables in the food court, they didn't see Kalbach. The two found a table on the edge of the dining area and waited.

Kalbach was fifteen minutes late, explaining as he arrived that he had checked to make sure they hadn't been followed. He also made it clear that his concern was more for his own job than the safety of Pierson's son.

"Now that we're finally together, why don't you tell me what you've heard from your son. I don't think I need to remind you about the legal consequences of withholding information in a criminal investigation," Kalbach announced in a demanding tone. Howard Pierson almost got up and left.

"Come on, you two! We're here to talk, and to help each other—and Matt, if possible."

"Why should I trust you?" Howard demanded of Kalbach.

"The way I see it, you don't have any choice. Your son doesn't have any friends on the force and if he is innocent, he's going to need all the help he can get."

"What did you find out?" Dr. Pierson demanded.

Recognizing it would be futile to continue the debate over who should reveal what first, Kalbach conceded. "A fax came in today from the DEA saying that your son is wanted for drug trafficking and is a suspect in the murder of a DEA agent. The Fed's want him in a bad way. Detective McCallister wants him. I don't think anybody really cares how they bring him in, if you know what I mean. They're not taking any chances with someone with your son's background. Better a dead suspect than dead cops. It's as simple as that."

"They're a bunch of damn liars!" Howard exploded, momentarily drawing the attention of diners from a nearby table.

"Dad, tell Steve what you know. Maybe he can help," Rosetti pleaded.

"Look, Steve, I don't know you from Adam. The only reason I'm talking to you is that Mike says I can trust you. If I tell you what I've learned, you can't say anything, to anybody. I have to have your word on it."

"You know I can't promise that."

"Then I have nothing to say," Howard concluded.

"Look, Steve, listen to what he's got to say, then make your decision, alright?"

The three exchanged suspicious glances. Reluctantly, Howard began his confession. Beginning with the postcard, Howard explained what the family had learned so far, deliberately omitting the name of Pepper Adler or any other details that might lead the officer to his son.

At the conclusion of the disclosure, Kalbach's expression was severe. Howard wondered what he saw in the face of the young officer. Was it concern? Was it disbelief? More importantly, what would he now do? Together, he and his son-in-law waited to find out.

Kalbach shook his head slowly, thoughtfully. "You really think what this guy told you is true?" he asked, unnecessarily.

"I know my son," Pierson stated. Rosetti nodded his agreement.

"If it's true, I don't see how I can help you unless you let me tell Detective McCallister. He's in charge of the local investigation, maybe he could..."

"If you say anything, to anybody, we'll deny having any knowledge of this conversation or the details discussed. The best way for you to help us, for you to help my son, is to keep us posted on what the authorities know."

"So you can get a warning to him and he can escape? For cryin' out loud, I'm a cop! I can't do that!"

"Look. If what we've learned is true and Matt is arrested, he'll be dead. No trial. No defense. Just dead." Howard's eyes now bore into the young officer's. "I know what I'm asking you to do, I know what you'll be risking. Believe me, I'll even understand if you can't help us. But for God's sake at least don't say anything to anyone. I'd beg if it would help," he pleaded.

Kalbach turned his eyes to the table. Again, there was tension in the silence as they waited for the verdict. Finally, he lifted his eyes again and traded stares with the two men across the table from him. "I'll do what I can," he finally stated.

"What exactly does that mean?" Rosetti, the lawyer pressed.

"Don't push it, Mike!" Kalbach snapped. "It means I'll do what I can," he stated again while rising to his feet. "You keep me posted, too. Remember, it's a two-way street." With that he was gone.

"What do you think, Mike? Can we trust him?" asked his son-in-law.

"Doesn't look like we have much choice, but yeah, I think we can. He's a good guy."

April 14, 2004   **Minneapolis, Minnesota**

"You want to know what I think?" Jed Michaelson said, not really caring if they were interested or not. "The sooner people wake up from their fairy tales and realize there is no such thing as 'God' or 'the Force' or whatever the hell you want to call it, the better off the world will be. What *Goel* has done is nothing compared to the centuries of atrocities committed by people who firmly believed they were fulfilling the will of God." Jed shoved a huge bite of pizza into his mouth and continued his oration, hampered only by the need to chew between words. "Christian, Muslim, Buddhist, I don't give a rip. Marx was only partially right. Religion is the opium of the people – some people. For some it mellows them out, numbing them to the harsh reality that we are alone in this world and there is no meaning! But to others it's like crack and its gets them so jacked up with self-righteous fervor they'll do anything, kill anybody, cut the heads off their enemies or blow the crap out of anything," he concluded, jabbing his finger at the front-page article of the copy of U.S. News and World Report on the table. The article reported the beheading of an American truck driver who was kidnapped by a radical insurgent group in Iraq a week earlier.

"No one can argue that people of every religion have done bad things," LeToure countered, "but don't you have to concede that religion can bring out the best in people? And for those who are hurting, hopeless, needing a second chance?"

238

"Opium, darling, just opium...but you're right, under the right circumstances, opium can change a lot of things. It's just not real."

Kampo and Belcourt were listening with mild amusement as their colleagues locked horns, while Pat Knodell gently shook her head, knowing where this was heading. From the beginning, two things were clear; Michaelson was baiting them, trying to draw them into a winless philosophical argument that he intended to dominate. They had wisely refused the bait but LeToure willingly took it, hook, line, and sinker.

"Then how do you explain that people of every age and culture have believed in an afterlife, that there is more to this world, this life, than what we can see and touch? Is everyone else wrong and you, Jed Michaelson, are the only one 'enlightened' enough to realize the truth?" LeToure countered.

"So if enough people believe in something it must be true? Listen, Brenda, a bunch of brainwashed people believing a fairy tale does not make it real."

"It's not that everyone believes the same, it's that there is something in us as humans that instinctively knows there is something more. I think it says in Ecclesiastes that 'God has placed eternity in the hearts of men.' It's not the details of what people believe that are universal, but the longing in our hearts."

"Ah, so now we know," Jed announced for the whole pizza parlor to hear, "the lady partakes of the opium herself!" Inside Jed was fuming. How dare she quote the Bible at him! "You know what I long for?" He caught himself before allowing his wrath to explode. "I long...to take a piss," he declared, glaring across the table at LeToure as he rose and stormed toward the restrooms.

LeToure caught Kampo as he tried to suppress a grin, earning him an irritated frown in return. "It's not funny!" she said, though she suddenly began to recognize the humor in

239

her valiant though hopeless attempt to have a meaningful conversation with Jed.

"Girl, you sure don't back down from a fight, do you?" Susan Belcourt said.

Brenda shook her head. "Ever since he's been back it's like he's been trying to pick a fight with me. "I honestly don't know what I did to get him so upset with me, but I made up my mind that I'm not going to back down from him. I'm sorry, I didn't mean to ruin our lunch."

"It's not you. It's who you represent that he's attacking. He thinks that because you're a Christian you are automatically one of those finger-pointing hypocrites," Kampo interjected.

"Sure, Bill, there are Christians who act that way but have I ever come across that way to you?" she asked, addressing the question to her colleagues.

"No," Susan answered. "But it doesn't matter. I think Jed made up his mind about you when he first read your file. You didn't have a chance. And I don't think a full frontal theological assault is going to help anything," she added, knowing that there was enough stress and frustration among the member of the *Go-el* Task Force without adding theological controversies into the mix. Long days and no progress in the hunt for *Go-el* was straining each of them.

Brenda looked across the table at Belcourt and nodded. "I hear you," she said, accepting the rebuke with a humility that surprised and impressed the veteran agent.

"Don't take it personally, Brenda," Pat Knodell said in an attempt to soothe the wounds. "You're having the privilege of seeing Jed at his worst, but deep down, he's really a pretty good guy. I'll talk to him."

"You don't need to defend me, Pat, I can take care of myself," LeToure protested.

"Don't worry, I'm not going to tell him he should apologize to you. I'm just worried about him. He hasn't been himself since he came back from Chicago." Pat Knodell excused herself from the table.

"The guy's just a jerk, that's his problem," Kampo said for LeToure's benefit, though she didn't respond.

Pat Knodell intercepted Jed Michaelson as he was coming out of the rest room. "Come on, Jed, we're going for a walk," she announced in her usual direct manor.

"You gonna scold me for being rude?" he said with thick sarcasm.

"No, I want to talk to you, so move!" she ordered.

They left the suite, found their way to the elevator, and exited the building. Though the sky was overcast, no rain was falling, at least not yet. The two walked another half block before either spoke.

"Okay, Pat, spill it. What do you want to talk to me about?" Jed asked, his sarcasm still evident though not as harsh.

"I want to know what's going on with you," Knodell answered, though it sounded more like an order. She half expected him to explode with anger or at least protest, yet instead, he just stopped walking and stared at her for what felt like an eternity.

"You want to know what's going on with me? Okay, I'll tell you," he snapped, turning from her and resuming his walk, though this time at a faster pace. "I'm sick to death of this damn assignment. I'm sick of wasting time, digging through files and evidence that dozens have already been through. I'm sick of reading the files of church personnel. We've spent two months working our asses off and we haven't gotten one step closer to *Go-el*. I'm just plain sick of this case!"

Pat Knodell's face grew stern as she listened. As Jed finished his defense, she grabbed his arm firmly, jerking him to a stop and turning him to face her. Though he was literally twice her size, she had absolutely no fear of him.

"So you're tired of this stupid case, are you?" she growled. "Well grow up, Jed, for Pete's sake. Do you think any of the rest of us aren't tired and frustrated? We're hunting a killer and until we find him, more people are going to die. You think that doesn't frustrate the hell out of me? Don't give me any more of this bullshit about being 'tired of the case'. I've worked with you before and you aren't acting like yourself. You're growling around like a constipated old bear and you've been taking it out on Brenda. Now, what the hell is going on?"

Like a school boy who had just been scolded, Jed turned his eyes to the ground. Knodell noted instantly that his reaction was not the anger she expected, but rather pain. She had just probed a very sensitive nerve in the thirty-four-year-old computer wizard.

"When I was twelve years old, my father committed suicide—blew his own head right off. The note he left told Mom and me that he had cancer and didn't want to be a burden on us or to make us watch him suffer. You know, even in the midst of the hurt and loss that I felt, I still respected him. Dad always looked out for us first, wanting to do what was best for Mom and us kids before thinking about himself. He died doing the same thing.

"But the afternoon of the funeral, back at our house, good ole Aunt Margaret comes up to me and Mom to give us a few words of comfort. You see, Aunt Margaret was a really religious person, 'born again' and all that bullshit. She told us that father was burning in hell because he took his own life and that we should give our lives to Jesus or we'd end up there, too.

"I suppose if someone were to say something like that to me now, I'd tear them apart, tell them where to go—something. But as a kid, all I could do was stand there and wonder. Why would God send my Dad to hell? I've hated the church ever since. All those hypocrites dressing up and going to church just so they can feel good enough about themselves to put everyone else down." He paused, ending his hurried pace. Abruptly he wiped a tear from his cheek. He withdrew a cigarette from his pocket, lit it and inhaled deeply, without once making eye contact with his associate, who was as close to a friend as he had, at least on the Task Force.

"So, Stan sends me to Chicago to do some digging into the lives of these hypocrites. Pat, you wouldn't believe the shit I found. Do you have any idea how many perverts there are who are pastors? How many have exploited money from the poor suckers in the pews? It's the sickest joke I've ever heard!" He spat out the words as though they were venom.

"But why take it out on Brenda?"

"I'm not taking anything out on anybody," Jed snapped back defensively.

"Come on Jed, everybody in the group has noticed. You're always snapping at her, and ripping her apart with your unique form of sarcasm. What did she do to you?"

"She didn't do anything," Michaelson fired his answer, turning away in disgust. "She didn't do anything— its more about who she is, what she represents."

"Oh, Jed, what are you talking about?"

"Think about it, Pat. She's an FBI academy grad, fresh out of school. She's got no experience—the only reason she's on this blasted Task Force is because she's one of them—nice, sweet, church-raised superficial hypocrite!"

Suddenly Pat Knodell began to laugh, much to the antagonism of the angry agnostic beside her. "Jed, I never knew you were so prejudiced!" she said mockingly.

"I'm not prejudiced! What the hell does that have to do with anything?"

"Think about it, you bonehead! The way you've been treating Brenda, the reasons behind it, it's exactly the thought pattern of a bigot—prejudging an individual on the basis of stereotypes and generalizations which may or may not be

243

true. Have you ever given Brenda a chance? Have you ever bothered to get to know her as an individual, as a person?"

Again Jed's posture assumed the position of a scolded school boy. With his eyes on the ground, he shuffled his feet nervously, waiting for the lecture to continue; wanting to protest, but knowing that his colleague was absolutely right. Jed had the strange feeling that he had somehow been violated, his behavior and motives suddenly exposed. The sarcastic, introverted computer analyst wanted to protest, wanted to hide but he was being confronted with the truth and he could do neither. Slowly an ironic smile spread across his face. "You know Pat, it really sucks when you can't argue with someone because you know they're right," he sighed. "I guess we better get back, we've got work to do," he conceded, turning and walking back toward headquarters.

Instinctively, Knodell knew that that was as close to an admission and confession that she would ever hear from Jed and she playfully grabbed his arm and tugged, pulling his arm under her own. "Come on, you big Teddy Bear," she teased. "We've got to catch the Boogie Man."

LeToure was waiting in the lobby when Jed and Pat returned to the building that housed their offices. Jed looked at her suspiciously, ready to resume their debate. Knodell excused herself and took the elevator to their floor.

"Hey, Jed, I'm sorry about the way I was talking to you back there," Brenda said softly, cautiously, not knowing what type of reaction she would get, not even knowing what type of reaction she desired.

Jed stopped in his tracks, turning his head so he could see her face. He studied her, waiting for the "But..." to fall, searching for some sign of pious satisfaction, yet finding none. "No problem," he said flatly, turned and resumed walking.

*   *   *   *   *   *   *

244

Arriving at the office complex they had converted into an investigative operation center, they were met immediately at the door by Torvick. "Hope you enjoyed your pizza 'cause there's not going to be any pizza where you're going. Michaelson, LeToure, you're flying to Honduras to do some more digging into the Lehman hit. I don't expect you'll learn anything more about the actual abduction but I want you to find out about Lehman himself. If these hits are about retribution, then he's got some dirt somewhere. Find it. Your flight leaves at 1533 hours, so get packing." Handing the unlikely companions their tickets, he turned to Susan and continued his orders. "Susan, you and Stan are heading to Capitol Hill to get the dirt on Rackl and Deshaw. We know Deshaw was under investigation. Find his connection to Rackl and the other two. Your flight leaves at 16:00. Check in twice a day and keep your cell phones charged," he added unnecessarily.

"Bill, you, Pat and I will hold down the fort and continue digging from here. People, you are looking for one thing: the link that ties *Go-el* to his victims. These hits are about retribution, so the connection is there. You're gonna find it," he ordered, locking eyes with his team.

Chapter Fourteen

April 17, 2004   **Bogotá, Colombia**

Five days in Tegucigalpa, Honduras—the site of General Lehman's abduction and murder—had revealed little to the mismatched investigators of the *Go-el* Task Force. Though no one at the embassy nor at the Honduran Intelligence Office were forthcoming enough to say it outright, General Lehman was not a popular man. It was alluded that he approached matters of diplomacy with blatant indifference and militarily looked with scorn on the Honduran soldiers he was responsible to train and support. At the U.S. military base ten miles outside of Tegucigalpa, the General received a more balanced review. There were some who spoke so defensively of him that LeToure began to suspect the Lehman had something in his past that had caused concern. Those who expressed reservation betrayed few details yet their evasions only served to fuel her suspicions.

After boarding the privately chartered twin turbo prop plane, LeToure tried to express her concerns to Michaelson over the loud drone of the engine. The plane taxied to the head of the runway and the pilot throttled up and sent the eight-seat plane racing down the strip, using as much of the tarmac as he could to gather the necessary speed to gain altitude in the heavy tropical air. Much of Michaelson's annoyance, the plane wasn't heading north. LeToure had lobbied Torvick into allowing them to follow a lead – more like an uneducated hunch, according to Michaelson – that was now taking them to Bogotá. In his anger, he had refused speak to her since the decision had been made.

"Listen, Jed, didn't you notice how the ambassador hesitated when we asked about the type of military operations Lehman had run down here? It was clear that he did not like the man. And what about the clerk at the Intelligence Office? She didn't give us any details, yet she all but accused him of dictating the target lists for the Honduran army – and I don't think she approved of the choices."

"Look, I know you're trying to develop your 'investigator's intuition', but like everything else we've been doing these last two months we are wasting our time down here, and I don't think we're going to learn anymore in Colombia. Sure, Lehman wouldn't have won any popularity contests, except maybe with a few of those Special Forces hard-cases, but tell me honestly, do you have one lead, one piece of evidence, one new question to ask when we repeat this drill in Bogotá?" LeToure still annoyed him, still seemed to him the "little church girl" pretending to be an FBI agent. To his amazement, his insult didn't have the effect he had hoped. Instead of the annoyed and slightly hurt look he had seen in her eyes on other occasions, she was grinning back at him – not the innocent smile that even he had to admit was attractive. This was a grin that proclaimed that she was a step ahead of him. "What?" he snapped.

"You're right, that's where I need you to step up to the plate. You're going to access the deployment records for every OP Lehman ran down here. I'll do the interviews and yes, I've got quite a few more questions for the people in Bogotá. You do what you do best and I'll do my job. By the way, pay attention the next time you interrogate someone with me. You might learn something."

Michaelson set up shop in a hotel room with an adjoining door with LeToure's. Immediately he went to work tracking down the necessary links that would eventually lead him to the data base for the Joint Colombian/U.S. operation records during the three years of Lehman's command. Meanwhile, LeToure, working next door, poured over the personnel rosters of the embassy staff and the list of "who's who" in the Colombian intelligence, police, and military, as well as the latest information from the DEA on the current players in the drug cartels.

This morning, LeToure left Michaelson to his computer hacking and headed for the U.S. embassy in Bogotá, arriving completely unannounced and asserting every bit of authority she possessed. By lunch, she was near completing her fifth interview of the morning, this one with Debra Smette, administrative assistant to the ambassador.

"Thank you for your help, Miss Smette. I'm about ready for lunch, but before we break, tell me about Richard Maier. I understand he was the Military Affairs Liaison here at the embassy until roughly six months ago." LeToure couldn't make out Smette's reaction. Her head turned away, the fingers on her left hand drew into a tight fist, the muscles in the fifty-four-year-old's face tensed noticeably. When she turned her head back to LeToure, tears were welling in her eyes.

"What do you want to know?" she answered, trying to control her voice.

"My records indicate that he resigned his post here at the embassy for personal reasons. Why don't you start there."

"Personal reasons had nothing to do with it," Smette snapped. "If that's what your 'records' say, you had better check your sources."

"My records," LeToure countered, her voice rising just enough to reestablish authority, "indicate that as of last week Richard Maier was on the government payroll through this embassy. They also indicate that roughly six months ago he was abducted, tortured, and returned to the gates of this embassy the next day. Why don't you start by telling me about the abduction?" Again, the woman's reaction seemed to betray conflicting emotions. Grief? Anger? Fear?

"I don't know very much about his abduction," she began tentatively, nervously, "he just didn't show up at the embassy that morning. We were still trying to determine what had happened to him the next day when suddenly a car screeches to a halt in front of the barricades at the main gate and the driver pushes him out of the car and speeds away." Now there were tears in her eyes as she paused to withdraw a tissue from the dispenser on the end table between their chairs. "I saw him when they brought him in and began administering first aid. It was horrible."

"What happened to him then?" LeToure asked, keeping the pressure on.

"They took him to the hospital with a Marine security detail to protect him until we could determine what had happened. We never saw him again. The ambassador held a briefing for all the embassy staff and informed us that Dick had suffered a breakdown as a result of the torture he endured and that he had been sent back to the States to get psychiatric help. He said he doubted that Dick would be able to return to his duties. He assured us they were investigating the abduction and reviewing security arrangements for all personnel living outside the embassy compound. None of us were reassured."

*   *   *   *   *   *   *

Back at the hotel, Jed was following orders and doing what he did best. By four in the afternoon, he had identified the links and channels necessary to obtain the information he needed to examine and had already hacked through the security protocols of the Colombian Intelligence Agency's database. After quickly locating his targeted files, Michaelson downloaded the information for later dissemination. After retrieving nine files containing classified records of contacts and communications between Colombian authorities and U.S. military and State Department personnel, Jed was entering into a hypoglycemic state which adversely affected his already morose mood. It was time for a snack. He was already pushing his chair away from the hotel-room desk when his eyes caught something displayed on his LCD screen. It flashed by in an instant as the document continued scrolling as it downloaded to Jed's flash-drive. "Whoa, there, Momma," he muttered, pounding the keys of the laptop to interrupt the download. "Now where were you..." he mumbled, searching the document. "Hello."

$$* \quad * \quad * \quad * \quad * \quad * \quad *$$

LeToure returned to the hotel after 19:00, exhausted from a day of interviews that had led nowhere, or at least nowhere in Colombia. The only lead she had to follow up on would take her to a psychiatric hospital in Lupic, Pennsylvania. Unlocking the door to her room, she tossed her attaché case onto the chair and threw herself on the bed. She needed a moment to collect herself before facing Michaelson and his sarcasm. She began the day with the self-confidence that she would have a breakthrough by the end of the day, some vital piece of information that she could shove back in his face.

Suddenly there was pounding on the door that adjoined their rooms. "Oh great, he heard me come in," she muttered. Pulling herself to her feet, she unbolted the door and was greeted by a Jed Michaelson she had never met.

"Hey, Brenda, I've been waiting for you to come back," he said with an enthusiasm that immediately made her suspicious. He pushed by her and spread printouts across her bed. "Look at this!" he announced, kneeling by the bed and stabbing his finger at one particular page.

LeToure snatched the page from the bed, her eyes scanning the page, locking in a moment on the name that had caught Michaelson's eyes two hours before: Bartle. "He was here!" she said.

"And not only Bartle," Jed announced, grabbing another page. "There," he said, pointing to an entry near the bottom of the page. "Lehman," they said in unison.

"There's our connection," Jed announced as though the discovery had somehow validated his efforts on the Task Force. "Remind me to listen to you the next time you use your intuition."

The compliment caught LeToure off guard and she suddenly felt a surge of affection for the colleague she could easily have strangled on many occasions. "Why Jed, I do believe that is the nicest thing you have ever said to me," she answered truthfully.

"I know," Jed grunted. "I'll try not to make a habit of it."

April 20, 2004   Lupic, Pennsylvania

They rose early the next morning to begin a series of airport hops that would eventually land them in Lupic, Pennsylvania. By the time they arrived at the psychiatric hospital that housed Richard Maier, it was 19:30. Michaelson was famished, which meant that much of the ground he had gained in making peace with LeToure was slipping away and in his present mood he didn't care. She was on a mission. She had to see Maier today. Not in the morning, not after dinner. Today, now.

Parking in the nearest available visitors spot, LeToure overheard Jed's muttering as she reached for her briefcase. "Hopefully this won't take long and I'll take you to dinner as soon as we finish." Jed grunted. "You know, I bet they have food here and when they hear you muttering to yourself that way, I'm sure they'd be happy to take care of you."

"Cute," Jed snapped. "Let's get this over with."

Since their visit was unannounced, outside visiting hours, and after dark, only the combined authority of FBI and CIA credentials gained them access to the patient. As might be expected in a mental health institution, rumors and paranoia quickly spread from the staff to the patients and soon the mismatched pair of investigators were absorbed into the paranoid delusions of the psychotics on Maier's floor.

LeToure met with Richard Maier in a small office behind the nurses' station, while Michaelson stood watch outside the door. LeToure assessed the man across the table. He was average in height and appearance, muscular despite the roll around his middle. Though he appeared disoriented, his mouth slightly open, frequently licking his dry lips, his posture was erect, stiff, definitely military. Remnants of his dinner clung to the front of his hospital gown and his fingers drummed nervously on his legs, the chair, the desk, and whatever he touched. His glassy eyes bespoke heavy doses of anti-psychotic medication. LeToure greeted him with a friendly, reassuring smile which Maier returned without much enthusiasm.

His current existence and the very fact that he was still alive resulted from an insurance policy he had created for himself in case any of his former associates in the State Department and Military ever turned on him. After his abduction and torture, Maier knew he would be considered a liability and so revealed to his co-conspirators that he had kept meticulous records of all of their illicit activities. Should he be killed or go missing, he had threatened the records would be turned over to the FBI. It had seemed a good protection at the time. He had never imagined that his former colleagues did not need to kill in order to silence him. Regularly administered psychotropic drugs reduced his cries of conspiracy to the ravings of a lunatic.

"Why do you want to talk to me?" Maier opened the conversation, his words slurred as they rolled over his swollen tongue.

"We understand that you used to work for the State Department and spent some time in Colombia. Is that true?"

His eyes seemed to clear and narrow at the question, as though the memories they triggered were calling him back from the drug-induced fog. Slowing his fingers stopped drumming. "Who is asking?" he said clearly.

"My name is Brenda LeToure. I'm with the FBI," she said, showing her identification.

"What do you want to know?"

"While working out of the Bogotá office, did you ever have dealings with Admiral James Bartle? He was with Naval Intelligence at the time."

"Dealings? An interesting choice of words," he said with a chuckle that grew into laughter. "That's a good one, Dick, that's a good one. She's a funny lady, funny, funny funny."

LeToure appraised him as his chuckling turned to incoherent muttering. "Did you ever have business with General Lehman?"

"Admirals and Generals, yes, yes, yes. Big men and bigger men. So big you think their heads will blow up!"

"Mr. Maier, you seem to recognize the names I mentioned. What type of business did you have with them?"

"Secret business, always secret. I won't tell, I won't tell no one. They trust me, they do. I don't say nothing to anybody. No sir," he said with a juvenile voice, shaking his head exaggeratedly to emphasize his point.

"What kind of secret business?" LeToure tried to ask innocently, hoping that Maier would let something slip.

"Oh, smart lady, very smart lady. Pretty lady tries to trick me, she does. No, no, no. I don't talk to no one about business, no business, no talk, no tell." He looked up to the ceiling, his head moving from side to side, his eyes seeming to fixate on the light fixture, his fingers again drumming on his legs.

*   *   *   *   *   *   *

Outside the door, Jed Michaelson had captured the interest of a young woman, a resident of the institution. With an intriguing combination of shyness and flirtation, she introduced herself to him as Eve. Hungry, highly uncomfortable being in a psychiatric hospital, and unaccustomed to the flattery of flirtation, Jed quickly began to perspire as the feeling of being trapped began to consume him.

"We've met before," she said, bashfully looking into Jed's eyes, then quickly away.

"I don't think so," he answered gruffly.

"I know it's been a long time, but I'm sure that you'll remember. Don't you remember our walks in the garden, the flowers and trees…"

"No, really, I think you have me confused with someone else."

She was undeterred. She leaned in close to him, placing her hand on his chest. "You remember how we never wore clothes back then," she whispered seductively.

*   *   *   *   *   *   *

"Mr. Maier, before you left your post in Bogotá, you were abducted from your home. I understand that the kidnappers tortured you. I want you to know that I am sorry about what you suffered."

254

Maier's gaze slowly moved from the ceiling fixture to meet LeToure. "Yes, they tortured me," he said with sudden clarity.

"Can you tell me anything about who did that to you?"

"I told, I told a hundred times. Nothing more to tell. Others want to know, too. Dead ones want to know. He scares them. He scares me." Maier's voice was almost a whisper and tears were filling his eyes.

"I'm sorry to have upset you. We are trying to catch the man who did those terrible things to you. I was hoping that by coming to you and asking you myself, I might learn something – you might remember something – that will help us bring him to justice." LeToure was patient, waiting for him to speak again.

He stared at her and started rocking gently backwards and forwards in his chair. "Pretty lady asking questions, pretty lady gonna die, pretty lady asking questions, pretty lady gonna die," he began to repeat. She leaned back in her chair and continued observing, aware of the chill that ran down her spine. Suddenly the rocking stopped and he looked straight into her eyes. "Pretty lady ask me questions, now I gonna die," he said with a tone of finality. "I'm finished talking with you," he said, rising to his feet and heading for the door.

*   *   *   *   *   *   *

LeToure followed Maier through the office door and stepped into a scene both tragic and comical. A woman was desperately clinging to Jed while two of the psychiatric aides were prying her off. All the while she kept crying out, "No, Adam! No, don't let them throw us out of the garden again!" Finally tearing himself free, Jed's face clearly expressed the emotions he was feeling. Loss of control, panic, fear, embarrassment. He looked toward LeToure just as she came

255

through the door. He saw the smile appear on her face. "Not a word!" he snapped, and began walking down the hall toward the gated exit. Stopping at the gate to wait for the security officer, LeToure caught up to him. Again he glanced at her and again he caught her smirk. He wanted to get angry at her but all he could manage to say was to repeat, "Not a word."

"Okay, not a word... Adam," she said and immediately broke into laughter.

Jed flushed as the wave of anger and irritation quickly swept over him, yet suddenly, he found himself smiling as well, then laughing with her. The security officer reached the door and gave them a disapproving look. "Settle down," he said as he unlocked and opened the door.

Composing themselves as they exited the building, the moment of levity quickly gave way to matters at hand. Briefly she recapped her interview with Maier. By the time they reached the car, the humor they enjoyed for those few moments was gone, replaced by the feelings that followed the words, "Pretty lady gonna die." Before unlocking the car, she turned and looked at her partner. "Jed, I'm getting the feeling we've backed our way into something and I don't think we're going to like where all this is leading."

Jed stopped by the passenger door of their rented sedan and looked over the roof. "As much as I hate to admit it, I'm learning to trust your intuition and I don't like what its saying. But do you think we could maybe have dinner before we get ourselves killed? I hate to die on an empty stomach," he said with a grin.

"Alright, I'll take you to dinner – I'll even buy... Adam." Their eyes met and for the first time in their relationship, they smiled at each other with genuine affection.

*   *   *   *   *   *   *

From a window overlooking the parking lot, a psychiatric aide watched the car leave the driveway. Informing his coworkers that he was taking a break, he left the ward and headed down the hall to the employee lounge. Finding it deserted, he went to his locker and retrieved his cell phone. Again, checking the area, he dialed the number and delivered the message that would earn him ten thousand dollars and his own death sentence. Unbeknownst to him, the people who paid him did not allow loose ends.

May 1, 2004   **Seattle, Washington**

The daily delivery and distribution of mail at the Seattle Lutheran Bible College was a highlight of the day for many students. Each day brought the expectation of letters or cards from family or friends back home and perhaps another check from loving and providing parents.

At 1:30 p.m. in the afternoon on every mail day, students would gather at the east end of the recreation hall where the student mail boxes were located, waiting for the office administrator of the college or often a fellow student, to place the coveted correspondence in their own numbered box. As many times as Angela Hotchner had sorted the mail, it always surprised her how certain students received mail almost daily, while others rarely received even the most common junk mail.

This Thursday's mail was no exception, as she commented to her volunteer assistant. "This is the fourth letter for Shelly today!" she said, holding up the letter for Tim Parnel to see. Tim smiled. "Hardly seems fair, does it?"

The process continued. Each would grab a handful of mail from the plastic basket provided by the local post office, sort through it, and place each piece in its appropriate box.

"Well, here's a surprise!" Angela suddenly exclaimed.

"What's that?"

"Here's a letter for Jeff Atkins. I don't think I've ever put anything in his box!"

Tim rushed over to her. "Let me see that," he said playfully, though he was deadly serious.

"It's just from some seminary. They're probably trying to recruit him," she answered without showing the letter.

"Let me see it," he said again, this time with a little too much edge on his voice.

She gave him a strange look and handed him the letter. "You sure seem interested in Jeff, considering that the two of you don't seem to get along very well."

Tim ignored the remark while studying the letter. The return address and emblem announced that it was from the Lutheran Theological Seminary of the Pacific in Berkeley, California. Tim wondered what its contents would reveal.

Suddenly he was aware that Angela was staring at him—not the admiring stare he had grown fond of, but a curious, suspicious stare.

"I'm sorry," he said, snapping back to the present. "When you said it was from a seminary, I got curious. I... I've been thinking about going to seminary myself lately. I was just wondering which one he was interested in," he lied, trying to cover his tracks.

Playfully she punched him in the arm. "And how long have you been thinking about seminary? How come you never mentioned anything about it to me?" she said, trying her best to look hurt.

"Oh, actually I had never thought about it at all 'til recently." This time he was telling the truth, in a manner of speaking.

It had taken many days to make the cross-country drive, but much longer to summon the courage to make it. Following his conversation with Pastor Olafson, Pierson had made up his mind to make the trip and confront his past. Yet like many decisions in life, committing was only half the battle. Until completed, doubt and second guessing wage constant war against every good intention. Many times before he had thought to go, only to be stopped by guilt and fear. Pulling the compact car to the curb, he parked and rolled up the windows. Now was the moment of truth.

Though only spring, the weather in Savannah, Georgia had been unseasonably warm. Though technically not an island, the Isle of Hope neighborhood of southeast Savannah was one of the historic city's most desired districts. Surrounded by water on three sides, it was populated by some of Savannah's elite as well as young couples and families aspiring to live the better life and climb the social ladder. Parking four driveways down the street from his destination, Pierson noted this particular street definitely was born of old money. Stepping out of the car, he stretched, trying to loosen his travel-weary muscles. A cooler late afternoon breeze from the east seemed to refresh him after seven hours in his mobile sauna, yet it wasn't the heat that had troubled him during the drive.

Nine months after that awful night, it was time to face a nightmare he had carried in his mind and soul. The memories haunted him more fiercely than ever as he came closer to his destination, closer to the greatest challenge he had ever faced.

Intuitively he surveyed the comfortable neighborhood. The houses were large with well-groomed yards. It was a neighborhood of the upper middle class, each house complete with accompanying toys – expensive cars, boats, RV's. With his eyes alert, he looked at each house, taking in details, drawing conclusions, alert for any sign of danger. The sound of a lawn mower hummed from half a block away. Sounds of splashing and the laughter of children revealed that a backyard pool was hidden behind one of the nearby houses.

The area was as safe as he could have hoped but he hesitated, taking a few extra precious moments. In truth, he really only wanted to delay the confrontation with his past for a little longer. Finally, he drew a deep breath as if to summon his courage and began walking.

He had deliberately parked four houses away and now began closing the distance toward his destination. He could feel his pulse racing, his mind ordering him to retreat before it was too late, his soul pushing him forward.

Reaching the door, he rang the bell immediately, robbing himself of the last opportunity to escape. He knew the person he had come to see was home. He had watched her pull into her driveway only moments ago after a long day at work and a quick trip to the grocery store, evidenced by her weary posture and the grocery bags she juggled in her arms.

The door opened slightly, enough for the thirty-one-year-old widow to see her visitor. A brass security chain prevented the door from being opened farther without force. "Can I help you?" Marie Claypool asked with a kind, though tired voice.

Though he had rehearsed his introduction many times and in many ways, suddenly the warrior found himself at a loss for words. He looked at the woman's partially concealed face and was at once transported back to another time. He could hear the screaming as clearly now as then.

"Excuse me? Can I help you?" she asked again, her voice puzzled.

As if being pulled back to the present, the visitor seemed to shudder for a moment, then their eyes met. "Yes,

I'm sorry, yes, you can help me. I was just distracted for a moment," he answered awkwardly.

"Well, what can I do for you?" She was becoming uncomfortable and slightly suspicious. Though she was sure she did not recognize him, there was something almost familiar about him. She realized she was slightly afraid, though she had no idea why.

"I..., I need to talk to you about your husband," he blurted out clumsily, his rehearsed introduction lost forever. He watched as the woman's face change instantly. Suddenly she looked years older as the lines of grief seemed to distort her face.

"What is it?" she asked, the trembling in her voice further betraying her pain.

"I have some information you deserve to know. I think we need to talk. May I come in? You don't need to be afraid."

After a moment of hesitation, the widow closed the door. He could hear her free the security chain, then slowly the door opened and the woman cautiously invited the familiar stranger in, closing the door behind him. Her right hand was concealed behind her back, holding a compact Glock 43 9mm pistol. Without inviting him to sit, she faced him. "Who do you represent?" she asked in a demanding tone.

The question caught him off guard. Again, he found himself struggling to find words. He remembered the last time he had seen her face. Her hands were secured behind her back with zip-ties, the gag in her mouth secured with duct tape. Members of his team were lowering her and the other non-combatants from Mantazar's yacht on to one of the drug lord's speed boats. When all were on board they set the boat adrift and scuttled the big yacht. "I don't represent anyone. Just myself. Your husband was murdered in Colombia, almost ten months ago, am I right?" He needed no answer, the tears in the widow's eyes answered for her.

261

She turned her head away, unwilling to let the stranger see her pain.

"What do you know about him?" she finally asked with a shaky voice.

"For one thing, I know who killed him, and if you are willing to let me ask you a few questions, I might be able to tell you why."

She turned quickly, staring intently at the stranger, her eyes suddenly reflecting more anger than pain. "Who did it?" she snapped.

Pierson looked away to avoid her penetrating eyes. "The hit was conducted by a United States Navy SEAL team," he answered in a matter-of-fact tone that surprised even him.

She stared at him in disbelief, trying to absorb what she had heard. "Are you saying that the Navy had my husband killed?"

"Not exactly... Look, maybe we better sit down. We've got a lot to talk about." She nodded and guided the stranger into the kitchen, still keeping the pistol hidden behind her back. She motioned for him to have a seat at the table. Once both were seated, the stranger continued.

"The orders for the hit on your husband came from a man named Bartle, Admiral James Bartle. At that time he was the commanding officer for Naval Intelligence. The SEAL team that attacked...that killed your husband was briefed by him personally. They were told that your husband worked for a powerful member of the drug cartel who had been threatening to launch a terrorist campaign on U.S. targets. The mission's rationale was simple—take out the drug dealer before he had a chance to act—a preemptive strike. They were shown reconnaissance photos and diagrams of Rodrigo Mantazar's yacht. They were given three targets: Mantazar himself, Jose' Gutierrez, his commanding officer, and your husband, though the team was told his name was Miguel Sanchez. They said he was

262

Mantazar's security and intelligence advisor. The team did as they were ordered, just like they were trained to do."

Across the table, the widow stared suspiciously at the stranger, studying him. "Who are you?" she suddenly demanded.

The former SEAL turned his eyes away, lowering them toward the table. "My name is not important. I'm just here because I thought you deserved to know the truth about your husband's death."

She continued to study him. Suddenly her eyes flashed with recognition and realization. "You were there! You were the one who..." Pierson looked up and locked eyes with the woman whose husband he had murdered. Her eyes seemed to pulsate between anger and fear. "You were the one! You were the one who..." Swiftly she brought forth the pistol and aimed it at the intruder's face. He didn't flinch, but looked past the barrel into her eyes, as though ready to accept his fate. She saw the stranger had tears in his eyes. Suddenly she burst into tears, her gun hand dropping into her lap.

She shook her head and drew in a gasping breath. "You bastard! Why did you come here? What were you looking for? Forgiveness? Did you want me to soothe your troubled conscience? You murdered my husband!" She glared hatefully across the table at the man with the eyes she now clearly remembered. "I think it's time for you to leave. Get out of my house!" she ordered, but the man with tear-filled eyes didn't move. "Get out!" she shouted.

"Mrs. Claypool, though your forgiveness would mean more to me than you could ever know, I didn't come here expecting to receive it. I came to help you understand why your husband was killed, why I was sent to kill him. I know this is painful and if you don't want to hear, I'll leave, I promise."

Across the table the widow said nothing, still glaring with hatred at the man who was no longer a stranger, but a murderer.

"Your husband worked for the State Department, and was sent to Colombia to work out of the embassy in Bogotá, is that correct?" He was answered with icy silence. She nodded slightly. "Did you know why he... why the two of you were sent to Colombia?" Again, she stared at him in silence. "Officially his job was to be the liaison for the embassy with the Colombian anti-drug forces. Unofficially, he was to sent to investigate Colombian government complaints of U.S. personnel involvement in drug trafficking. Were you aware of this?"

She said nothing, but her anger was being held in check by her desire for answers and understanding. She shook her head and managed to utter the word, "No."

"Mrs. Claypool, my team was sent in to take out your husband because his investigation threatened some very powerful, very influential people."

"I think you mean, 'murder,' don't you? You 'take out' the trash, you 'take people out to dinner!' You murdered him, and I saw you do it!"

"Yes, ma'am," Pierson said, the widow's words striking his heart. "I did."

She stared at him, her emotions in turmoil, hating him, yet confused by the hint of compassion she felt toward him, and then hating herself for allowing it. "Who did it?" she finally said. "Who was behind the orders you received?"

"Admiral Bartle, General Lehman. Recognize those names?"

She stared at him, suddenly paralyzed with fear, for the first time realizing that she herself might be in mortal danger. "That was you? You killed them?"

"No," he shook his head. "Those were the names I was able discover, but I know it goes much higher and is not limited to military leaders. Mrs. Claypool, I came to you for

264

two reasons. First, I believed you deserved to know that your husband was a good man who got in the way of some very bad people. I also want to say," he looked down at the table, seeing his own wringing hands. "I want you to know that I am sorry for my part in this." He looked up to see her crying. "I'm sorry. I'll leave. You don't need to worry, I won't bother you again." He pushed away from the table and made his way to the front door. He was turning the knob when Marie caught up to him.

"You're not in the Navy anymore, are you?" she suddenly asked.

Surprised by the question, he turned to face her. "No, ma'am. That night, after what happened on the yacht... I knew something wasn't right. I asked questions, lost control. I was court-martialed." He opened the door and stepped out.

Still wrestling with the emotions warring within her, Marie called to him. "I'll be honest with you. I don't know if I will ever be able to forgive you for what you did to Michael, but I will try. I will try."

He turned back to face her. Finding no words to respond, he simply lowered his eyes and nodded in appreciation. It was more than he had hoped. As he walked back to his car, he realized that a weight had been lifted from his shoulders.

*　　*　　*　　*　　*　　*　　*

She dead-bolted the door behind the stranger after watching him walk away. Though she realized it was naïve, she no longer feared him, but the memories he stirred reawakened fears she had been fighting to conquer since that awful night. Suddenly she knew she needed to call her uncle, actually Michael's uncle. Returning to the kitchen, she found her address book and dialed the number for the home of Senator Glen Barnell.

A preview of

In Such a World

Book Two

Cross Paths

Chapter One

A cluster of rock stood on the left side of the trail about a hundred meters up ahead. *I can make it to those rocks*, Pierson told himself as he willed his burning legs to continue pumping. It was a skill he had developed in his BUD/S training. Don't focus on the end, set smaller goals along the way and keep moving through them. Never quit. He was running a trail that most would find challenging to simply hike.

After his conversation with Marie Claypool, Pierson knew he had to make some important decisions about his future. He also knew he needed exercise and a challenge. Two nights after leaving Savannah, he used his laptop in his hotel room to research trail runs in the area. The Black Mountain Crest Trail Run caught his attention. The website claimed it was the toughest trail run in the world. He accepted the challenge on the spot and the next morning drove to Burnsville, North Carolina.

Only four miles up the steep path leading to the peak of Mount Mitchell, he was already chastising himself. Two more miles of brutally steep trail lay ahead of him. He had started at too fast a pace, blowing by three groups of hikers. He had underestimated how strenuous the Black Mountain Crest trail would be— an over 6,500 foot climb in six miles. Besides, he had let himself get out of shape. His weeks living off the grid and his cross-country road trip had taken its toll.

Legs rubbery, lungs burning, he reached the rock landmark he had chosen as his goal and slowed his pace, eventually stopping and clasping his hands behind his head, sucking in air through his nose and expelling it through his mouth, shaking out his legs in the process. As his pulse slowed and breath returned, he slipped off his backpack and retrieved his water bottle, sipping a few gulps. He took a moment to look at the forest around him. He was nearing the tree line and already getting a glimpse of the views that awaited him. Uncharacteristically he stepped off the trail and began weaving his way through the trees, always preferring to avoid trails. He breathed deeply the rich smells of the forest. Safely out of sight from the trail, he allowed himself the luxury of taking a seat at the base of a large spruce tree.

His visits with Pastor Olafson and Marie Claypool and been his first steps toward reconciling with God and people, but his heart ached for those relationships beyond his control to reconcile. He could only imagine the fear and anger his family must have toward him. With changes to his appearance, a complete set of IDs—his new name Matthew Craige, a couple of credit cards, and the cash his friend had retrieved for him—he was free in a way few people experience. Yet a profound sadness suffocated whatever joy or excitement he might otherwise have felt. He was free to do everything but what he wanted most: to go home.

Perhaps fatigue allowed his mind to be haunted by a growing sense of déjà vu. Pierson knew that sights, sounds, smells can be triggers for memories long forgotten, waking them from the shadows of the subconscious, evoking a spontaneous smile or a gut twisting surge of grief, fear, guilt or shame. In this case, it was the smell of moist soil and decaying foliage of the forest that triggered the first memory from Matthew Pierson's past.

269

It was twelve years and a lifetime ago. Matt Pierson was a senior in High School and serving as an apprentice youth director of his congregation's Middle School youth group. Under the leadership and supervision of the congregation's associate pastor, the young Pierson and his youth directing partner, Jon, had taken the Middle Schoolers on a weekend retreat to Mount Gilead Christian Camp located in California's northern coastal hills about 15 miles west of Santa Rosa. Sharing the camp were Middle School groups from two other area congregations. Each church was to run their own programming and activities in their own areas of the camp.

Given the nature of Middle School youth, immediately the hormonally charged students began to check out the youth from the other congregations. Flirtations began immediately. Leaders from all three congregations gathered to discuss the situation and make plans. The camp was divided into the three sections. Boundaries were drawn and explained to every camper.

By midafternoon, members of all three youth groups had conducted reconnaissance missions into the areas of the camp occupied by the other church groups. Their efforts discovered that there were "hot" guys and equally "hot" girls in the varying youth groups. Plots for a late-night rendezvous were hatched and the word began to spread among their fellow campers.

Thinking themselves ever so clever, the youth of Pierson's congregation approached each other, in full hearing of their leaders, with all the subtlety they could muster given their level of experience with clandestine operations. With exaggerated winks and nods, they passed on the message. "The *game* will be at *1:00 tomorrow.*"

By sundown, Pierson, Jon, and their fearless leader Pastor Phil had broken their code and knew all their plans. The boys from one of the other camps were going to meet up with the girls from their group at 1:00 a.m. by the camp's fire pit and amphitheater. As the commanding officer, Pastor Phil issued the proclamation. "I don't think we can let this happen." He then began laying out his plan for the ambush.

Pierson smiled to himself as the memories of his first ambush replayed through his mind. So many years ago, he, Jon, and Pastor Phil had lain on their bellies in the woods along the dirt road that connected two sections of the camp, their faces inches from the moist ground, the smell of earth filling their nostrils. It was the smell that had awakened the distant memory. They waited in silence for the boys from the other group to cross the no man's zone. In buckets beside them, each was armed with ten carefully prepared water balloons. The three leaders had snuck out of their own cabins after making sure their youth were sound asleep. By 12:45 a.m. they were in position and the young Pierson experienced his first lesson about springing a successful ambush. Patience.

They waited 'til 1:00 a.m., checking their watches often, their adrenalin pumping, their hands gently squeezing the water balloons they held. The road below them was empty and silent. 1:05. 1:08. 1:12. 1:15 a.m. "I don't think they're coming," Jon whispered from his position on Pierson's right. Pastor Phil was stationed on his left. He would be the first to fire. The seconds rolled into minutes and all three began wondering if the "enemy" would show.

Was their intelligence wrong? Had the kids caught on to their plans? Had they been suckered? Were the kids right now gathering in another part of the camp? The three church leaders were just about to give up their planned ambush and return to their cabin when Pastor Phil whispered excitedly, "They're coming!"

Seven youth from the other camp were approaching just as anticipated, only not on foot, but on bicycles. They were in no hurry as they made their way toward their appointed meeting. Were they deliberately procrastinating, letting the girls camp wait, Pierson wondered? Silently Pastor Phil let fly his first balloon. Matt and Jon followed suit and suddenly out of the blackened forest a silent barrage of water balloons began hailing down on the unsuspecting youth.

As the balloons began exploding on their bikes, their bodies, and the ground around them, one word rang out among the other exclamations of shock and surprise. "Shit!" Instantly they wheeled their bikes around and pumped their pedals as fast as their Middle School-aged legs could work them. They were defeated and escaping to the protection of their part of the camp! The ambush had been an amazing success.

Pierson smiled at the memory, for a moment relieved that his sense of déjà vu was satisfied. Yet the relief was short lived as the fond memory was replaced by another, far more sinister event. Again, it was the aroma of the soil and forest that allow the second memory to eclipse the first. He shut his eyes tightly as if to squeeze back the dark recollections of his past, but it was too late. It was the night of his first kills.

Deep in the rain forests of northern Colombia, Pierson was deployed with his four-man unit from SEAL Team Four. They were to provide rearguard support for the *heavy hitters*—an eight-man squad dispatched from Development Group Six. They would perform the actual hostage rescue. As the newest member of the team and still a *virgin* in that he had no confirmed kills to his credit, it was decided without words that his unit would be placed where he could do the least amount of damage if the shit were to hit the fan.

In the Teams, especially in the field, rank meant little compared to experience and reputation. Though a Lieutenant, Pierson didn't protest, but inside he hungered for the opportunity to prove himself. Not only green, in BUD/S he had been saddled with the nickname, *Preacher*, due to the Bachelor's Degree in religious studies he had earned before receiving his Naval commission. For many in the Teams, religion equaled ethics which equaled hesitation. Pierson knew what all the veterans in his platoon wondered about him. Would he pull the trigger when needed or have that split second of hesitation of ethical doubt? Though he admitted it to no one, he wondered the same thing about himself.

Their mission that night was special. Locals in nearby villages had been complaining of atrocities at the militia's hands following recent regional votes in favor of anti-cartel candidates. Though normally such operations as tonight's would be either turned over to or conducted with Colombian national forces, this particular band of militia had abducted several western journalists, specifically CNN's Colombian affiliate reporter Camila Laureano and her film crew. When the mutilated body of her videographer washed

273

ashore on the west bank of the Cauca River just north of Cali, the Joint Special Operations Command had decided to take matters into their own hands.

Another eight-man squad from SEAL Team Four was position three kliks down river to the east, prepared to provide a distraction and ambush to draw militia forces away from the compound and annihilate them while the DEVGRU boys did their dirty work. The plan had been that by morning, Camila Laureano would be freed and every member of the militia dead.

Positioned approximately fifteen meters apart, Pierson and his unit were deployed in a square with a small trail running down it's middle, one man on each side, one pair guarding the trail from the east, the other from the west. All four were hidden in the foliage, waiting for their mates to launch the distraction, each frustrated that, as on other missions, they would be on the sidelines while others got the action. They had been in position for two hours and their muscles ached for motion.

Then Pierson heard voices coming from the forest to the west of him. He whispered into the microphone of his in-ear conduction headset. "We've got company. No visual. At least two bogies," Pierson concluded, detecting at least two distinct voices. His eyes strained through his night vision binoculars but he could see nothing through the dense jungle undergrowth.

"Copy that," the man on his starboard side whispered first, followed in sequence by the two others to the east. Each man knew they could not let anyone pass their position. They had no idea the size of the force coming their way nor even if they were militia or civilians. Whatever the case, they were in the wrong place at the wrong time.

As trained, Pierson and his forward teammate let the first two pass by. They wore farm worker clothes and were whispering too loudly to each other as they past. Each had an AK47 slung over his shoulders; sloppy and undisciplined. Definitely militia. Two more followed ten paces behind, also whispering to each other, completely unaware they were about to die.

There didn't seem to be any more coming. Pierson tensed his muscles as though a snake coiling to strike. He listened for the sound behind him that his rear teammates were engaging their targets. Two spits, two thuds as the bodies collapsed to the ground. Instantly Pierson fired his SIG-Sauer P226, the weapon making a sharp spit as it sent the bullet through the attached sound suppressor. The militiaman's head snapped back sharply as the bullet exploded through the opposite side of his skull. Instantly the SEAL to his right fired and the fourth militiaman was blown off his feet and thrown to the ground, the body landing just two meters from Pierson.

Each SEAL remained concealed, silent again, ready to engage if more militia appeared on the trail. A tension-filled five minutes passed before Pierson whispered into his microphone. "Morales, hold position. Rayes, Daw, get the bodies off the trail."

As ordered, Rayes and Daw broke cover and dragged the first two bodies from the trail, concealing them beneath the undergrowth. They returned for the second pair.

"Contact," Pierson whispered urgently. Four more militia suddenly appeared on the trial, bunched together, jogging as though trying to catch up to their comrades, AK47s cradled in their arms.

Rayes and Daw dropped the bodies and instantly sank to a squatting position, unable to shoulder their weapons for fear of being seen. But it was too late, they had already been spotted. The joggers almost collided with each other as the first militiaman saw them and froze in his tracks.

With his sound-suppressed M4 pressed firmly into his shoulder, Pierson fired twice, the bullets striking center mass, throwing the first militiaman back into the others. Shifting to his second target, Pierson fired again, two more quick shots, another tango down. His third target was starting to turn to run away, his face awash with panic. Again, Pierson fired twice. The man staggered back but did not fall, momentarily blocking Pierson's view of his fourth target. The fourth militiaman, fully panicked, spun and began sprinting down the trail he had just moments ago traveled. Rounding the bend in the trail, he disappeared from Pierson's view.

"We've got a runner. I'm going after him," Pierson huffed into his com unit as he sprinted after his prey. Drawing his combat knife, closing the distance between them, he saw the man look back over his shoulder. Pierson saw the terror in his eyes. The gap between them closed and Pierson tackled the militiaman, wrapping his leg around his victim's legs, his left arm grabbing the man's head and yanking back violently, exposing the man's neck. With the knife in his right hand he slashed the man's throat so deeply it nearly beheaded him. Blood erupted and sprayed Pierson's face and soaked into his uniform. Clutching the dying man,

276

he felt every tremor, heard every sound of his final gurgling breaths as his victim died in his arms.

Years ago, yet as the memory so engulfed him, he could remember every detail; the smells of the rain forest, cordite and blood. He remembered his consciousness protesting and the deliberate decision to shut it down and silence it. He remembered the next morning, when one of the DEVGRU guys approached him. "Five confirmed kills, not one bullet wasted. Not bad for a preacher," he said with a devilish grin. It was the first time he met then Chief Warren *Pepper* Adler, who would go on to recommend him for the selection process for DEVGRU.

Voices from the trail snapped his attention back to the present. Through the trees, he caught glimpses of one of the groups of hikers he had passed. Three men, two women. Mid-thirties he estimated.

Perceiving no threat from them, he rose and began quietly weaving his way between the trees, working his way up the mountain away from the trail, his pride not willing to let the hikers realize they had passed him. Ten minutes later he returned to the trail, ahead and out of sight of the hikers. Rested now, he immediately resumed his run up the mountain. He paced himself better and made the summit without further stops. His mind was preoccupied, no longer with his past, but with his future.

By the time he made it back to the valley floor, one thing was clear. It was time to move on. The dual memories the day's outing had stirred reminded him of the contrast between the two chapters of his life. When he had walked with God in his youth, he remembered having an underlying peace about his future. Having walked away from God, he now knew guilt and the uncertainty of whether he'd even live through each day. "Okay Lord, if you'll have me back, I'm going to put my trust in you." He whispered his simple prayer. He remembered the suggestion Pastor Olafson had made during their visit. Then it had seemed a mere fantasy, but now… Maybe, just maybe. He would have plenty of time to think about it as he made his way cross-country, back to the west coast. If not home, at least closer to it.

About the Author...

T.J. Hux earned his MDiv degree from Pacific Lutheran Theological Seminary in Berkeley, California. He has a wife, three sons, and one daughter-in-law. His passions include his faith, free-diving for abalone on the northern California coast, fishing, and hunting.

Made in the USA
Lexington, KY
17 January 2017